THE SHŌWA ANTHOLOGY 2

THE
SHŌWA
ANTHOLOGY
Modern Japanese Short Stories

2
1961–1984

Edited by
Van C. Gessel
Tomone Matsumoto

KODANSHA INTERNATIONAL LTD.
Tokyo, New York, and San Francisco

ACKNOWLEDGMENTS

The editors wish to thank the following authors for graciously allowing the translation and publication of their stories: Ibuse Masuji, Ishikawa Jun, Abe Kōbō, Yasuoka Shōtarō, Kojima Nobuo, Yoshiyuki Junnosuke, Shōno Junzō, Shimao Toshio, Kurahashi Yumiko, Inoue Yasushi, Minakami Tsutomu, Endō Shūsaku, Abe Akira, Shibaki Yoshiko, Ōba Minako, Kōno Taeko, Kanai Mieko, Kaikō Takeshi, Ōe Kenzaburō, Tsushima Yūko, and Nakagami Kenji.

In addition, the estates of the following have granted permission for the use of the included works: Hori Tatsuo, Dazai Osamu, and Kawabata Yasunari.

Concerning works previously published elsewhere, the editors gratefully acknowledge the following:

International Creative Management, for permission to use a slightly revised version of the translation of Abe Kōbō's "The Magic Chalk," which appeared in Asia Magazine, translated by Alison Kibrick. © 1982

Peter Owen, Ltd., for permission to reprint "The Day Before" by Endō Shūsaku, from *Stained Glass Elegies*, translated by Van C. Gessel. © 1984

Columbia University Press, for permission to reprint a slightly revised version of "Bad Company" by Yasuoka Shōtarō, from *A View by the Sea*, translated by Kären Wigen Lewis. © 1984

Japan P.E.N. Club, for permission to reprint "The Silent Traders" by Tsushima Yūko, from *Japanese Literature Today* (no. 9, March 1984), translated by Geraldine Harcourt. © 1984

Publication of this anthology was assisted by a grant from the Japan Foundation. The in-house editing was done by Stephen Shaw.

LCC 85-40070
ISBN 0-87011-747-5
ISBN 4-7700-1247-0 (in Japan)

First edition, 1985

CONTENTS

II

The Immortal
by Nakagami Kenji (1984)   412

Notes on the Translators

Selected Bibliography of English Translations

I

昭和短篇小説集

2

THE MONASTERY

Kurahashi Yumiko

Translated by Carolyn Haynes

Kurahashi Yumiko was born in 1935 in a rural area surrounding the city of Kōchi, which has been a remarkable breeding ground for modern writers (others include Yasuoka Shōtarō and Ōhara Tomie). Initially Kurahashi planned to pursue her father's career in dental hygiene, and she received her license to do so, but she had become interested in French literature on the side and enrolled in that department at Meiji University. In this she has something in common with another contemporary experimental writer, Abe Kōbō, who turned to the writing of fiction as soon as he received his medical degree.

In 1960, the year she graduated from Meiji University with a thesis on Sartre, Kurahashi published the short story "Parutai" (Partei; tr. 1982) and created a literary sensation comparable to the discovery of Ōe Kenzaburō just two years previously. From the outset of her career as a writer, Kurahashi has been influenced by Sartre, Camus, and Kafka, and her declared intention is to be an anti-realist. This she achieves marvelously through a blend of native sensitivity and a strikingly rich and fluent experimentalism. She may, in fact, possess the most fertile literary imagination in Japan today. But it is an imagination that has been tempered by accusations of "plagiarism," a year of creative writing study in Iowa in 1966, and a period of silence following the publication of her most interesting works to date: Sumiyakisuto Q no bōken (The Adventures of Sumiyakist Q, 1969; tr. 1979), Yume no ukihashi (The Floating Bridge of Dreams, 1971), and Hanhigeki (Anti-tragedies, 1971). More recently she has returned to active

participation in the literary world with the publication of Otona no tame
no zankoku dōwa (*Cruel Fairy Tales for Adults, 1984*).

*The present story, "Kyosatsu," was written in 1961 and is a product of
Kurahashi's early, somewhat indecisive experimentalism, but her intriguing views of reality and unreality and the fluidity of human relationships
are expressed in this story with the same vigor and skill to be found in her
other works.*

*   *   *

The early walk Father and I take along the flagstone path was interrupted
today by the unanticipated arrival of K. The sloping path we were about
to descend, winding from one building to the next, was aglow in the still
dormant light of the summer morning when K, the traveler K, came
bounding up with that extravagant agility of his. He presented my father
with a letter of introduction from some university. I cannot describe his
vacant but intoxicating looks, which have a quality one sees in dreams;
I cannot even say from what planet this traveler might have come. According to his own account, which is of course unverifiable, K is a scholar
of art just recently appointed to an educational institute. Even more
dubious is his claim to be a poet—dubious because of the ambivalence
of that term itself. In spite of this, or perhaps indeed because of it, Father
ushered K into our temple with a startling burst of scathing comments—
both witty and self-mocking—and a familiarity bordering on enmity which
seemed inappropriate in a priest of our sect. My hand, extended in
greeting, was clasped in K's, which trembled with enthusiasm, a chilly
excitement, and in that moment my eyes were seared by the fire in K's
rude gaze. Taking this in with the acuity of his years, Father approached
me and, as if in ridicule, muttered that name—your name, my betrothed.
I am not sure whether the giddiness I felt was caused by the worn
familiarity of that name or by the flicker of passion I had discerned in K.

I suppose K will stay at Temple H.

Having promised to see him again despite complex reservations, I served today as K's cheerful, intimate guide. We embarked on an enthusiastic tour of the monastery buildings, from the reliquary pagoda to the winding verandas and on to the ancient wooden storehouse. Drawn by some mysterious attraction, we walked behind the old abandoned belfry and took a small path that twisted and turned like a labyrinth through the grove. We seemed to be following the tracks of time, spiraling down into the interior of our spirits. Despite the encroaching heat, the grove had trapped cool, green air in its web of foliage. We wandered along the wooded path, avoiding the menacing sun which shone like an old bronze dish above us. The thicket of maple and beech trees interlocking above a cover of hawthorn and andromeda ended shortly, and we entered a wood of cedars rising perpendicularly. Hundreds of parallel shafts of sunlight streamed through the trees to pierce our bodies. I kicked off my shoes to let the moss caress my feet, and, shaking off K's admonishing voice which rang with shrill foreboding, I ran between the cedars like a snake through grass. K ran after me. We kept up this strange game, drawing together only to lose sight of one another, the thread of pursuit becoming more and more entangled, until we were suddenly greeted by two limpid springs. They were seductive traps the earth had laid for us, staring blue eyes our bare feet wounded as we scurried over the shifting pebbles. In silence we endured the permeating cold. After a long interval, K and I abruptly thrust out our hands in an act of plunder until they intertwined, my hand with K's, and from this moment of plantlike union we surrendered to the artifice of our burning fingers, that through our hands' embrace each might draw the other into the greedy receptacle of his own being.

This afternoon I sought refuge from the violence of the midday heat. My bare legs stretched at full length on the floor of an old pavilion in the dense green shade. I gave in to the numbing lure of drowsiness, and with the distorted precision of a hallucination, I relived from the previous day the still vivid imprint of K's caress, an embrace and connection that was purely spiritual—the contact of our hands no more than the inevitable closing of a circuit.

In the same way that it is hard for me to remember your body, I cannot even attempt a faithful description of K's physical form. I know only that your imposing, convex figure is an entity more solid than the very buildings of this monastery, the central pillar of my existence; whereas K's concave figure, an almost defiantly meager presence, seems merely hollow, the negation of a soul possessed of such ill-fated magnetism.

Until now I was the pure and innocent daughter of this kingdom, the mistress of a vast monastery—the great and small halls and the winding galleries that connect them, the scores of temples with their earthen walls, the gates, the storehouse, the grove concealing innumerable springs and streams. Yet had I ever truly seen them before? My walks with K these past few days have shown me this. I am now seeing this temple complex through K's eyes. Emulating K, sharing his sentiments, I am tying myself to this place with bonds of affection, tasting the delight of a pilgrim from a foreign land. Yet this sharing of covert pleasure is very like the uncertain solidarity of traitors.

Despite the cruelty of the afternoon sun, I set out for the spring that lies deep in the grove, to join K in a scheme he shyly proposed several days ago. He was already at the spring, standing like a ghost bathed pale in the fairy-tale light of midday. But the sight of me invariably turns K transparent and makes him drip with sweat. I clasped his hand, a hand like a bunch of red-hot rays (I can find no better words to describe this mundane contact, which is so ruinous for K, so like a secret rite to me), and we undressed in the shade of the moss-covered rocks. Then, urged on by the accord each read in the other's eyes, we set off like brave stallions on our expedition to the cave, an adventure presaged days before. Eagerly tracing the course of the water that bubbled from the spring, we struggled to breathe air heavy with the fragrance of summer grasses, until we found the funnel-shaped depression leading to a subterranean river which we had come upon the other day. Here water from the spring lapped gently against the rocks before being sucked into the bowels of the earth.
Standing at the rim of the funnel, I watched K slide into the passage, leaving an unearthly, startled cry in his wake; then I too slid my naked body into the opening in the rock, colder to the touch than reptilian skin.

The pain of rocks scraping my belly blotted out the fear I felt at crossing this threshold into the unknown. The chill gloom of the nether world hung in the air. We walked along a narrow arcade formed by columns and ledges of rock. The sound of dripping water was everywhere; the subterranean waterway coursed through its channel like a gentle vein, swollen by a host of tributaries. Our excited voices rang out in the dark as we sought to pierce the suffocating gloom; our cries were like the shrieks of bats in flight, rising to a thin pitch of fear and fascination—pathetic screams tearing at the membrane of our souls. Suddenly the cavern was filled with a faint glow. Concealed beneath the high vaulted ceiling, a mosaic of waters in every shade of blue had formed a small, mysterious lake, and a shaft of silver light, seeping through a crevice in the vault, now cleft the surface of the pool. With an inner luminescence, the stunning color of the water seemed to dye even the air of the cavern the same lustrous hue; in chill ecstasy we clasped our arms about our bodies, which had themselves become a plantlike blue. Then, without warning, K dived like a fish into the water and disappeared. The calm was shattered, and the pool, disturbed by K's agitated movements, dissolved into a thousand glittering mineral flakes and scattered its radiance throughout the cavern. I realized that I was biting my lips violently, chilled by the water which sent a shuddering but agreeable sensation through my body. Then K bared his white teeth in a shout and pulled me into the water. His arms sought my body, slippery as a fish, in a fierce, defiant embrace. Obsessively he caressed my hair, which floated like strands of seaweed on the water, but the next moment I was swimming, guided by the light, toward the opening to the world outside.

Our eyes were momentarily blinded by the light, and then we saw an awe-inspiring scene. The water flowed slowly out of the cavern and trickled in a narrow cascade down a perpendicular cliff. From its base stretched a distant world etched in hieroglyphs of rocky precipices and barren valleys, a desolate, bizarre world unmistakably not our own. I stood with my fingers twined in K's, caught in a trance yet wanting only to flee. But K's white body heeded its own impulse and scrambled down like a lizard toward this world of fierce sunlight and stone. It was a forbidden zone to me, and I was left to return despondent, plunging more recklessly than a madman back into the darkness of the cavern and on to the haven of the monastery.

I am ill. But I am confident that by your return this illness will have left me. Ultimately, my steady progress toward recovery will mean a closing of the doors for me, as I resume my life as daughter of this monastery. I cannot bring myself to forsake the inheritance of this kingdom's worldly objects, you among them. There remains only one seed of anxiety—my sorrow in knowing that K, that rootless wanderer, would also confine himself here.

Your carefully announced arrival—though it should have been an eagerly awaited homecoming—seems to have dealt a harsh blow to the sentiments that K has bottled up inside him. The first chivalrous encounter between you and K occurred, according to some exquisite, unconsciously devised scheme, at the middle gate early this morning. No visitors had yet come to the gallery where K and I stood ringing the wooden pillars playfully with our fists. My father had sent you off as his representative, and now you were returning with the fruits of your mission packed in a mundane leather case. Still clad in your dazzling black robes, you approached at a near gallop from the massive main gate, sounding the flagstones on the path as you came. As you neared us K, despite ample foreknowledge of your return, was thrown into a panic at this sudden meeting and dashed his head against the glass wall of formality that stood between you, heedless of the injury he caused himself, and scattering brilliant fragments on the ground. Like a sister trying to gloss over her younger brother's blunder, I reddened in confusion, and as I reached for your heavy case, I tossed a mocking remark in K's direction.

My cruelly lighthearted introduction must have been more painful for K than the most violent condemnation. Let it be so . . . I am satisfied for your sake. You, my betrothed, with your pendulous fleshy earlobes like the stone Buddhas, a priest epitomizing the perfect fusion of transcendence and ego, you who are to succeed my father after our marriage and become abbot of this vast temple complex—throughout my introduction you stood confronting K, that incarnation of irrefutable re-

223

ality, and bit by bit you undermined his already tenuous existence. I too reverted in your presence to an unwarranted condescension toward K, acting as if he were a mere traveler, or an effete and possibly bogus artist. All the while K used this opportunity to take in my hair, my neck, especially my eyes with avid glances; but this you must not mind, for the fruits of his admiration are for you, not I, to savor.

In any event, it is natural that K should feel respect and goodwill toward you, since you are my betrothed. You both are satellites revolving in opposite orbits around the magical power that I am privileged to wield.

K will not leave the temple. Like one seeking a site for some unspeakable crime, he spends day after day probing every inch of this labyrinthine complex, every corner of its rotting buildings, its temples and refectories, the white walls of the bathhouse, the maze of paths and streams in the forest. I am no longer his guide; K's remoteness precludes the resumption of those summer walks which so resembled pilgrimages, but this stems no doubt from the good-natured jealousy he feels toward you. K seems bent on spiriting away this enormous kingdom piece by piece, absorbing its three dimensions—nature, human artifice, and power combined—through his wide-open eyes. He has even decided not to return to his research position in the autumn. So now he is nothing. I cannot explain from what world K came to intrude on ours, or imagine what will become of this oddly childlike trespasser. . . That is something only you can know, because you are a peerless gentle seer, who understands the web of karmic relations.

As the summer wanes, tilting its chalice of light with increasing swiftness, K's presence here has dwindled into insignificance as we sit behind our walls of calm conventionality; but I wonder if it isn't nurturing some dangerous cancer all the same. Precisely because I want more than anything to abandon resistance to that destiny he has set in motion here, I fear that it will continue slowly to decay, poisoned by the curse it bears within itself, until it ends in catastrophe.

I am dazzled by the sovereignty over you and K that my sex bestows on me. When the two of you have placed me at the heart of a conversation, addressing each other in silver tones while your eyes duel venomously, I conduct the swelling strains of the dialogue with a counterpoint of queenly majesty and innocent coquetry. Then why do you still refuse to acknowledge the iridescent, unplumbed bond of sympathy that has begun to grow between myself and K?

You know, you should kiss me in front of K. He wants to see it, too.

The days, each indistinguishable from the next, consume the autumn sunlight. An interminable drought has dried up almost all the springs on the temple lands; only the underground river that K and I explored that summer day supplies the secret cavern with a shallow flow of water. The sun adheres to its daily round, leaving a masterpiece behind—an arc of melancholy yellow that makes the cluster of wooden halls and the shroud of dust raised by visitors shine like gold in the autumn sky.

K has left the temple—for the time being; which is to say that he and I have a tacit understanding that his absence will last only as long as it takes us to contrive some mutually desirable scheme. He will definitely return, summoned by the mesmerizing bell on the big clock, like a traveler plunging into the snare that destiny has set for him.

As autumn enters its swift, inevitable decline, I cannot check my own descent, each day a little deeper, into a singular anguish. K's absence has become too painful, like a gaping hollow inside me. You must surely have noticed: when I look into the mirror I am startled by the morbid gray circles beneath my eyes.

In consultation with Father, you have advanced our wedding date by five months, presumably so that this change of plans and the busy days before the ceremony should redeem me.

This entire monastery is run as a single administrative unit, and it is you who are to head it next. And I am to be your wife. You will never fully possess me, though; at most you will have only that half of me which has already hardened. The vessel you know as me—unfailingly cheerful but visibly transparent—contains absolutely nothing, as befits a vessel of misery. For the present it is imperative that I have your practical concern, your affection (though no one knows better than I that you love me), and your constant touch.

K will miss the wedding. . . I set out today for the sacrifice like a maiden sent to consort with the statues that have stood in that great hall, absorbing the debris of time, for a thousand years. That was the pact we made for the sake of this great monastery.

Matrimony and its attendant rites of the flesh have worked no change in me. The void inside me is too immense, a void that cries out for another, false partner, the husband of my fantasies.

Then today K returned, coated in fatigue, to complete that obscure circuit. It must be passion that has caught him in its net. If you would give your blessing, the three of us could share a love so abundant that none need ever go hungry; yet K does not want that.

I am at a loss how to receive this bridegroom in funeral dress.

K told me this: that both he and the light of the spell that controls his fate dwell in my eyes.

You and K toss the concept of death back and forth between yourselves like a bouncing ball in a child's game. This constant dialogue on death—of course it is death by one's own hand that is at issue—is harmless and even wholesome for you, but it is mortal sport for K. Each time you toss him that smooth ball, K's whole body is stabbed by deadly thorns invisible yet as painful as if he had embraced a cactus. Again today, in the face of your eloquent refutation he pursued this passionate debate on death. I shudder with a sweet anxiety.

Still halfheartedly stirring the embers of yesterday's strange discussion on the aesthetic suicide, you and K were busy sorting through the storehouse collection of old scrolls and rare *gigaku* masks, urns fashioned as dragon heads, and swords. Shoulder to shoulder you toiled like the most amicable of twins. Recklessly I put on one of the large demon masks and wedged myself between the two of you, digging my hands into the dust. My hand brushed a sensitive fork of flesh, but whose fingers they were I couldn't tell. . . At this point K grasped the plain blade of a sacred sword. Turning to you with savage, icy composure, he made a request you could not deny him: that he be allowed to borrow this sword to protect himself on his journey.

You know, don't you, that I do not want to set K free. The cool, damp caverns of K's existence are now one more force protecting the equilibrium necessary to keep me bound to you. As if draining a cup, I have swallowed the absurd fantasy that K is my younger brother, or that I will marry him off to a friend in order to keep him close to me.

You will be tolerant, I know, and permit me these foolish dreams. And yet you scrutinize me with your contemptuous eyes, deliberately silent about my feelings for him, as if you wanted to underscore his existence and suffocate me by assiduously avoiding sarcasm.

You were instructed by my father today to take part in the secret rite of penance for the sins of the world. On this occasion, as on every other, K occupied a symmetrical position, with me as your axis (I inevitably pretend not to see your well-suppressed indignation at the impropriety of this, but would you yourself prefer that he be allowed between us?); and with only a hint of irony he presented his congratulations as though he were a perfect stranger. You returned his salutations with an air of polished cordiality: the perfect priest personifying the world and its canon of conduct. Forced into the armor of this deceitful goodwill, K treats you with brutal respect. If I radiated an almost hostile cynicism then, it was not directed at you. You have every right to display those civil, antagonistic teeth in your smiling face.

I finally passed sentence on K; with only some faint justification, I condemned him to desist indefinitely from any visit when he might possibly run into us. . . Raising his exhausted, yellow face, K listened to my decision, shreds of despair still lodged between his teeth. Then he lashed out at me, brutally, incoherently, arming himself with all the polished craft and cunning of his crime. Volleying word after word of stinging praise, he reiterated his unshaken admiration for your genius for theater and my acting skills. While this bitter barrage flew from his tongue, I threw back my head, swallowing like a lethal dose of some powerful drug his claim that you and I are in league against him.

K is still away today.
You are performing the rite of repentance. I cannot see you, either.

There was still snow on the ground at noon, but I was bathed in an unseasonably abundant February sunlight when I went to the refectory to observe your ritual meal. Milk-white light streamed over the seats of the eleven ascetics, and strict silence reigned from the ringing of the bell, when a white-robed monk began to serve the simple fare, to the blessing that signaled the end of the meal. With your glasses you stood out as the freshest, handsomest figure among those men assembled in prayer, but the tiny glint they gave off alarmed me, for it was then that I caught sight of K, standing motionless outside the hall.

From dusk onward, an incredible number of spectators and groups of foreigners began swarming about the Kannon Hall. I stood below in the tall forest of pillars supporting the veranda, in a spot where my hair and eyes risked being scorched by flying sparks, and awaited the beginning of the fire ceremony. As if in keeping with this esoteric drama, which has been repeated for a thousand years, heavy, gentle snowflakes began to fall. At the same moment, the ascetics gave an unearthly cry— reverberating from antiquity down through the ages—though in their midst one could detect the boyish timidity of the younger monks. Then they thundered wildly up the steps and into the hall. On their shoulders they bore great torches of fiercely burning cedar. The eleven torches, thrust one after another beyond the railing, blazed in cones of fire and light, swirling above my head in a dance of savage, frenzied spirits. The dance described an unfinished ring of fire, scorching the dark sky. I opened my mouth and disgorged all self-awareness so that I could drink in the sparks that rained around me. It happened then: a hand like an electrically charged hook seized my neck from behind—and instantly, in a jumble of recognition, I knew it to be K. Turning, I pressed my lips against his, lips salty as a bewitching wound glistening with blood; but still the violent shower of snow and fire cooled my face and singed my hair as if to prevent the breach before betrothal, the estrangement before union of these two insubstantial souls. I had not seen K's face, for my breasts had ripened amorously in a sudden rising of sap, and our exchange of poisonous fluids had drowned me in an intense, almost mortal pleasure. This, the entire beginning, was the end.

You see it all now, don't you: the kiss K and I shared last night, the fine tapestry of saliva lingering on my lips, the mysterious bond that brings two people's lips together. With mouth agape I await the final act.

When the black hand of night had come to rest over the monastery and gray mist began to rise from the springs and river, a messenger from K suddenly appeared. He was a novice from Temple H, and he handed you K's note. You eyed me gravely, arresting the cry on my lips and the flood in my eyes with your almost comical self-possession, that icy composure of yours. The message it bore . . . I knew was word of his fatal departure. But you cold-bloodedly tore it up, instructing me in a voice more ponderous than the tolling of a bell to bring the short sword to the messenger. Those words sent the battlements around me crashing to the ground, yet you turned to the novice with a ruthless smile—still innocent, it seemed—and asked him to convey your wishes for the safety of K's journey. The ancient sword vibrated in my palm with a metallic sound—three lines, perhaps, of delicate musical notation. My teeth chattered like dozens of rattling stones, so loud you turned in disbelief. With a cruel effort, I clenched my trembling teeth and mutely handed the novice the murder weapon, in obedience to your calm behest.

You took it all in, didn't you—my face swollen to bursting point with its burden of tears and choked sobs, my eyes sunk deep in sharply creviced flesh. . . I turned my face abruptly away, so violently it almost broke my neck. A low moan escaped my clenched jaws like a drop of despair, a single, concentrated bead of emotion, and I fled the room. In the bedroom, imprisoned by modern walls and oppressive curtains, I flung myself onto the bed, bent over double—I did not weep, for what solace could gentle tears of self-pity bring my charred spirit?—but my body stiffened unawares, deadened by the curse that had already begun to envelop K. Time made its faint footsteps echo inside my sensitized skull, pacing threateningly back and forth, and drew me little by little into abstract numbness.

In a shuddering trance I dreamed of K ripping himself open with a blade of transparent ice. Offering me his lips, where the traces of that blasphemous kiss still lingered, K mutilated his own white flesh, severing that consciousness which burned like blood in a rose-colored blaze. . . Suddenly I heard a long drawn-out cry, followed by the sad tremolo of a soul plummeting from this world.

Soon the abbot of Temple H, drawn to the discovery of K's act by that intolerable cry echoing around the globe, came with his face distorted by shock to tell you of the tragedy. Without a sound I paled and collapsed before you, yet I managed a faint satisfied smile at this blow which seemed a vengeance on you.

Rushing to Temple H, we found K lying senseless in a pool of blood. No hand could save him now. His ashen face was masked in this atrocious, pagan death. Beneath the burden of dense nothingness his dying spirit sought its final release, spewing in a cone of red mist through the hole gouged in his throat, whistling like the strains of a flute more plaintive than the sorrowful ocarina.

Suddenly a voice rising in prayer froze me to the spot. It was you; you stood motionless, a statue of hardened, bitter salt, chanting a spirited sutra in your sonorous voice.

Funeral arrangements were summarily completed; the ceremony was little more than a purging of the violent death of a sinful outsider. While the corpse was being washed according to Father's instructions, I too was washed in salty, bitter tears. The innumerable wounds held for me an attraction even greater than the flesh surrounding them, and I covered the white corpse with imaginary kisses. The pallbearers passed through woods frozen the color of white bones and out through the rear gate, drawing away into the distance unaccompanied by even an attendant monk or relative. Behind the slow procession of gravediggers and professional mourners trailing their attenuated shadows, the last spasmodic throes of the sun dyed the evening haze blood red, and presently the procession was engulfed like the intermittent line of a river on the distant, undulating horizon of dust-colored sand and stones.

UNDER THE SHADOW
OF MT. BANDAI

Inoue Yasushi
Translated by Stephen W. Kohl

Inoue Yasushi is one of the established deans of modern Japanese literature, a "dean" being defined as the owner of a house around which Japanese newspaper reporters gather like vultures once every year before the Nobel Prize for Literature is announced in Sweden. Inoue certainly can boast of one of the most enduring and successful careers in modern letters in Japan, and the variety of his work has earned him many devout supporters in his country's literary circles. He chaired the international meeting of the P.E.N. Club in Tokyo in May 1984, and was elected an international vice-president of that organization.

Inoue was born in Asahikawa on the island of Hokkaido in 1907. His father was an army surgeon, and the frequent transfers that his parents endured contributed to their decision to send him off to live with his grandmother, an experience that finds literary expression in scores of his isolated heroes. Although Inoue had difficulty dedicating himself to his studies as a youth, the single-minded devotion he displayed for physical and spiritual discipline in pursuits such as Judo was later mirrored in his near-scholarly passion for literature. Inoue kept himself aloof from the many philosophical disputes of the 1930s; aesthetics was his main interest when he enrolled at Kyoto University. After graduation in 1936, Inoue joined the staff of reporters on the Mainichi. He was drafted a year later, but illness forced him to leave his army division in North China after only a few months. When he returned to the Mainichi, Inoue was assigned to cover religious and artistic news, a task that gave him the opportunity to deepen his knowledge of Buddhism and the classical arts, two realms that play a central role in his fictional writings.

By 1947, Inoue had attracted attention not only as a poet, but as the author of two exquisitely poetic short stories, "Tōgyū" (Bullfight) and "Ryōjū" (The Hunting Gun, tr. 1961); the former was awarded the Akutagawa Prize for literature. Within three years, Inoue had resigned from the newspaper and was devoting all his time to his creative endeavors. His journalistic eye for detail and sense of audience enabled him to produce a string of popular novels, but Inoue did not find his niche until he began publishing historical works, many of them set in China. A succession of novels such as Tempyō no iraka (The Roof Tile of Tempyō, 1957; tr. 1975) and Tonkō (Tun-huang, 1959; tr. 1978) set the tone for Inoue's literature—the examination of the faintest ripples of cultural interchange between Japan and the outside world, ripples often created by lonely individuals who remain essentially nameless and faceless in the annals of official history. Most recently Inoue has returned to that examination of cultural interplay in Wadatsumi (God of the Sea, 1977), a detailed study of Japanese emigration to the United States. In 1981 he published Honkakubō ibun (Papers Left by the Priest Honkaku), a sensitive, ghostly account of the death of the medieval tea master, Sen no Rikyū. "Kobandai" (1961), translated here, is one of the most prominent of many Inoue stories combining meticulous historical research, a restrained, scholarly style, and an empathy with the muted details of human tragedy which are often lost amidst the larger calamities of nature.

*   *   *

In those days the road from Kitakata to Hibara was a journey of some fifteen miles. By leaving Kitakata around eight o'clock in the morning and proceeding at a leisurely pace, one could be in Hibara by two or three in the afternoon. On the way, however, one crossed the Ōshio Pass just beyond Ōshio village. For some distance on both sides of the summit there was a difficult stretch that wound its way through sharp outcroppings of rock. Yet teamsters with pack animals passed this way in both directions virtually every day, and for these sturdy working men the trip was no hardship. The road, called the Yonezawa Highway, went from Wakamatsu through Kitakata and Hibara and on to Yonezawa. Now that the railroad has gone through, the highway has been largely abandoned. But in the last years of the nineteenth century, in fact, on July 13, 1888, when I set out from Kitakata to make the journey over the mountains, the road was rather crowded. Horses and travelers were frequent because of the many sawmills around Hibara which cut wood that was then hauled to Wakamatsu for use in the lacquer trade. The number of freight wagons carrying logs for that purpose alone was increasing daily, it seemed to me.

Though traveling on official business, we were not in a hurry, and from the very outset our excursion had a festive, holiday air about it. At the time I was working as a tax collector. Of course everyone supposes a tax collector is someone who goes around extorting money from poor people, but that was not really the case. Today we would call someone with my job a tax assessor or a surveyor of crop production.

Ours was the county office responsible for collecting taxes, and every year we were required to survey the amount of land under cultivation by the villages within our jurisdiction and to assess taxes on any land that had been cultivated since the previous year. Making that assessment was my job . . . but perhaps first I should explain that the town called Kitakata did not yet really exist. Instead, there were only the villages of Odatsuki and Koarai, which were separated by the Tazuki River; I worked for the county office located in Odatsuki. Back then the work we did was called "land production surveying." On the trip I am describing, our purpose was to survey the north flank of Mt. Bandai, which fell within the administrative district of Hibara village. My job was to survey the land that was being farmed by the many tiny villages scattered about the region popularly known as the "back side" of Mt. Bandai.

I was accompanied on the journey by two assistants, Tomekichi and Kinji. Tomekichi was of an age where his hair was beginning to be flecked with white. He was in his late forties, thin, and very serious. He walked with his kimono tucked up behind to allow greater freedom of movement. His spindly legs gave the impression that he was a pretty weak traveler, but in reality none of the rest of us could match him when it came to trekking through this wild north country. Kinji was a reticent young man of thirty who tended to be rather gloomy. He also wore his kimono tucked up and straw sandals on his feet. I was the only one of the group dressed anything like a modern tax assessor. I had dark blue work pants and a windbreaker, but like the others I wore straw sandals and had an extra pair tied to my belt.

Although I was the leader of the group, at age twenty-eight I was also the youngest. From the time I was twenty I had worked as a customs inspector for foreigners in Yokohama, so I had some knowledge and experience in the work of assessment; which is probably why, even at my age, I had become a person of authority in this rural county office. Tomekichi was not a professional assessor; he had originally come to the county office as a part-time employee, but over the years he had helped with the business of assessment and eventually joined the staff of the assessor's office. I believe he felt quite satisfied with the position he occupied. Kinji was a clerk who had only recently been employed in the Kitakata office. His handwriting was very neat and clear.

Our trips were usually scheduled to last ten days and we always made certain we had plenty of spare time. On our first day we planned to follow the familiar route from Kitakata to Hibara, and since it would hardly impress the villagers if we arrived in Hibara too early in the day and just lazed around, we made a point of loitering at tea shops along the road, and even paused for a nap under the shade of the trees once we reached the pass. Our clerk Kinji, who had only been married for about a month, dozed every time we stopped to rest, and was teased endlessly by Tomekichi.

The weather grew very warm and sweat bathed our bodies the moment we started walking, but whenever we paused to rest, the dry wind on our skin felt refreshingly cool. This was indeed the best time of the year to be traveling in this part of the country. The rainy season had been late and it was early July before we had any days that were completely cloudless. The weather was quite unusual that year and some people were concerned about the effect this would have on the crops. Since the weather had only just cleared, we had been accustomed to seeing a dull, overcast sky for days on end. But now the vital, green vegetation covering the mountains, the clean air that settled the dust, and the cloudless, deep, translucent blue sky all greeted us as we set out on our trip. We looked forward eagerly to days of pleasant traveling.

On that first day we finally arrived in Hibara around four o'clock. On the way, there was an incident so trivial it is probably not worth mentioning, except that I had reason to remember it afterward. We were walking along the bank of the Hibara River after coming down from Ōshio Pass when we met a woman going in the opposite direction, a woman dressed as a pilgrim making the rounds of the Sixty-six Holy Sites. For a moment she stood in silence blocking our way, until we saw that she appeared to be trying to say something. We clustered around, peering intently at her face and trying to catch her murmured words. She was muttering some sort of warning to us, saying "Go back. Go back. You will be in danger if you go any further." The woman appeared to be about forty and was dressed in the gray clothing typical of a pilgrim. A gray knapsack was on her back and she wore leggings and mittens to match. In one hand she carried a small bell. Her complexion was dark and made even darker by the liver spots of advancing age. She seemed to be a strong-willed and ill-tempered woman. She gazed steadily at us when she spoke, and I noticed that her eyes glittered with an unnatural brightness. She was no ordinary person.

Kinji and I both pushed past the woman, ignoring her words, but when Tomekichi tried to follow, she moved left or right several times, blocking his way, until finally he had no choice but to shove her aside. Having done that, he hurried to catch up with Kinji and myself, muttering, "Crazy woman! How unpleasant!" Nevertheless, Tomekichi seemed to have been disturbed by what the woman said, for as we walked along he turned back two or three times to look in her direction, and seeing that she was still watching us, he murmured something about this encounter being a very unlucky sign.

So, this was one of our experiences, but we were on the first day of our trip and were relieved at not having to face the drudgery of our usual office duties, and our spirits remained high. Later that day we felt several mild earthquake tremors. Once a jolt came just as we were crossing a bridge. It was not a suspension bridge, but the support beams began to creak, and we could see cracks appearing where the boards joined together. "It's an earthquake," said Tomekichi, and even before he spoke,

I knew it was a strong one. Over the course of the previous month we had become quite familiar with earthquakes. Even in the region around Kitakata it was common to have two or three tremors a day that were sharp enough for a person to feel, so we had grown used to them and saw no cause for alarm.

Thinking about it later, it occurred to me that the warning the mad pilgrim woman had given us should not have been laughed off. Indeed, if we had listened to her and turned back at that point, most likely we would each be leading our appointed lives without ever having experienced the tragedy and sadness that soon befell us. When you come right down to it, man's intellect is a pretty shallow thing, and we never know what the future holds. So, as it turned out, we continued on our way, taking ourselves step by step unwittingly toward the gates of Hell.

Hibara, as I said earlier, was a village of some fifty houses located along the Yonezawa Highway. In earlier times it had been called Hinoki Yachi. The village was surrounded by groves of cypress called *hinoki*, so the original name of the place meant "valley choked with *hinoki*." The village lay in the shadow of Mt. Bandai, to the west of Mt. Azuma, and on the flank of Mt. Takasone. It was surrounded by mountains, and not only was there very little level ground in the region, hardly any of what was level had been brought under cultivation. In that sense, it was not a productive area. The people of the villages there preferred to make their living cutting wood or stripping bark for use in making paper, or by driving their packhorses over the mountains.

There were three inns in the village. Were one to continue along the road from Kitakata directly northeast and cross the pass at the county border, in another seven miles one would reach the village of Tsunagi; and from there it was another seven miles or more to Yonezawa. Hibara was indeed a tiny mountain settlement, but it was situated on a corridor used, much more then than at present, to spread the new Meiji enlightenment, and just four or five years earlier a troupe of Sumo wrestlers had passed through this region on their way to Yonezawa and Yamagata. We were guided by the village headman to the entry hall of an inn where we removed our traveling sandals. I noticed the inn sported an enormous sign announcing that it was here that the Sumo tour had stayed. Apparently the sign had been made soon after the wrestlers' visit.

It was our plan on the following morning to leave the Yonezawa Highway on which Hibara was located. We were to turn due south and follow the Nagase River through the forests that covered the lower slopes of Mt. Bandai. About four miles from Hibara was a hamlet of seven houses called Hosono, and a couple of miles further on was the village of Ōsawa, consisting of some twenty houses. At Ōsawa one stood directly beneath Bandai. It was only a couple of miles from Ōsawa to the hot spring resorts of Nakanoyu and Kaminoyu, located midway up the slope of Mt. Bandai; the road went straight up the side of the mountain. Several miles from Ōsawa toward the northeast flank of Bandai stood the village of Akimoto, which was composed of twelve households.

Our job on this trip was to survey these three villages—Hosono, Ōsawa, and Akimoto. We had postponed our survey in Hibara, thinking that since there was a village headman living there, we could conduct it any time. We decided to survey the three small villages buried deep in the mountain forests during the brief period between the end of the rainy season and the onset of really hot weather in midsummer.

That night, by previous arrangement, we had a meeting at our Hibara inn with the people from the village headman's office. We received support for our plan from the three members of the headman's staff, namely, Shuntarō, Kume, and Shinshū. Shinshū, of course, is an odd name, but everyone kept calling him "Shinshū, Shinshū," and soon I was following their example. Both Shuntarō and Kume were men in their sixties. Shuntarō was a rather reserved, aristocratic man, with large ears and a cheerful expression. Kume was quite the opposite, being somewhat impulsive and loud by nature. He had sunken eyes and prominent cheekbones. Shinshū was a small, intelligent man who managed all the details of the office work with a voluble tongue and vivid gestures. It was difficult to judge his age from his features; he might have been in his thirties or forties.

These three men were eager to have the land survey carried out and agreed to accompany us to the actual survey sites. Barely twenty years had passed since the Meiji Restoration and many local citizens thought we were trying to cheat them when we described the system of levying land taxes. And so we had to marshal a force of workers at least this large to persuade a mere forty households to consent to the annual survey.

Early the following morning, July 14, the six of us were ready to depart. The three local men, Shuntarō, Kume, and Shinshū, had the skirts of their kimonos tucked up like Tomekichi and Kinji. We all wore leggings and straw sandals and used towels to protect our faces from the sun. Just as we had all assembled in the earthen-floored hallway of the inn to set out on our journey, we felt the first earthquake of the day. This was the most severe of the many tremors we had experienced recently, and all of our group as well as the maids at the inn quickly spilled out into the road.

As we were leaving the village, we came to a bridge and from there proceeded along the left bank of the Nagase. Here the road curved gently in a southerly direction and passed through an open area of stony ground. No sooner had we come to that rocky place than we felt another tremor. This one was milder than before and we supposed it was merely an aftershock of the previous jolt. None of our party made any comment, but it did give us reason to pause. I noticed that the ground was littered with small stones and the morning sunlight touched these stones, glinting off the blades of grass that grew between them. Even though it was still early, the sunlight sent up shimmering heat waves which promised a hot day ahead. To be watching something as insubstantial as this haze of heat and at the same moment to feel the ground begin to tremble filled me with uneasiness, as though even the earth itself were not to be relied upon. But the tremor passed in an instant, like the shadow of a bird sweeping over the ground, and though an ominous feeling flickered through my mind, as soon as the trembling stopped I forgot all about it.

After leaving the flat land along the river we found ourselves confronted by the three massive peaks of Daibandai, Kobandai, and Akahani. Gazing at these lofty summits, we were deeply impressed by their grandeur. I had often heard people speak of the beauty of this region in the shadow of Mt. Bandai, and I now realized that it was in fact more magnificient than I had been told. From the lower slopes of the great mountain down to the river plain stretched large natural forests of cypress, oak, zelkova, and maple, which gave a dark, almost gloomy aspect to the landscape. The slopes of Bandai itself were covered with stands of red pine, white birch, and other sorts of trees. From where we stood on the riverbank the whole view was one vast wooded panorama. It was hard to believe that the three villages we planned to visit were somewhere out there beneath that sea of living trees. Indeed, it was a bit frightening to think that people spent their whole lives beneath the canopy of that seemingly endless forest.

Just before reaching Hosono, the road forked. One branch went along the lower slopes of Mt. Naka Azuma, and the other, the road we would follow, led in the direction of Mt. Bandai. We took the fork to the right and soon came to a long, log bridge that crossed over to the right bank of the Nagase River.

As we passed over the bridge, the clerk, Shinshū, noticed a swarm of toads moving beside the river.

"Look at all the toads down there among the stones. They must be migrating.", Shinshū's comment prompted the rest of us to notice that what appeared to be stones beside the river was in fact a vast army of toads on the move. They followed one leap with another without a moment's pause, and since the ones behind kept surging forward, those in front had no choice but to keep moving. There was an odd single-mindedness in this moving, living mass. I had the feeling they were all intent on a single goal, allowing nothing to divert their attention.

We all commented on this remarkable sight and stood for a time entranced by it. Shinshū said that in the spring when the snow begins to melt he had seen groups of toads mating, but this was the first time he had ever seen so many of them migrating. Kume replied that once, about ten years ago, he had seen toads fighting in this area. Apparently one group had a dispute with another group from further up the river, and they had waged a toad battle to settle the issue by force. He was sure that was what these were up to as well.

"Come on! Let's get going. We'll never get our survey done if we just stand here," said Tomekichi. At this the rest of us turned away from the toads and continued on our way.

Around ten o'clock we reached the village of Hosono. I call it a village though it consisted of no more than seven households. They were nice, sturdy houses clustered together on a narrow piece of land closed in on the east and west by the peaks of Hachimori and Tsurugigamine. The encroaching hills seemed to crowd into the village on both sides. This was truly a mountain hamlet. The main work of the men there was logging, and each of the houses had a small shed attached which looked something like a chicken coop. Here the family kept a wood lathe or two. The farming was left to the women, and when we arrived at the village there was no sign of them because they were all out in the fields.

Tomekichi was taken by one of the villagers to the mountains behind the settlement so that he could get a view of the layout of the fields, while the rest of us passed the time in desultory conversation with an old man who had once been a logger. There was another small tremor during our talk.

While waiting for Tomekichi to return, we met some of the men of the village and made preliminary arrangements for the survey we would be conducting during the next few days. Having accomplished that much, we left Hosono and headed on. Beyond the village the land suddenly opened out into low, rolling hills. A broad plain spread east and west, and standing in the middle of it we had an unobstructed view of Mt. Bandai.

After leaving Hosono our route turned away from the river we had been following for so long. Ōsawa was a couple of miles further along this road, which ran through virgin forests. Actually the path was so narrow it could hardly be called a road. We passed places called Kiyomogihara and Ōfuchi, but they were merely names, for we did not see a single dwelling. At Kiyomogihara we met a group of people, including some women, who were coming down from one of the hot spring resorts on Mt. Bandai. The group consisted of a man and his wife who were in their fifties, their youngest son who was fifteen or sixteen, the wife's younger sister who was in her thirties, and two young men from the village of Shiobara near Hibara who were serving as guides to the group.

The man was a merchant from the Niigata region who had gone to the resort of Nakanoyu for a month's treatment, but they had cut short their visit by a full week and were now hurrying down the mountain, having formed the uneasy impression that the mountains were somehow different from usual.

The husband had the sallow complexion one associates with the chronically ill and he remained silent in a sullen, bad humor. The woman's face was tight with emotional strain of the sort seen in hysterical people, and she rattled on like a person unable to stop talking. According to her story, four or five days earlier they had been surprised to find that the amount of hot mineral water flowing down from Kaminoyu had dropped off significantly. Also, the quantity of steam that issued from among the rocks had inexplicably increased in both volume and pressure. Although Nakanoyu still had plenty of water for the baths, in the past couple of days it had become so hot no one could bathe in it. In addition, the mountain had been rumbling for the past four or five days and the rumbling had grown more ominous each day. This morning the sound was so fierce it seemed the mountain itself might burst. Then, of course, there had been the tremors. The woman said they made a habit of coming to this resort every year, but this was the first time anything strange had occurred, and they thought something alarming was going to happen.

In concluding their story the wife said, "There are many other people besides ourselves who are frightened and leaving the mountain. And now we meet a group like yourselves going in the opposite direction. I suppose it takes all kinds." She estimated that there were still some thirty guests at the Kaminoyu hot spring and about twenty each at Nakanoyu and Shimonoyu.

One of the young guides from Shiobara said that for the past ten years people had often predicted that Mt. Bandai was about to blow its top, but it never had. Still, given the recent events, he thought it might blow this year after all. Last night there had been a light sprinkling of rain on the mountain, but today on the way down he had noticed that the small lake at Numanotaira had completely dried up. His view was that this sort of thing could be a frightening sign if one chose to interpret it that way, and yet it might not mean anything at all. On Mt. Bandai he felt that such signs were cause for alarm. The young man explained all this to us falteringly in the local dialect. Judging from what he said, he might have had reason to be worried, and then again, maybe not. But his fear was evident in the inconclusive way he spoke. He finished by saying, "What can one do, anyway?" Motioning for the rest of the group to follow, he led them quickly down the mountain. The young man had used the odd phrase, "blow its top," suggesting that it might erupt, but in the local dialect this literally meant that the whole top of the mountain would blow off.

We were a bit disturbed by these stories from the family from Niigata, but we did not feel all that uneasy about getting any closer to the mountain they were fleeing. After parting with the merchant and his family, the normally reserved Shuntarō said, "In all my life I have never seen so many snakes as we've seen today. I, too, believe something odd is going on." I had also noticed the snakes, but since this was my first trip to the area, I thought perhaps this was just a place where they were unusually common. After leaving Hosono we saw any number of them crossing the road with their heads raised. Every time we stopped to rest and looked around before sitting down, we saw something long and thin slither off silently into the bushes. The fact that Shuntarō, a local resident and a man not much given to expressing his opinions, commented on the matter seemed to be all the more significant. Then, in response, Kume tilted his head to one side and said, "I haven't been aware of the snakes particularly, but I have noticed that the doves and pheasants seem upset. I've hunted for years, but I've never seen birds as worked up as this." Kinji, who had hardly said a word all day, had a frightened look on his face, and in ominous tones said, "Yesterday, we met that pilgrim just below the pass. Do you remember what she said?" He turned to Kume as he spoke.

At the same moment, from the other side Tomekichi said, "Kinji!" ordering him to be quiet in a surprisingly harsh tone of voice. "Don't talk about that rubbish!" This outburst was strange coming from the usually taciturn Tomekichi.

Shinshū was the only one in the group who appeared to be totally unaffected by the atmosphere of tension that had developed. "Sometimes the mountains rumble and the snakes and birds move about. What's wrong with that? If you start letting yourself get excited about every little thing you'll have another stroke, Shuntarō. And you, Kume, to hear you talk, one would think you're getting senile as well as bald." He made a joke of the situation, but what he said had been instructive as well. I realized for the first time that Shuntarō's usually phlegmatic attitude toward things was due to the fact that he had once had a stroke. As for

Kume, I had thought he kept his head shaved, but after Shinshū commented on his baldness, I noticed that in fact he had small wisps of hair growing here and there on his head.

It was one o'clock when we arrived in Ōsawa. The village was composed of several parts with names such as Oshisawa, Osusawa, and so on, and there was no way of knowing for sure which was the original name. Various people had from time to time made different entries in the county register, calling the place by different names. I suppose it didn't much matter what its real name was, since everyone within the boundaries of the forest, whether they lived in the village itself or elsewhere, referred to it simply as Ōsawa. There were twenty houses and some two hundred people living there. They had a splendid view of Mt. Bandai from dawn to dusk.

We asked the people there to provide us with lodging for the night, and then, since the sun was still high in the sky, we set out for Akimoto, which was a couple of miles further on to the northeast. We had planned to begin our survey there the following morning, so we wanted to have a look at the site today and talk a bit with its inhabitants. Just beyond Ōsawa the Nagase River turned sharply east, making a wide sweep around the base of Mt. Bandai. As everyone knows, this is the river that flows into Lake Inawashiro on the front side of Mt. Bandai. In the area where we found ourselves, the river was flanked on both sides by broad, flat plains. After leaving Ōsawa we followed a road upstream along the river. About a mile from the village we came to the spot where the Ono joined the Nagase. From that point onward, the Nagase became a wide stretch of water. Another mile further on was the confluence of the Ogura. Akimoto consisted of a dozen houses located several hundred yards from where the two rivers ran together.

The lower slopes of Mt. Bandai between Ōsawa and Akimoto were carpeted with thick forests broken occasionally by high meadows and rolling hills. A clump of white birch crowned one hill, and here and there were broad open spaces overgrown with dwarf bamboo and reeds taller than a man. These open, brushy spaces created striped patterns across the flank of the mountain.

As we traveled from Hosono to Ōsawa, the peak known as Kobandai was directly in front of us, while on the right and left were Akahani and Daibandai. These three together formed the massif known collectively as Mt. Bandai. The peaks had towered before us for a long while, but when we reached the village of Akimoto, the view of Mt. Bandai had assumed a new aspect. Up until then Kushigamine, which was actually some distance to the left, seemed quite close to the three peaks of Bandai and appeared to be a fourth in the group, but from Akimoto we could see that there was a considerable distance separating them, and that Bandai was a different mountain entirely. It was, at any rate, a beautiful view.

At Akimoto we were served tea at one of the farmhouses, and while enjoying this new view of Mt. Bandai we made arrangements with the local people to begin our survey the following morning. As we sat together on the long veranda of the house discussing these matters, we felt the jolt of yet another earthquake. The old farmer who owned the house thought it was perfectly natural that the people of Ōsawa were upset by so many earthquakes. He suggested that we would be safer if we finished our work in Ōsawa as quickly as possible and came here to his village.

It was from this farmer that we learned for the first time that the wells of Ōsawa had gone dry and that the tremors had been especially sharp there, with the rumbling of the mountain reaching unusual proportions. The people of Ōsawa had been living in constant fear, and had not been able to work in their fields for the past ten days, wondering among themselves whether they should evacuate their homes or not.

Akimoto and Ōsawa were both in the shadow of Mt. Bandai, but there were several long swales running north of the mountain in such a way that they set Ōsawa apart. It was a common belief that whenever anything strange happened on the mountain, Ōsawa alone felt the effect of it. The people of Akimoto were quite unconcerned, treating Ōsawa's misfortunes as though they were standing on one bank of a river watching a city burn on the opposite shore.

When we heard all this, we did not feel much like spending the night at Ōsawa, and wondered how the people there must feel at having to provide hospitality for us while they themselves were frightened for their lives. Still, we had already asked them to arrange lodging for us for that night, and the following day we would be free to make other plans, so with this in mind we decided to return.

On reaching the place where the Nagase and Ono rivers met, we came across a young man and woman dressed much more fashionably than other people in the region. Even seeing them from afar we could not imagine they were locals, and since we were walking at a faster pace we soon overtook the pair. They were probably in their early twenties and everything about them suggested the sophistication of city-dwellers. At first glance the man appeared to be a student of some sort; he was wearing casual Western clothing and carrying a Western-style umbrella. The woman had a pale complexion and a round, feminine face. Her head was covered by a shawl, and judging from her hairstyle and elegant, striped kimono we could only suppose that she came from a fashionable Tokyo neighborhood.

When I asked the pair where they were heading, the man mentioned the Kaminoyu hot spring, but the only luggage they had was a single cloth-wrapped bundle which the woman carried. Although they were obviously travelers, it seemed unlikely that they were typical guests at a local spa. Shinshū asked when they expected to reach Kaminoyu, yet neither of them could reply. In fact, they did not know where exactly Kaminoyu was, or which road to take, or how far it would be; they seemed to be just strolling casually about the fields and meadows on the lower slopes of Mt. Bandai.

I all but insisted that they spend the night with us at Ōsawa. Under the circumstances it appeared to be the only solution, since they seemed almost in a daze. The woman hesitated and looked as if she wanted the man to refuse, but he seemed rather weak-willed and finally, as though making a concession to me, he agreed to go with us.

The young couple were considerably slower than we were, so I paused from time to time to let them catch up. As I waited I had occasion to inspect the woman. She was extraordinarily attractive. Though she was not strikingly beautiful in the traditional sense, there was a purity and innocence in her face, in the way she walked and in the smallest movement she made, that impressed me more deeply than any other woman I had seen.

Eventually we made our way back to Ōsawa along with our two new companions, and Shinshū had no trouble arranging accommodation for them as well. As it turned out, I stayed in one house with the young man and woman while the other five stayed across the road. The village well had dried up so we were not able to have a bath that night, but otherwise we were treated with remarkable hospitality by the people of the village.

As we had learned in Akimoto, the people here were frightened by the earthquakes and the rumbling of the mountain and were all ready to flee, but our hosts seemed to take courage from our presence and from having additional people to share the house with them.

Both the house where I was lodged and the one where Tomekichi and the others stayed were occupied by large, extended families which included people of several generations. Not just in Ōsawa, but in Hosono and Akimoto as well, there were many households with large numbers of children; apparently eight or nine per family was normal around here.

All the homes were built in the same pattern, having a large room with a sunken hearth and wooden floor that faced a dirt-floored hallway. Beyond the room with the hearth was a smaller living room, and beyond that a wooden door which led to a back room. The living room looked out on the front garden, and the back room faced the rear gate; both were bordered by a small veranda. It was decided that I would sleep in the living room, the young couple would have the back room, and all the members of the large family would sleep together in the room with the wooden floor and sunken hearth.

After deciding who would sleep where, the young couple and I joined the rest of the family around the hearth where we were served dinner. As we ate, the farmer and his wife told us of several unusual happenings. This year's snow had been deeper than usual but had melted off early, and recently the people from Tsuchida had gone into the swamp to cut walnut trees. They had heard a loud report like the sound of a tree trunk snapping, but it had come from deep within the earth so the people had been frightened and had run away. Also, at about nine o'clock in the evening on April 15, a pale blue flame had flared from the peak of Mt. Bandai and flashed across the sky, followed a few moments later by a great rumbling sound. As the parents related these stories, the children sat in a cluster gazing intently at their faces, and whenever I interrupted with a comment, they all turned in unison to stare at me. I noticed that the young man and woman hardly said a word all evening, and they seemed so preoccupied with their own thoughts I was worried about them. They replied in monosyllables when spoken to, but they never initiated a conversation.

As we were eating dinner, another guest arrived at the house. He told us he had set out from Hibara at about noon that day. Sitting on the edge of the raised floor by the hallway unlacing his straw sandals, he spoke with great animation, saying this was the first time he had made the trip from Hibara and that he had found the road bad and it had been farther than he thought, and that altogether he had had a rough time of it. He was completely uninhibited as he talked on and on. When at last he approached the hearth where the rest of us were seated and the light of the lamp fell on his face, he appeared to be a salesman of some sort, about forty years old, with surprisingly pleasant features.

Somehow we all knew right away that he would end up telling us the story of his life even though no one asked to hear it. He said he came from a certain village on the front side of Mt. Bandai. As a young man he had left home and gone to Osaka where he had been successful in the fish-cake business. Over the years he had saved a little money, and now for the first time he was on his way back to his village for a visit. He planned to sponsor an elaborate memorial service for his parents who were now dead, but his real purpose in returning to his birthplace was to surprise the people there, and to watch their mouths drop open in amazement when they saw how successful he had been.

Since his home was on the other side of Mt. Bandai, the normal route would have been by way of Inawashiro, which was closer and easier. But he was not taking the usual road, and indeed the fact that he had decided to approach the mountain by way of Hibara and make a surprise return to his village seemed typical of a small-time entrepreneur who had achieved some measure of success. He was clearly easy prey to flattery and somewhat proud and boastful, but hardly to the point of being disagreeable. There was also a good side to his nature and I found it admirable that he had been thrifty and industrious enough to save some of his money for the sake of this trip.

Until this man's arrival the people of the household had told us only the most gloomy and discouraging stories about Mt. Bandai, but once this lively character appeared, the tone of the conversation changed completely. From that point on sounds of laughter burst out time and again from the group gathered around the hearth. And yet even while we were talking we felt one slight tremor and heard the mountain rumble twice. The tremor was very mild, but it filled our hearts with dread nonetheless, and the small children clung desperately to their parents with frightened faces and began to cry. The other sounds I merely took to be the wind, and when I learned they came from the mountain, I realized that I had already heard them several times that day. The rumbling of the mountain was quite different from the earthquake tremors in that the children neither cried nor clung to their parents. Rather, I thought I could detect signs of extraordinary intensity in their innocent faces as they strained to follow the sound as it died away somewhere deep within the earth. It seemed cruel that these youngsters had to endure such dread and anxiety.

That night, after we had finished dinner, all of us including the family members retired to bed early. The fish-cake merchant from Osaka ended up sleeping in the living room with me and we arranged our quilts side by side. No sooner had his head touched his pillow than he was sound asleep and snoring loudly.

I also was soon asleep, but I slept lightly and was awakened a short time later. The moment my eyes opened I heard the faint noise of the shutters being slid open in the back room. The sound lasted only a moment, then stopped, but after a brief silence it was repeated. I had an idea that these cautious noises had been going on for some time. I strained my ears trying to hear what was happening in the back room and presently I heard footsteps and the rustle of clothing. Judging from the sounds, I determined that the young couple were leaving the house by way of the veranda. Somehow, ever since going to bed I had had a feeling that something like this might happen, and I realized why I had been sleeping so lightly. In any case, now that I was aware of what was going on, I knew I could not simply ignore the situation.

Without hesitation I threw open the shutters of the living room and stepped down into the garden in my bare feet. The moonlight made the scene outside as bright as midday. I could clearly make out the leaves of the nandina bushes at the bottom of the garden. I went around the side of the house to the back and followed a path that passed beside the well and came out in a corner of a field that was terraced up one level higher than the garden. The wild plants and the tassles of the pampas grass shone silver in the moonlight, stretching away into the distance. Far across the field I could make out the figures of the young couple as they walked away from the farmhouse.

The situation did not seem critical enough to require that I dash after them, so I merely quickened my pace and began to catch up. When I got within fifty yards of them they turned around and I called out, "Don't be fools! Where do you think you're going?" I tried to make my voice sound as loud and peremptory as possible. The woman looked as if she was ready to break into a panicky run, but quickly gave up with a slump of resignation. She hid her face behind her sleeve and began to weep. The young man seemed utterly incapable of doing anything, and from the moment I called out, he just stood there dazed.

The woman was dressed in a different kimono from the one she had worn earlier. It was of a deep purple fabric, and in the brilliant moonlight her pale face contrasted sharply with its color. I had a suspicion that she had had death in mind when she put on her finest clothes.

Her face was tear-stained as she looked up and said, "Neither of us is prepared to go on living." I ignored her and merely told them to go back to the house, setting out in that direction myself. When we reached the well at the rear I stopped to wash my feet. They both followed my example and washed theirs too. Since I had no shoes to put on, I entered the house through the back room and from there returned to my own bed in the living room. For a while I heard the woman softly sobbing, but I paid no attention to this and was soon asleep.

The following day, July 15, I was woken by a loud rumbling in the earth. It was shortly before six o'clock. I knew the time because the fish-cake merchant also rose from his bed at the same moment. From somewhere on his person he produced an enormous, gold pocket watch, and holding it up to a ray of bright sunlight that had slipped through a crack in the shutters, he announced the time.

Since neither of us could get back to sleep again, we opened the shutters and seated ourselves on the veranda, where we each smoked a cigarette and felt the cool morning air on our skin. As we sat there, we heard the shutters of the back room and the room where the family had slept being opened. Apparently everyone had been woken by the sound of the mountain, though of course this was not such an early hour for a farming family to be getting up. It looked as though the people in the house across the road had been awake for some time. I saw Tomekichi and Shuntarō in the front garden discussing something as they laced up their traveling sandals. Moments later Kume, Kinji, and Shinshū also appeared; they were getting ready to start the survey. Since I still had to eat breakfast I decided to delay my departure and set off a little behind them.

I was watching their movements without really paying much attention when Tomekichi happened to look over in our direction. Apparently he caught sight of me, for he waved. He gestured to indicate that they would go on ahead, and I watched as they set out from the garden and disappeared from sight: Kume, Shuntarō, Tomekichi, Shinshū, and Kinji, in that order.

About thirty minutes after the others had left the house across the road, I started after them with the fish-cake merchant and the young couple. The woman was dressed in the same purple kimono she had worn the night before, which led me to suspect that they had not yet given up the idea of taking their lives; the thought irritated me.

"I'm going on to Akimoto from here," I said to the couple. "You had better come with me. I can find someone there to accompany you as far as Inawashiro."

The man nodded slightly in acknowledgment, but the woman kept her eyes on the ground and said nothing. From their expressions I had the feeling that the man had already abandoned the idea of suicide and that it was only the woman who was still determined to carry out their plan. Perhaps, I thought, the man had never really been interested in killing himself and had only been led unwillingly to these alpine meadows by his companion. If that were the case, the woman's desire to take her life seemed especially poignant.

We set out along the river, the same road I had taken to Akimoto the

251

day before. Just as on the previous day, the sky was delightfully clear: a limpid, pale blue unmarred by clouds. A short distance out of the village of Ōsawa the road crossed a small stream flowing down from the Kobuka marsh. Just beyond the stream the road forked, one branch going to Akimoto and the other to Kawakami and Nagasaka.

There the merchant parted company with us and went off along the upward sloping road, half hidden by the scrub bamboo. All we could see of him was his white shirt, the cloth bundle in which he carried his spare clothes, and a small knapsack. He walked away from us with disagreeable swiftness, and soon even his white shirt was lost from sight.

Accompanied by the silent couple from the city I set off toward the confluence of the Ono River. After parting from the merchant, we had hardly gone any distance at all before we saw about ten children from the village standing on an outcrop at the top of a low hill that flanked our road. The youngest was perhaps five or six and the oldest about ten years old. Apparently they had come from the village looking for a place to play. There was certainly no school playground in such a remote village, and no doubt once these youngsters were a little older they would be busy doing chores around the house, but they were not yet old enough for that. It was just the height of the silk-making season, and to keep them from being underfoot, the younger ones were sent out every morning to play by themselves in the open fields.

They stood clustered together on the outcrop above and solemnly gazed at us as we passed along the road below. I looked up at them and wondered if any of them belonged to the family in whose home we had spent the night. All these farm children looked more or less the same to me; they were the same faces I had seen masked with fear as they sat around the hearth when the earthquake had struck, the same faces I had seen straining to hear the receding sound of the rumbling mountain. I could not distinguish the children of one family from those of another, but felt that if any of the group had been in our house, I would like to call out some word of greeting.

It was at that precise moment that everything happened. At exactly 7:40 the earth gave a great heave and shudder. This was different from the tremors we had felt before, much more violent, and I was knocked to the ground. I could not tell if it came from the mountain or the ground beneath me, but I heard the most terrifying sound issuing from the bowels of the earth. I saw the young woman lose her balance, stagger, and fall to her knees. I scrambled to my feet only to be thrown down again by a second violent jolt. This time I used my right arm to brace my body against the bucking earth. I glanced up at the outcrop to see if the children had also been thrown down, but there was no sign of them. All I could see was a swirl of dust slowly rising in the air.

By this time I knew better than to try and leap up again, but after the second quake subsided, I carefully rose to my feet. Beside me I saw that the young man had reached out a hand and was helping the woman up as well.

At the same moment, I saw two or three small heads poke up above the edge of the outcrop. Soon all the heads appeared in a row and I heard one of the children cry out in a loud voice, cadenced almost as though he were singing, "Blow, mountain, blow! Give it all you've got!" Soon several of the others joined in, shouting with all their tiny might, "Blow, mountain, blow! Give it all you've got!"

Their chant—or scream of defiance, whatever it was—was scarcely finished when in thunderous answer a roar came rolling back over the earth. It was a blast so powerful that I was lifted off my feet and hurled to the ground several yards to my right. On and on went the roar while the earth heaved in convulsive spasms. Later, when I tried to recall the exact sequence of events, I was never sure just when it was that I happened to catch sight of Mt. Bandai, but I know I saw a huge column of fire and smoke rising straight up into the clear tranquil sky; like one of the pillars of Hell it rose to twice the height of the mountain itself. The whole mountain had literally exploded and the shape of Kobandai was blotted out forever. It was only much later, of course, that I realized what had occurred.

I cannot say with any certainty how I survived the explosion. The entire north face of Mt. Bandai came avalanching down in a sea of sand, rocks, and boulders. I remember it now as a nightmare vision, as something so terrifying as to be not of this world. The avalanche obliterated the forests that covered the lower slopes of the mountain. The wall of debris swept down with terrible speed and force. I saw the purple kimono swirl up in the air like a scrap of colored paper, and in a flash it was swept away in that tide of mud. I do not know exactly where or when it was that the kimono disappeared from sight. The air was so thick with clouds of ash and pebbles I could not tell whether it was day or night. I staggered along the bank of the Ono River and sought refuge on the high ground north of Akimoto. That alone saved my life. If I had fled in any other direction I would simply have been whisked away without a trace.

Within an hour of the time Mt. Bandai exploded, the villages of Hosono, Ōsawa, and Akimoto were all swept away, and whatever remained was buried under yards and yards of stone. As most of my readers will know, it was not just the north slope that was affected; many villages on the east side of the mountain also met the same tragic fate.

Many accurate and detailed studies and reports have been published regarding the eruption of Mt. Bandai, and I certainly have nothing to add to them. My intention here has been quite different, for it was a personal experience of the eruption that I wanted to relate.

What remains indelibly burned upon my memory and ringing in my ears is the defiant challenge—"Blow, mountain, blow! Give it all you've got!"—uttered by those brave children, who could do nothing else in the face of the mountain's awesome power.

And one more thing: officially, 477 people died that day, but for the sake of accuracy I believe at least three more casualties should be added to that number. Although their names are not known, I feel that when we honor the victims of this disaster we must also mention the departed souls of that young man and woman and the fish-cake merchant from Osaka as well. Today Hosono, Ōsawa, and Hibara are all buried beneath the large lake that formed when the stones and mud of the eruption blocked the Nagase River. Akimoto lies at the bottom of another such lake. Though I have related this story in some detail, the fact is that I have never gone back to visit the area, and it is unlikely that I ever shall. The region today, they tell me, is noted for its pristine alpine lakes, but who can say what terrible memories would revive if I were to go there again and gaze upon them. No, I shall never revisit the countryside that lies in the shadow of Mt. Bandai.

MULBERRY CHILD

Minakami Tsutomu

Translated by Anthony H. Chambers

Minakami Tsutomu's career as a writer did not really get under way until he was forty. During the first thirty-nine years of his life, he went through thirty-six different occupations, ranging from Buddhist acolyte to clerk in a geta shop, peddler, manager of a mahjong parlor, and journalist.

The second son of a shrine carpenter, Minakami was born in 1919 in the village of Okada, Fukui Prefecture, which is the setting for "Mulberry Child." When he was ten years old, his parents, desperately poor and eager to reduce the number of mouths to feed, sent him to the famous Zen monastery of Shōkokuji in Kyoto, where he took his vows in 1930. In 1937, a layman once again, he was enrolled briefly at Ritsumeikan University and began his multifarious succession of careers.

After the war he studied with the novelist Uno Kōji (1891–1961), under whose influence he wrote his first novel, the autobiographical Furaipan no uta *(The Song of a Frying Pan), in 1948. But Minakami was unable to support himself by writing until 1959, when he published an extremely popular mystery entitled* Kiri to kage *(Mist and Shadow). In 1961 he won the Mystery Writers' Club Prize for* Umi no kiba *(The Fangs of the Sea), which deals with Minamata Disease, caused by environmental pollution.*

Dissatisfied with his reputation as a writer of social-problem mysteries, however, Minakami turned to the experiences of his youth for Gan no tera *(The Temple of the Wild Geese), which brought him the Naoki Prize in 1962. In* Gobanchō Yūgirirō *(The Yūgiri House in Gobanchō, 1962), he treats the burning of the Golden Pavilion from a different point of view than Mishima Yukio had in his* Kinkakuji *(The Temple of the Golden Pavilion, 1956), that of a young prostitute from the Japan Sea coast. The element of local color becomes even stronger in* Echizen takeningyō *(The Bamboo Doll of Echizen), which won high praise from Tanizaki Jun'ichirō in 1963.*

An exceptionally prolific writer, Minakami has published a number of historical novels, biographies, travel accounts, and autobiographical essays. His biography of his mentor Uno Kōji won the Kikuchi Kan Prize in 1971, and his study of the fifteenth-century Zen master Ikkyū was awarded the Tanizaki Prize in 1975.

"Mulberry Child," written in 1963, demonstrates Minakami's characteristic blending of autobiographical elements with Buddhism and local color in a sweet-sad portrayal of the lives of the very poor in rural Japan.

*   *   *

"Do you know the story of the mulberry child, the child born out of a mulberry patch? It's probably nothing new to a writer like you. In the poor villages of the north country, only so much land is available for fields and paddies, and when there get to be too many children, well, all the people can do is abandon them, starting with the third or fourth boy. 'Thinning,' it's called, and it was tolerated until about 1900. Mothers would come right down to the police station and report, 'It was a boy, so I wet a towel and covered his mouth, and killed him. Please don't be too hard on me.' Well, the officer would pretend he didn't know anything, and arrange it so the higher-ups never found out. In the village where I was born, too, a lot of thinning went on."

This is how old Tarokichi began his story.

Every year, in the Second Month by the old calendar, a curious observance called "Shaka Shaka" took place in the Ōi District of Wakasa Province.

Wakasa is a narrow strip along the Japan Sea coast between Echizen and Tamba. The towering mountains on the border of Shiga Prefecture send a series of ridges, like the teeth of a comb, down toward the sea, where they end as promontories and peninsulas. The coastline looks like the blade of a saw, so that the highway from Tsuruga to Maizuru passes through one short tunnel after another and skirts the coast so closely it is showered with spray from the waves. The villages that nestle in the valleys running from the sea into the mountains are isolated from each other by the ridges between them. Each village has its own customs and dialect.

Ōi District, where Tarokichi was born, was in one of these valleys; and the observance of "Shaka Shaka" survived only in the hamlet of Okada, at the far end of the deep valley. It was a remarkable custom, one not to be seen in any other village.

Well, "a remarkable custom" may sound a little pretentious, Tarokichi added. This is how he described it.

After midnight on the fifteenth of the Second Month, all the village children from six to fifteen would gather before the Kannon Hall, deep in the forest behind the village. At the first light of dawn they formed a procession and walked through the village, rapping softly at the door of each of the sixty houses. In groups of three, four, five, and six, the children rapped on the doors at dawn. As they went they called "Shaka, Shaka-a," over and over.

"Shaka Shaka" probably refers to Lord Shakyamuni—the Buddha— and Tarokichi thought that the observance might be a demonstration of faith in the temples in the area. In any case, the children went from door to door, knocking and crying "Shaka, Shaka-a." At each house, someone would get out of bed and open the door just enough for a hand to pass through.

"Who is it?" a grown-up voice would ask from inside.

The children would give the hereditary names of their houses and their personal names. In Ōi District, most of the house names ended in "-zaemon" or "-emon," and so a child would identify himself by shouting something like, "I'm so-and-so from Taroemon's." Thereupon the grown-up, hiding behind the door, would thrust out a hand and say, "Open your bags."

The children would loosen the strings on their large cloth sacks, pull the mouths open, and hold them toward the crack in the door. The grown-up's hand would shoot out and drop sweets and roasted beans into the bags.

By the time they had made the rounds of all sixty houses, the children would barely be able to stand up any longer, and their bags would be swelling with all manner of sweets and beans.

All of this took place early in the morning. That night, the men and women over sixty gathered at the Kannon Hall, where a votive lamp had been lit. The hall was equipped with a sunken hearth, in which pine roots and large branches were burned. The old men and women would spread mats around the hearth and, with the oldest ones nearest the fire, pray to Amitabha and talk through the night. The children sat with them.

Among the old people there were some who chanted "Shaka, Shaka-a," which suggests that this gathering, too, had to do with Shakyamuni.

Tarokichi didn't know what the fifteenth of the Second Month signified in Buddhism, but he said he had a feeling that it was the date of the Buddha's death and Nirvana, and that the activities of the children and the old people were by way of a memorial service for his soul.

Each household, then, as it prepared sweets and beans and put a handful in each child's bag, was performing in its own way the ceremony known as *Segaki*, or "Feeding the Hungry Ghosts." And for their part, the children—who are often called *gaki*, or "hungry ghosts"—accepted the food offerings that day in deference to Lord Shakyamuni. Likewise, when the old men and women gathered at the Kannon Hall to light a fire and pray to Amitabha, they were comforting Shakyamuni's soul. In the snow country, lighting a fire was the warmest form of hospitality. And so the old people entertained themselves around the fire with stories of the departed who had gone to join the Buddha.

Tarokichi was born in the hamlet of Okada, in a house known as Katsukichi. Katsukichi had been his grandfather's name, and was assumed in turn by his father. Tarokichi turned six that year and joined in the Shaka Shaka observances for the first time.

Tarokichi couldn't sleep on the night of the fourteenth. He was happily anticipating the hour when he would finally be able to join the other children and walk in the Shaka Shaka. A child of five could not join them; but when he turned six his parents would tell him, "Now you can go with the others in Shaka Shaka." Thus from the age of five—or even four—children waited eagerly for their day to come.

It snowed on the fifteenth of the Second Month. In Wakasa the snow was heaviest during the Second Month; at times it would fall steadily for a week. The houses had steep, triangular roofs of thatch, from which the snow slid to form high walls around each house. Reeds that had been cut and stored in advance were stretched around each house to soften the fierce winds, rendering the interiors still darker.

Tarokichi waited sleeplessly for morning. At about five o'clock, he heard a child's voice at the entrance to the Katsukichi house: "Shaka, Shaka-a."

"Who is it?" asked Tarokichi's mother.

"It's Yasuke from Kanzaemon's," came the voice from outside.

"All right," said Tarokichi's mother, opening the door a crack.

The wind came in, bearing white, powdery show. His mother, wrapped in a short robe, felt the icy blast on her knees. Exclaiming at the cold, she took a handful of roasted beans from a bucket she had ready by the door. "Here, for Yasuke from Kanzaemon's," she said, and gave the beans to the child as he waited in the blizzard with his bag open.

Yasuke from Kanzaemon's was seven. Pulling the string to close his round-bottomed bag over the roasted beans, he said, "Hey, Tarokichi. Tarokichi, where are you? Do you want to come with me?"

Tarokichi was up and ready to go, without even washing his face. The strap was around his neck and the bag dangled against his chest as he concentrated on tying the cord of his baggy cotton pants.

"Yasuke from Kanzaemon's. Will you take him with you?" his mother asked.

"Yes," came the reply.

Hearing this, Tarokichi was at the door in a flash and bounded out into the driving snow.

"Yasuke, take me with you for Shaka Shaka."

"All right, follow me. When I say 'Shaka Shaka,' you say it too."

Yasuke was one year older than Tarokichi. Walking along the village roads in the snow, he called "Shaka, Shaka-a." In no time the two children were white with the powdery snow.

Oddly enough, the child one accompanied on one's first Shaka Shaka always became a close friend. Tarokichi became Yasuke's friend. If Tarokichi had waited silently at the door when Yasuke called his name in the snow, then Yasuke would have had to go on by himself. Yasuke had invited Tarokichi with friendship in mind, and Tarokichi had agreed; and so they made the rounds together.

For two hours, Tarokichi and Yasuke ran through the snow-covered village, filling their bags. When the Shaka Shaka was over, they played together all day and promised to go together to the Kannon Hall that night.

The Kannon Hall was the village community center. The tile roof that covered it was just adequate to ward off the elements; the walls had collapsed, and the posts and beams had begun to tilt. A large stone, on which visitors left their footwear, lay in front of the square building, and just inside was a large, plank-floored room. Facing the entrance was an altar, containing a small, boxlike shrine. The doors of the shrine were opened only on this day; in the dim interior stood an image of the Bodhisattva Kannon, about three feet tall and covered with dust.

There was nothing unusual about the image, except that the gold leaf had fallen off, exposing the grain of the wood. One arm hung to about the navel; the other was bent at the elbow, the thumb and forefinger joined to form a circle. On the candlestand in front of the image flickered a "one-pound candle." Mats had been spread over the planks, and a fire had just been lit in the hearth. Smoke billowed from the damp wood. That year there were thirty-two men and women over the age of sixty in the village of sixty houses, but several who had passed ninety were unable to negotiate the snowy path to the hall. Those who could walk with the aid of a staff would join the assembly. But when Tarokichi and Yasuke arrived, the hour was still early, and only old Shōza from Kamimura was there.

"Shōza" was short for Shōzaemon, the name of his house. When Tarokichi and Yasuke looked inside they saw old Shōza seated by the hearth, poking at the smoldering wood.

"Has it started to burn?" they asked as they stepped inside.

The old man was popular with the village children. They liked some of the old people of the village and disliked others. Shōza was one of their favorites. He often had strange stories to tell them.

"Who's that? Ah, Tarokichi from Katsukichi's, and Yasuke from Kan-zaemon's."

Rubbing his bleary eyes, he glared in their direction. He was past seventy and hard of hearing.

"Yes, Tarokichi and Yasuke," replied Yasuke.

The two boys sat at the hearth. Shōza eyed them.

"The mulberry child from Kanzaemon's," he said out of the blue.

Yasuke was startled. "What's a mulberry child? What's a mulberry?" he asked.

Tarokichi pricked up his ears, too. What a funny thing for Shōza to come out with, he thought.

"You don't know what 'mulberry child' means, Yasuke? Tarokichi? You're the child of a mulberry patch, Yasuke. You were born from a hole in a mulberry patch."

Old Shōza grinned broadly; his one or two remaining teeth were a grimy yellow, and his gums showed purple. He fixed his sunken eyes on Yasuke. Tarokichi could not look Shōza directly in the face. He was frightened. Though he didn't know what the old man meant, he thought that Shōza was insulting his new friend Yasuke by calling him a mulberry child.

"I wasn't born from a hole in a mulberry patch. I was born from my mother," shouted Yasuke, about to cry.

"Yasuke, you don't know," said Shōza, trying to explain. "You're a mulberry child. You'll understand when you grow up. You were born from the mulberry patch."

Yasuke was on the verge of tears, but he fought them back. He didn't want the young Tarokichi to see him cry, and he was loath to give in so easily to old Shōza, who said such scornful things about him. Stoically he clenched his teeth.

The old people began to gather in front of the hall. Removing their wooden geta and boots and shaking the snow off their hoods and blankets, they came inside. Seeing old Shōza poking at the fire, they would say, "Good work, Shōza. So it was your turn to build the fire this year. Thank you."

Proceeding to the shrine, each one would pull from his sleeve the incense sticks he had brought, light the tips at the candle, and push the sticks into the damp ashes that filled the incense burner. Then each would join his hands and begin to chant the prayer to Amitabha:

Nan Amida Butsu, Namu Amida Butsu,
Namu Amida-a Butsu, Namu Amida Butsu.

The chanting of the old men and women swirled with the smoke toward the low ceiling of the Kannon Hall. Tarokichi and Yasuke, oppressed by the heavy odors of hair oil and perspiration, soon went outside.

It was snowing. From the hall came the voices of the old people praying to Amitabha. Tarokichi walked ahead. Behind him, Yasuke said quietly, "Mulberry child. . ."

Tarokichi looked back; Yasuke was glaring at him furiously. Tarokichi saw contempt in his face. Feeling a surge of anger, Tarokichi began to run, kicking the snow as he went.

Why had Yasuke changed so, after old Shōza called him a mulberry child? Tarokichi did not understand until he had grown up.

They had become friends by doing Shaka Shaka together, but from that day on Yasuke never came to play with him. It was very strange.

"Only recently did I understand why Yasuke looked so dejected and angry." Tarokichi continued his story.

"Yasuke was Kanzaemon's third boy. They were a poor family. That makes it sound as though my family was rich, but we were poor, too. The difference is that Yasuke's family had a lot of children. There are extra expenses when you have a lot of children, and so they were that much poorer. Yasuke's father, Kanzaemon, and his mother—her name was Okane—were both hard workers. Yasuke was born in the late autumn of 1899. Okane was busy one evening, harvesting beans on a terrace in the farthest fields at Tanida, when her term came full and she began to feel labor pains. Farmwives used to go on working right up through the last month—they weren't able to check into a clinic and give brith with the help of a nurse or a midwife, as they do nowadays. When Okane felt the pains, she held her stomach and started back toward the house at Okada. The house was empty—Kanzaemon was a carpenter and had probably gone off to help on a construction job somewhere. On her way home, Okane, still holding her stomach, met up with Shōzaemon.

"Seeing Okane covered with oily sweat and her veins bulging as she walked toward him, he asked, 'Is it the baby, Okane? Is the baby moving?' Without answering, Okane fell to her knees at the side of the road. The pains were getting worse.

"'Okane. What are you going to do with so many children?' asked Shōzaemon. 'You have two boys. This will be your third. How do you think you can raise it? Shall I help you? Let it be a mulberry child. Let it be a mulberry child, and pray for its happiness on the other side.'

"There were no passersby that evening on the mountain road. Okane must have thought of Shōzaemon as the Buddha himself, as he helped her up from behind.

"'Shōza. Please help me. Just do what you think is best.' Okane was groaning with pain as she spoke.

"Shōzaemon nodded and said, 'All right.' He helped her lie down on the grass at the roadside, loosened her sash, and began to rub her stomach. The baby came right away. It gave a big cry. Okane, clutching some plantain roots by the road, had exhausted her strength and fainted. When she came to, much later, Shōza and his wife had put her to bed in the storeroom at home. The baby she had given birth to was nowhere to be seen. When he saw that Okane had opened her eyes, Shōza spoke.

"'It's a mulberry child now. I left it in a mulberry patch. If it isn't alive tomorrow, I'll bury it. Don't worry, Okane. I'll take care of everything for you.'

"I wonder when the custom started. Around that time, many of the families were raising silkworms for the extra income, and mulberries grew in most of the fields at the edge of the village. I remember from my childhood that, when the leaves were full, the fields would be covered in green; and when the leaves fell, the mulberry fields would look like Needle Mountain in Hell. Okane gave birth to Yasuke in late autumn, when the big mulberry leaves were swaying in the ocean breeze. I went into the mulberry fields many times. When the red fruit ripened—in May, was it?—I would stuff myself with mulberries. The village children would roam the fields from morning to night, hunting for the tastiest berries. Once I came across a hole, and it gave me a fright. As I recall, it was in the middle of a field, at the farthest point from the surrounding walkways.

It was shaped like an urn; the sides had been carefully tamped with a mallet. At first glance, the place looked as though an urn *had* been buried there. The hole was about a foot across, and quite deep—I had to lie down and peep over the edge to see the bottom. I could make out lots of something that looked like rope, all glistening and slimy. Most likely it was weasels and rats that had gone down to drink the rainwater that collected there, and died, unable to climb up the hard-packed sides. There was a peculiar smell—yes, like the smell of a dead cat or dog. The children were afraid of these holes. When they saw one, they'd say, 'A tochinampin hole!' and run away. A *tochinampin* is a giant flying squirrel in our dialect. When I saw that hole in the mulberry field, I asked my parents, 'What's that hole for?' 'It's a tochinampin hole,' they told me. 'The tochinampin stores dead mice and cats in there to eat in the winter. Don't go near it. If you fall in, you'll never get out. You'll be eaten by the tochinampin.'

"All the children in the village ate mulberries, and all of them asked their parents about the frightening holes. When they did, they were told that those were tochinampin holes.

"The sad truth is that Okane, with Shōzaemon's help, had put her third boy out as a mulberry child. In other words, he was left in a tochinampin hole."

"But that's not the end of the story. As I said at the beginning, a 'mulberry child' was a child *born out of* a mulberry patch. That's right: it's a child who crawled out of the hole he had been left in. The day after a newborn infant had been left in a hole, someone from the family would go to make sure it was dead; and they say that sometimes there'd be a strong child who had crawled out of the hole and was found crying under the dew-covered mulberry leaves. A very strong and lively child, that must have been. When a baby was found still alive the next morning, they would take it home and rear it. I suppose the people figured that such a strong child would be sure to grow up into a good worker who could help with the family business.

"Yasuke from Kanzaemon's was born at the roadside and abandoned by old Shōza; but the next morning, when Shōza went back to the mulberry patch to look, he was sleeping peacefully under the mulberry leaves. It was remarkable. The grown-ups said that Yasuke was a prodigy, the first 'mulberry child' in the village, and they gazed at him in astonishment.

"That night in my sixth year—on the fifteenth of the Second Month, at the hearth in the Kannon Hall—when old Shōza called Yasuke a mulberry child, he wasn't being insulting.

"He was saying to Yasuke, 'You are the strongest boy in the village.' Come to think of it—early one morning, about ten days after I joined in Shaka Shaka for the first time, before the snow began to melt, when the village saw blizzards day and night, old Shōzaemon suddenly died.

"The old man's words—'mulberry child'—still ring in my ears; but Yasuke, the mulberry child, died of cholera when he was thirteen. It's hard to forget your childhood friends. Yasuke was taller and stronger than I was; his pug nose was always running, and he called 'Shaka, Shaka-a' in the blizzard as he led me by the hand, walking through the village to get our sweets. I can see him even now."

ONE ARM

Kawabata Yasunari

Translated by Edward Seidensticker

In his Nobel Prize acceptance speech of 1968, Kawabata Yasunari (1899–1972) wrote: "The snow, the moon, the blossoms, words expressive of the seasons as they move one into another, include in the Japanese tradition the beauty of mountains and rivers and grasses and trees, of all the myriad manifestations of nature, of human feelings as well." This ability to fuse the distinctions between the human realm and the domain of nature is a distinctive and intoxicating feature of his writings. In renowned works such as Yukiguni (Snow Country, *1948; tr. 1956) and* Yama no oto (The Sound of the Mountain, *1954; tr. 1970), Kawabata displays a true poetic genius for describing the human situation in terms of the subtle movements of flora and fauna, of mountain rumbles and winter landscapes bathed red by fires and passions.*

These elements have endeared Kawabata to the Western reader, who recognizes in him a prolongation and fulfillment of the traditions of classical Japanese literature. That aspect is indeed strong in Kawabata. Equally forceful, however, are the insurmountable distances that Kawabata places between his characters. Often it seems as if the men and women in his stories belong to opposing magnetic fields: however much they may think they want one another, something in their basic natures always drives them apart. Yet this very unattainability (or at times an unconscious desire to be alone) creates that element of unsullied purity which hovers over many of the women characters. Yōko in Snow Country—*first seen not directly, but in a mirrored reflection—retains her attraction for Shimamura because he can never obtain her. Kikuko in* The Sound of the Mountain *preserves both her purity and her fascination for Shingo because she is his daughter-in-law. These distant encounters can be traced all the way back to Kawabata's "maiden" work, "Izu no odoriko" (*The Izu Dancer, *1926; tr. 1955).*

Another aspect of Kawabata's writings which figures prominently in stories such as "Kataude" (One Arm, 1963) is a strong element of surrealist fantasy, a product of Kawabata's early training as a modernist. Indeed, with all of Kawabata's late fascination with makai *(the demon world), madness, and bizarre use of imagery, "One Arm" could be called one of the more typical examples of his work as it is known in Japan.*

*   *   *

"I can let you have one of my arms for the night," said the girl. She took off her right arm at the shoulder and, with her left hand, laid it on my knee.

"Thank you." I looked at my knee. The warmth of the arm came through.

"I'll put the ring on. To remind you that it's mine." She smiled and raised her left arm to my chest. "Please." With but one arm, it was difficult for her to take the ring off.

"An engagement ring?"

"No. A keepsake. From my mother."

It was silver, set with small diamonds.

"Perhaps it does look like an engagement ring, but I don't mind. I wear it, and then when I take it off it's as if I were leaving my mother."

Raising the arm on my knee, I removed the ring and slipped it on the ring finger.

"Is this the one?"

"Yes." She nodded. "It will seem artificial unless the elbow and fingers bend. You won't like that. Let me make them bend for you."

She took her right arm from my knee and pressed her lips gently to it. Then she pressed them to the finger joints.

"Now they'll move."

"Thank you." I took the arm back. "Do you suppose it will speak? Will it speak to me?"

"It only does what an arm does. If it talks I'll be afraid to have it back. But try anyway. It should at least listen to what you say, if you're good to it."

"I'll be good to it."

"I'll see you again," she said, touching the right arm with her left hand, as if to infuse it with a spirit of its own. "You're his, but just for the night."

As she looked at me she seemed to be fighting back tears.

"I don't suppose you'll try to change it for your own arm," she said. "But it will be all right. Go ahead, do."

"Thank you."

I put her arm in my raincoat and went out into the foggy streets. I feared I might be thought odd if I took a taxi or a streetcar. There would be a scene if the arm, now separated from the girl's body, were to cry out, or to weep.

I held it against my chest, toward the side, my right hand on the roundness at the shoulder joint. It was concealed by the raincoat, and I had to touch the coat from time to time with my left hand to be sure that the arm was still there. Probably I was making sure not of the arm's presence but of my own happiness.

She had taken off the arm at the point I liked. It was plump and round—was it at the top of the arm or the beginning of the shoulder? The roundness was that of a beautiful Occidental girl, rare in a Japanese. It was in the girl herself, a clean, elegant roundness, like a sphere glowing with a faint, fresh light. When the girl was no longer clean, that gentle roundness would fade, grow flabby. Something that lasted for a brief moment in the life of a beautiful girl, the roundness of the arm made me feel the roundness of her body. Her breasts would not be large. Shy, only large enough to cup in the hands, they would have a clinging softness and strength. And in the roundness of the arm I could feel her legs as she walked along. She would carry them lightly, like a small bird, or a butterfly moving from flower to flower. There would be the same subtle melody in the tip of her tongue when she kissed.

It was the season for changing to sleeveless dresses. The girl's shoulder, newly bared, had the color of skin not used to the raw touch of the air. It had the glow of a bud moistened in the shelter of spring and not yet ravaged by summer. I had that morning bought a magnolia bud and put it in a glass vase; and the roundness of the girl's arm was like the great, white bud. Her dress was cut back more radically than most sleeveless dresses. The joint at the shoulder was exposed, and the shoulder itself. The dress, of dark green silk, almost black, had a soft sheen. The girl was in the rounded slope of the shoulders, which drew a gentle wave with the swelling of the back. Seen obliquely from behind, the flesh from the round shoulders to the long, slender neck came to an abrupt halt at the base of the upswept hair, and the black hair seemed to cast a glowing shadow over the roundness of the shoulders.

She had sensed that I thought her beautiful, and so she lent me her right arm for the roundness there at the shoulder.

Carefully hidden under my raincoat, the girl's arm was colder than my hand. I was giddy from the racing of my heart, and I knew that my hand would be hot. I wanted the warmth to stay as it was, the warmth of the girl herself. And the slight coolness in my hand passed on to me the pleasure of the arm. It was like her breasts, not yet touched by a man.

The fog yet thicker, the night threatened rain, and wet my uncovered hair. I could hear a radio speaking from the back room of a closed pharmacy. It announced that three planes unable to land in the fog had been circling the airport for half an hour. It went on to draw the attention of listeners to the fact that on damp nights clocks were likely to go wrong, and that on such nights the springs had a tendency to break if wound too tight. I looked for the lights of the circling planes, but could not see them. There was no sky. The pressing dampness invaded my ears, to give a wet sound like the wriggling of myriads of distant earthworms. I stood before the pharmacy awaiting further admonitions. I learned that on such nights the fierce beasts in the zoo, the lions and tigers and leopards and the rest, roared their resentment at the dampness, and that we were now to hear it. There was a roaring like the roaring of the earth. I then learned that pregnant women and despondent persons should go to bed early on such nights, and that women who applied perfume directly to their skins would find it difficult to remove afterward.

At the roaring of the beasts, I moved off, and the warning about perfume followed me. That angry roaring had unsettled me, and I moved on lest my uneasiness be transmitted to the girl's arm. The girl was neither pregnant nor despondent, but it seemed to me that tonight, with only one arm, she should take the advice of the radio and go quietly to bed. I hoped that she would sleep peacefully.

As I started across the street I pressed my left hand against my raincoat. A horn sounded. Something brushed my side, and I twisted away. Perhaps the arm had been frightened by the horn. The fingers were clenched.

"Don't worry," I said. "It was a long way off. It couldn't see. That's why it honked."

Because I was holding something important to me, I had looked in both directions. The sound of the horn had been so far away that I had thought it must be meant for someone else. I looked in the direction from which it came, but could see no one. I could see only the headlights. They widened into a blur of faint purple. A strange color for headlights. I stood on the curb when I had crossed and watched it pass. A young woman in vermilion was driving. It seemed to me that she turned toward me and bowed. I wanted to run off, fearing that the girl had come for her arm. Then I remembered that she would hardly be able to drive with only one. But had not the woman in the car seen what I was carrying? Had she not sensed it with a woman's intuition? I would have to take care not to encounter another of her sex before I reached my apartment. The rear lights were also a faint purple. I still did not see the car. In the ashen fog a lavender blur floated up and moved away.

"She is driving for no reason, for no reason at all except to be driving. And while she drives she will simply disappear," I muttered to myself. "And what was that sitting in the back seat?"

Nothing, apparently. Was it because I went around carrying girls' arms that I felt so unnerved by emptiness? The car she drove carried the clammy night fog. And something about her had turned it faintly purple in the headlights. If not from her own body, whence had come that purplish light? Could the arm I concealed have so clothed in emptiness a woman driving alone on such a night? Had she nodded at the girl's arm from her car? Perhaps on such a night there were angels and ghosts abroad protecting women. Perhaps she had ridden not in a car but in a purple light. Her drive had not been empty. She had spied out my secret.

I made my way back to my apartment without further encounters. I stood listening outside the door. The light of a firefly skimmed over my head and disappeared. It was too large and too strong for a firefly. I recoiled backward. Several more lights like fireflies skimmed past. They disappeared even before the heavy fog could suck them in. Had a will-o'-the-wisp, a death-fire of some sort, run on ahead of me, to await my return? But then I saw that it was a swarm of small moths. Catching the light at the door, the wings of the moths glowed like fireflies. Too large to be fireflies, and yet, for moths, so small as to invite the mistake.

Avoiding the automatic elevator, I made my way stealthily up the narrow stairs to the third floor. Not being left-handed, I had difficulty unlocking the door. The harder I tried the more my hand trembled—as if in terror after a crime. Something would be waiting for me inside the room, a room where I lived in solitude; and was not the solitude a presence? With the girl's arm I was no longer alone. And so perhaps my own solitude waited there to intimidate me.

"Go on ahead," I said, taking out the girl's arm when at length I had opened the door. "Welcome to my room. I'll turn on the light."

"Are you afraid of something?" the arm seemed to say. "Is something here?"

"You think there might be?"

"I smell something."

"Smell? It must be me that you smell. Don't you see traces of my shadow, up there in the darkness? Look carefully. Maybe my shadow was waiting for me to come back."

"It's a sweet smell."

"Ah—the magnolia," I answered brightly. I was glad it was not the moldy smell of my loneliness. A magnolia bud befitted my winsome guest. I was getting used to the dark. Even in pitch-blackness I knew where everything was.

"Let me turn on the light." Coming from the arm, a strange remark. "I haven't been in your room before."

"Thank you. I'll be very pleased. No one but me has ever turned on the lights here before."

I held the arm to the switch by the door. All five lights went on at once: at the ceiling, on the table, by the bed, in the kitchen, in the bathroom. I had not thought they could be so bright.

The magnolia was in enormous bloom. That morning it had been in bud. It could have only just bloomed, and yet there were stamens on the table. Curious, I looked more closely at the stamens than at the white flower. As I picked up one or two and gazed at them, the girl's arm, laid on the table, began to move, the fingers like spanworms, and gathered the stamens in its hand. I went to throw them in the wastebasket.

"What a strong smell. It sinks right into my skin. Help me."

"You must be tired. It wasn't an easy trip. Suppose you rest awhile."

I laid the arm on the bed and sat down beside it. I stroked it gently.

"How pretty. I like it." The arm would be speaking of the bedcover. Flowers were printed in three colors on an azure ground, somewhat lively for a man who lived alone. "So this is where we spend the night. I'll be very quiet."

"Oh?"

"I'll be beside you and not beside you."

The hand took mine gently. The nails, carefully polished, were a faint pink. The tips extended well beyond the fingers.

Against my own short, thick nails, hers possessed a strange beauty, as if they belonged to no human creature. With such fingertips, a woman perhaps transcended mere humanity. Or did she pursue womanhood itself? A shell luminous from the pattern inside it, a petal bathed in dew— I thought of the obvious likenesses. Yet I could think of no shell or petal whose color and shape resembled them. They were the nails on the girl's fingers, comparable to nothing else. More translucent than a delicate shell, than a thin petal, they seemed to hold a dew of tragedy. Every day and every night her energies were poured into the polishing of this tragic beauty. It penetrated my solitude. Perhaps my yearning, my solitude, transformed them into dew.

I rested her little finger on the index finger of my free hand, gazing at the long, narrow nail as I rubbed it with my thumb. My finger touched the tip of hers, sheltered by the nail. The finger bent, and the elbow too.

"Does it tickle?" I asked. "It must."

I had spoken carelessly. I knew that the tips of a woman's fingers were sensitive when the nails were long. And so I had told the girl's arm that I had known other women.

From one who was not a great deal older than the girl who had lent me the arm but far more mature in her experience of men, I had heard that fingertips thus hidden by nails were often acutely sensitive. One became used to touching things not with the fingertips but with the nails, and the fingertips therefore tickled when something came against them.

I had shown astonishment at this discovery, and she had gone on: "You're, say, cooking—or eating—and something touches your fingers, and you find yourself hunching your shoulders, it seems so dirty."

Was it the food that seemed unclean, or the tip of the nail? Whatever touched her fingers made her writhe with its uncleanness. Her own cleanness would leave behind a drop of tragic dew, there under the long shadow of the nail. One could not assume that for each of the ten fingers there would be a separate drop of dew.

It was natural that I should want all the more to touch those fingertips, but I held myself back. My solitude held me back. She was a woman on whose body few tender spots could be expected to remain.

And on the body of the girl who had lent me the arm they would be beyond counting. Perhaps, toying with the fingertips of such a girl, I would feel not guilt but affection. But she had not lent me the arm for such mischief. I must not make a comedy of her gesture.

"The window." I noticed not that the window itself was open but that the curtain was undrawn.

"Will anything look in?" asked the girl's arm.

"Some man or woman. Nothing else."

"Nothing human would see me. If anything it would be a self. Yours."

"Self? What is that? Where is it?"

"Far away," said the arm, as if singing in consolation. "People walk around looking for selves, far away."

"And do they come upon them?"

"Far away," said the arm once more.

It seemed to me that the arm and the girl herself were an infinity apart. Would the arm be able to return to the girl, so far away? Would I be able to take it back, so far away? The arm lay peacefully trusting me; and would the girl be sleeping in the same peaceful confidence? Would there not be harshness, a nightmare? Had she not seemed to be fighting back tears when she parted with it? The arm was now in my room, which the girl herself had not visited.

The dampness clouded the window, like a toad's belly stretched over it. The fog seemed to withhold rain in midair, and the night outside the window lost distance, even while it was wrapped in limitless distance. There were no roofs to be seen, no horns to be heard.

"I'll close the window," I said, reaching for the curtain. It too was damp. My face loomed up in the window, younger than my thirty-three years. I did not hesitate to pull the curtain, however. My face disappeared.

Suddenly a remembered window. On the ninth floor of a hotel, two little girls in wide red skirts were playing in the window. Very similar children in similar clothes, perhaps twins, Occidentals. They pounded at the glass, pushing it with their shoulders and shoving at each other. Their mother knitted, her back to the window. If the large pane were to have broken or come loose, they would have fallen from the ninth floor. It was only I who thought them in danger. Their mother was quite unconcerned. The glass was in fact so solid that there was no danger.

"It's beautiful," said the arm on the bed as I turned from the window. Perhaps she was speaking of the curtain, in the same flowered pattern as the bedcover.

"Oh? But it's faded from the sun and almost ready to go." I sat down on the bed and took the arm on my knee. "This is what is beautiful. More beautiful than anything."

Taking the palm of the hand in my own right palm, and the shoulder in my left hand, I flexed the elbow, and then again.

"Behave yourself," said the arm, as if smiling softly. "Having fun?"

"Not in the least."

A smile did come over the arm, crossing it like light. It was exactly the fresh smile on the girl's cheek.

I knew the smile. Elbows on the table, she would fold her hands loosely and rest her chin or cheek on them. The pose should have been inelegant in a young girl; but there was about it a lightly engaging quality that made expressions like "elbows on the table" seem inappropriate. The roundness of the shoulders, the fingers, the chin, the cheeks, the ears, the long, slender neck, the hair, all came together in a single harmonious movement. Using knife and fork deftly, index and little fingers bent, she would raise them ever so slightly from time to time. Food would pass the small lips and she would swallow—I had before me less a person at dinner than an inviting music of hands and face and throat. The light of her smile flowed across the skin of her arm.

The arm seemed to smile because, as I flexed it, very gentle waves passed over the firm, delicate muscles, to send waves of light and shadow over the smooth skin. Earlier, when I had touched the fingertips under the long nails, the light passing over the arm as the elbow bent had caught my eye. It was that, and not any impulse toward mischief, that had made me bend and unbend her arm. I stopped, and gazed at it as it lay stretched out on my knee. Fresh lights and shadows were still passing over it.

"You ask if I'm having fun. You realize that I have permission to change you for my own arm?"

"I do."

"Somehow I'm afraid to."

"Oh?"

"May I?"

"Please."

I heard the permission granted, and wondered whether I could accept it. "Say it again. Say 'please.'"

"Please, please."

I remembered. It was like the voice of a woman who had decided to give herself to me, one not as beautiful as the girl who had lent me the arm. Perhaps there was something a little strange about her.

"Please," she had said, gazing at me. I had put my fingers to her eyelids and closed them. Her voice was trembling. "'Jesus wept. Then said the Jews, Behold how he loved her!'"

"Her" was a mistake for "him." It was the story of the dead Lazarus. Perhaps, herself a woman, she had remembered it wrong, perhaps she had made the substitution intentionally.

The words, so inappropriate to the scene, had shaken me. I gazed at her, wondering if tears would start from the closed eyes.

She opened them and raised her shoulders. I pushed her down with my arm.

"You're hurting me!" She put her hand to the back of her head.

There was a small spot of blood on the white pillow. Parting her hair, I put my lips to the drop of blood swelling on her head.

"It doesn't matter." She took out all her hairpins. "I bleed easily. At the slightest touch."

A hairpin had pierced her skin. A shudder seemed about to pass through her shoulders, but she controlled herself.

Although I think I understand how a woman feels when she gives herself to a man, there is still something unexplained about the act. What is it to her? Why should she wish to do it, why should she take the initiative? I could never really accept the surrender, even knowing that the body of every woman was made for it. Even now, old as I am, it seems strange. And the ways in which various women go about it: unalike if you wish, or similar perhaps, or even identical. Is that not strange? Perhaps the strangeness I find in it all is the curiosity of a younger man, perhaps the despair of one advanced in years. Or perhaps some spiritual debility I suffer from.

Her anguish was not common to all women in the act of surrender. And it was with her only the one time. The silver thread was cut, the golden bowl destroyed.

"Please," the arm had said, and so reminded me of the other girl; but were the two voices in fact similar? Had they not sounded alike because the words were the same? Had the arm acquired independence in this measure of the body from which it was separated? And were the words not the act of giving itself up, of being ready for anything, without restraint or responsibility or remorse? It seemed to me that if I were to accept the invitation and change the arm for my own I would be bringing untold pain to the girl.

I gazed at the arm on my knee. There was a shadow at the inside of the elbow. It seemed that I might be able to suck it in. I pressed it to my lips, to gather in the shadow.

"It tickles. Do behave yourself." The arm was around my neck, avoiding my lips.

"Just when I was having a good drink."

"And what were you drinking?"

I did not answer.

"What were you drinking?"

"The smell of light? Of skin."

The fog seemed thicker; even the magnolia leaves seemed wet. What other warnings would issue from the radio? I started toward my table radio and stopped. To listen to it with the arm around my neck seemed altogether too much. But I suspected I would hear something like this: because of the wet branches and their own wet feet and wings, small birds have fallen to the ground and cannot fly. Automobiles passing through parks should take care not to run over them. And if a warm wind comes up, the fog will perhaps change color. Strange-colored fogs are noxious. Listeners should therefore lock their doors if the fog should turn pink or purple.

"Change color?" I muttered. "Turn pink or purple?"

I pulled at the curtain and looked out. The fog seemed to press down with an empty weight. Was it because of the wind that a thin darkness seemed to be moving about, different from the usual black of night? The thickness of the fog seemed infinite, and yet beyond it something fearsome writhed and coiled.

I remembered that earlier, as I was coming home with the borrowed arm, the head and tail beams of the car driven by the woman in vermilion had come up indistinctly in the fog. A great, blurred sphere of faint purple now seemed to come toward me. I hastily pulled away from the curtain.

"Let's go to bed. Us too."

It seemed as if no one else in the world would be up. To be up was terror.

Taking the arm from my neck and putting it on the table, I changed into a fresh night-kimono, a cotton print. The arm watched me change. I was shy at being watched. Never before had a woman watched me undress in my room.

The arm in my own, I got into bed. I lay facing it, and brought it lightly to my chest. It lay quiet.

Intermittently I could hear a faint sound as of rain, a very light sound, as if the fog had not turned to rain but were itself forming drops. The fingers clasped in my hand beneath the blanket grew warmer; and it gave me the quietest of sensations, the fact that they had not warmed to my own temperature.

"Are you asleep?"

"No," replied the arm.

"You were so quiet, I thought you might be asleep."

"What do you want me to do?"

Opening my kimono, I brought the arm to my chest. The difference in warmth sank in. In the somehow sultry, somehow chilly night, the smoothness of the skin was pleasant.

The lights were still on. I had forgotten to turn them out as I went to bed.

"The lights." I got up, and the arm fell from my chest.

I hastened to pick it up. "Will you turn out the lights?" I started toward the door. "Do you sleep in the dark? Or with lights on?"

The arm did not answer. It would surely know. Why had it not answered? I did not know the girl's nocturnal practices. I compared the two pictures, of her asleep in the dark and with the lights on. I decided that tonight, without her arm, she would have them on. Somehow I too wanted them on. I wanted to gaze at the arm. I wanted to stay awake and watch the arm after it had gone to sleep. But the fingers stretched to turn off the switch by the door.

I went back and lay down in the darkness, the arm by my chest. I lay there silently, waiting for it to go to sleep. Whether dissatisfied or afraid of the dark, the hand lay open at my side, and presently the five fingers were climbing my chest. The elbow bent of its own accord, and the arm embraced me.

There was a delicate pulse at the girl's wrist. It lay over my heart, so that the two pulses sounded against each other. Hers was at first somewhat slower than mine, then they were together. And then I could feel only mine. I did not know which was faster, which slower.

Perhaps this identity of pulse and heartbeat was for a brief period when I might try to exchange the arm for my own. Or had it gone to sleep? I had once heard a woman say that women were less happy in the throes of ecstasy than sleeping peacefully beside their men; but never before had a woman slept beside me as peacefully as this arm.

I was conscious of my beating heart because of the pulsation above it. Between one beat and the next, something sped far away and sped back again. As I listened to the beating, the distance seemed to increase. And however far the something went, however infinitely far, it met nothing at its destination. The next beat summoned it back. I should have been afraid, and was not. Yet I groped for the switch beside my pillow.

Before turning it on, I quietly rolled back the blanket. The arm slept on, unaware of what was happening. A gentle band of faintest white encircled my naked chest, seeming to rise from the flesh itself, like the glow before the dawning of a tiny, warm sun.

I turned on the light. I put my hands to the fingers and shoulder and pulled the arm straight. I turned it quietly in my hands, gazing at the play of light and shadow, from the roundness at the shoulder over the narrowing and swelling of the forearm, the narrowing again at the gentle roundness of the elbow, the faint depression inside the elbow, the narrowing roundness to the wrist, the palm and back of the hand, and on to the fingers.

"I'll have it." I was not conscious of muttering the words. In a trance, I removed my right arm and substituted the girl's.

There was a slight gasp—whether from the arm or from me I could not tell—and a spasm at my shoulder. So I knew of the change.

The girl's arm—mine now—was trembling and reaching for the air. Bending it, I brought it close to my mouth.

"Does it hurt? Do you hurt?"

"No. Not at all. Not at all." The words were fitful.

A shudder went through me like lightning. I had the fingers in my mouth.

Somehow I spoke my happiness, but the girl's fingers were at my tongue, and whatever it was I spoke did not form into words.

"Please. It's all right," the arm replied. The trembling stopped. "I was told you could. And yet—"

I noticed something. I could feel the girl's fingers in my mouth, but the fingers of her right hand, now those of my own right hand, could not feel my lips or teeth. In panic I shook my right arm and could not feel the shaking. There was a break, a stop, between arm and shoulder.

"The blood doesn't go," I blurted out. "Does it or doesn't it?"

For the first time I was swept by fear. I rose up in bed. My own arm had fallen beside me. Separated from me, it was an unsightly object. But more important—would not the pulse have stopped? The girl's arm was warm and pulsing; my own looked as if it were growing stiff and cold. With the girl's, I grasped my own right arm. I grasped it, but there was no sensation.

"Is there a pulse?" I asked the arm. "Is it cold?"

"A little. Just a little colder than I am. I've gotten very warm." There was something especially womanly in the cadence. Now that the arm was fastened to my shoulder and made my own, it seemed womanly as it had not before.

"The pulse hasn't stopped?"

"You should be more trusting."

"Of what?"

"You changed your arm for mine, didn't you?"

"Is the blood flowing?"

"'Woman, whom seekest thou?' You know the passage?"

"'Woman, why weepest thou? Whom seekest thou?'"

"Very often when I'm dreaming and wake up in the night I whisper it to myself."

This time of course the "I" would be the owner of the winsome arm at my shoulder. The words from the Bible were as if spoken by an eternal voice, in an eternal place.

"Will she have trouble sleeping?" I too spoke of the girl herself. "Will she be having a nightmare? It's a fog for herds of nightmares to wander in. But the dampness will make even demons cough."

"To keep you from hearing them." The girl's arm, my own still in its hand, covered my right ear.

It was now my own right arm, but the motion seemed to have come not of my volition but of its own, from its heart. Yet the separation was by no means so complete.

"The pulse. The sound of the pulse."

I heard the pulse of my own right arm. The girl's arm had come to my ear with my own arm in its hand, and my own wrist was at my ear.

My arm was warm—as the girl's arm had said, just perceptibly cooler than her fingers and my ear.

"I'll keep away the devils." Mischievously, gently, the long, delicate nail of her little finger stirred in my ear. I shook my head. My left hand—mine from the start—took my right wrist—actually the girl's. As I threw my head back, I caught sight of the girl's little finger.

Four fingers of her hand were grasping the arm I had taken from my right shoulder. The little finger alone—shall we say that it alone was allowed to play free?—was bent toward the back of the hand. The tip of the nail touched my right arm lightly. The finger was bent in a position possible only for a girl's supple hand, out of the question for a stiff-jointed man like me. From its base it rose at right angles. At the first joint it bent in another right angle, and at the next in yet another. It thus traced a square, the fourth side formed by the ring finger.

It formed a rectangular window at the level of my eye. Or rather a peephole, or an eyeglass, much too small for a window; but somehow I thought of a window. The sort of window a violet might look out through. The window of the little finger, the finger-rimmed eyeglass, so white that it gave off a faint glow—I brought it nearer my eye. I closed the other eye.

"A peep show?" asked the arm. "And what do you see?"

"My dusky old room. Its five lights." Before I had finished the sentence I was almost shouting. "No, no! I see it!"

"And what do you see?"

"It's gone."

"And what did you see?"

"A color. A blur of purple. And inside it little circles, little beads of red and gold, whirling around and around."

"You're tired." The girl's arm put down my right arm, and her fingers gently stroked my eyelids.

"Were the beads of gold and red spinning around in a huge cogwheel? Did I see something in the cogwheel, something that came and went?"

I did not know whether I had actually seen something there or only seemed to—a fleeting illusion, not to stay in the memory. I could not remember what it might have been.

"Was it an illusion you wanted to show me?"

"No. I came to erase it."

"Of days gone by. Of longing and sadness."

On my eyelids the movement of her fingers stopped.

I asked an unexpected question. "When you let down your hair does it cover your shoulders?"

"It does. I wash it in hot water, but afterward—a special quirk of mine, maybe—I pour cold water over it. I like the feel of cold hair against my shoulders and arms, and against my breasts too."

It would of course be the girl again. Her breasts had never been touched by a man, and no doubt she would have had difficulty describing the feel of the cold, wet hair against them. Had the arm, separated from the body, been separated too from the shyness and the reserve?

Quietly I took in my left hand the gentle roundness at the shoulder, now my own. It seemed to me that I had in my hand the roundness, not yet large, of her breasts. The roundness of the shoulder became the soft roundness of breasts.

Her hand lay gently on my eyelids. The fingers and the hand clung softly and sank through, and the underside of the eyelids seemed to warm at the touch. The warmth sank into my eyes.

"The blood is going now," I said quietly. "It is going."

It was not a cry of surprise as when I had noticed that my arm was changed for hers. There was no shuddering and no spasm in the girl's arm or my shoulder. When had my blood begun to flow through the arm, her blood through me? When had the break at the shoulder disappeared? The clean blood of the girl was now, this very moment, flowing through me; but would there not be unpleasantness when the arm was returned to the girl, this dirty male blood flowing through it? What if it would not attach itself to her shoulder?

"No such betrayal," I muttered.

"It will be all right," whispered the arm.

There was no dramatic awareness that between the arm and my shoulder the blood came and went. My left hand, enfolding my right shoulder, and the shoulder itself, now mine, had a natural understanding of the fact. They had come to know it. The knowledge pulled them down into slumber.

I slept.

I floated on a great wave. It was the encompassing fog turned a faint purple, and there were pale green ripples at the spot where I floated on the great wave, and there alone. The dank solitude of my room was gone. My left hand seemed to rest lightly on the girl's right arm. It seemed that her fingers held magnolia stamens. I could not see them, but I could smell them. We had thrown them away—and when and how had she gathered them up again? The white petals, but a day old, had not yet fallen; why then the stamens? The automobile of the woman in vermilion slid by, drawing a great circle with me at the center. It seemed to watch over our sleep, the arm's and mine.

Our sleep was probably light, but I had never before known sleep so warm, so sweet. A restless sleeper, I had never before been blessed with the sleep of a child.

The long, narrow, delicate nail scratched gently at the palm of my hand, and the slight touch made my sleep deeper. I disappeared.

I awoke screaming. I almost fell out of bed, and staggered three or four steps.

I had awakened to the touch of something repulsive. It was my right arm.

Steadying myself, I looked down at the arm on the bed. I caught my breath, my heart raced, my whole body trembled. I saw the arm in one instant, and the next I had torn the girl's from my shoulder and put back my own. The act was like murder upon a sudden, diabolic impulse.

I knelt by the bed, my chest against it, and rubbed at my insane heart with my restored hand. As the beating slowed down a sadness welled up from deeper than the deepest inside me.

"Where is her arm?" I raised my head.

It lay at the foot of the bed, flung palm up into the heap of the blanket. The outstretched fingers did not move. The arm was faintly white in the dim light.

Crying out in alarm I swept it up and held it tight to my chest. I embraced it as one would a small child from whom life was going. I brought the fingers to my lips. If the dew of woman would but come from between the long nails and the fingertips!

THE DAY BEFORE

Endō Shūsaku

Translated by Van C. Gessel

There was a time when the name of Endō Shūsaku (1923–) was invariably introduced to Western readers as "the Japanese Graham Greene." Recently, however, enthusiastic critical reactions to translations of Endō's works into a dozen languages have prompted a critic to suggest that, by the twenty-first century, Greene may consider himself fortunate to be labeled the "British Endō." Six novels, a play, a short story collection, and a contemplative life of Jesus have been translated into English and many other languages, establishing Endō as the most accessible of contemporary Japanese novelists, not only because he deals with questions of Christian faith and human weakness that transcend national boundaries, but also because he writes with a simplicity and an eye for detail and structure that are rare qualities among his contemporaries in Japan.

Endō was baptized a Catholic at his mother's instigation when he was eleven years old. The influence of a strong but forgiving maternal figure has remained central to his writings and to his conception of God, as the critic Etō Jun has pointed out. This Madonna-Jesus figure was first sketched out in a series of short stories that Endō wrote after a long hospitalization in the early 1960s; his collection Aika *(Elegies, 1965), from which "The Day Before" (Sono zenjitsu) is taken, is filled with preliminary sketches for the larger themes Endō would paint with bolder strokes in novels such as* Chimmoku *(Silence, 1966; tr. 1969) and* Samurai *(The Samurai, 1980; tr. 1982). Even clearer portrayals of Christ as a compassionate mother figure may be found in the story "Haha naru mono" (Mothers, 1969; tr. 1984) and Endō's Iesu no shōgai (Life of Jesus, 1973; tr. 1978). The fumie that is a central image in "The Day Before" is yet another image of Christ—in this case, a copper or wooden likeness of Mary or Jesus which the Japanese authorities in the seventeenth century used to ferret out suspected Christians. Those who would trample on the sacred image were released, whether or not such an action reflected their true inner feelings. The fumie for Endō thus represents the dichotomy between outward behavior—cowardice, betrayal—and internal aspirations.*

After studying French Catholic fiction at Keiō University, Endō spent two and a half years in France, beginning in 1950 when he traveled to Europe aboard a merchant vessel in one of the first groups of Japanese students to go abroad after the Second World War. In Europe, the conflicts between Eastern and Western cultures, between Oriental pantheism and Occidental monotheism, seared his conscience and led him to write his first fiction, Shiroi hito (White Man, 1955), which was awarded the Akutagawa Prize. Endō followed this initial account of betrayal and brutality in occupied France with a study of moral corruption set in Japan, Kiiroi hito (Yellow Man, 1955), and created a sensation with his castigation of the Japanese moral conscience in Umi to dokuyaku (The Sea and Poison, 1958; tr. 1972).

Endō is also widely known in Japan as the author of lighter "entertainment" novels, many of which, like Obakasan (Wonderful Fool, 1959; tr. 1974), combine a comic exterior with a deeply compassionate, fundamentally religious core. The entire range and variety of Endō's literary output may, in fact, be viewed as a manifestation of his cautiously optimistic belief that the "mud swamp" of Japan may be transcended through acts of selfless charity, accompanied by a pained but bemused smile—the sort that the narrator of "The Day Before" is also to muster just before he faces possible death.

*   *   *

For some time I had wanted to get my hands on that *fumie*. If nothing else, I at least wanted to be able to see it. The image was owned by Fukae Tokujirō of Daimyō village, Sonoki, in Nagasaki Prefecture. A copper engraving of the crucified Christ was set in a wooden frame eight inches wide by twelve inches long.

It had been used during the fourth siege of Urakami, the final persecution of Christians in Japan. Use of the *fumie* was supposed to have been abolished by the U.S.-Japan Treaty of 1858, but apparently it was used again in this suppression, which occurred after the signing of the accord.

My desire to obtain the *fumie* was aroused when I read in a Catholic tract about Tōgorō, a villager from Takashima in Sonoki District, who apostatized during the fourth siege. The tract fascinated me. Its author of course confined himself to presenting the historical facts surrounding the suppression and said very little about Tōgorō, but my interest was riveted on him.

Father N, a friend from my school days, happened to be in Nagasaki at the time, so I wrote to him about my feelings concerning Tōgorō. In his reply he mentioned the *fumie*. Daimyō village was in his parish, he noted, and a Mr. Fukae from the village owned a *fumie* from the period. It seems that some of Fukae's ancestors had been among the officials who had carried out the supression

The day before I was due to have my third operation, arrangements were made for me to see the *fumie*. My friend Father Inoue was supposed to go to Nagasaki and bring it back with him. This was not merely for my benefit, of course; his assignment was to deposit the image in the Christian Archives at J University in Yotsuya. That was a disappointment to me, but I conceded the necessity of preserving such precious objects. Father Inoue telephoned my wife and let her know he would be allowed to give me a brief look at it before he turned it over to the university.

I dozed off in my hospital room as I waited for Father Inoue. Christmas was approaching, and I could hear a choir practicing on the roof—probably students from the school of nursing. Sometimes I would open my eyes a slit and listen to those voices in the distance, then close my eyes again.

I sensed someone softly opening the door to my room. It might be my wife, I thought, but she was supposed to be running around making all the arrangements for my massive surgery tomorrow. So I couldn't imagine it would be her.

"Who's there?"

A middle-aged man dressed in a fur jacket and a mountaineering cap peered in. I did not know him. I glanced first from his dirty cap to his fur jacket, then lowered my gaze to the large lace-up boots he was wearing. Ah, it must be someone from Father Inoue, I thought.

"Are you from the church?"

"Huh?"

"Father sent you, didn't he?" I smiled, but his eyes narrowed and a strange expression crossed his face.

"No. I asked 'em over in the ward, and they said you might wanna buy."

"Buy? What?"

"You get four for six hundred yen. I got books, too. But I didn't bring 'em today."

Not waiting for me to respond, he appeared to twist at the waist and pulled a small paper envelope from his trouser pocket. Inside the envelope were four photographs with yellowed borders, a result no doubt of cheap developing. In the shadowy prints the dim figure of a man could be seen embracing the indistinct body of a woman. A single wooden chair stood beside the bed in what appeared to be a dreary hotel in the suburbs.

"You don't understand. I'm being operated on tomorrow!"

"That's why I brought these." He had no words of sympathy to offer. Scratching the palm of his hand with the photographs, he continued, "Since you got an operation coming up, you can buy these as a good luck charm. Buy 'em and the operation's bound to be a success. How about it, captain?"

"Do you come around to this hospital often?"

"Sure. This is my territory."

It may have been a joke, or perhaps he meant it seriously, but he made the declaration to me with all the bravura of a physician talking to one of his patients. I took a liking to the man.

"No, no. These pictures don't interest me."

"Well. . ." He looked rueful. "If you don't like these, what sort of pose do you want, captain?"

He lit up a cigarette from the pack I held out to him and began to chatter.

Nowhere does a person get more bored and develop a greater desire to look at pictures and books of this sort than in a hospital. No location was more suitable to peddle such goods, since the police would never suspect. This fellow had divided up the territory with his colleagues and made the rounds of the city hospitals.

"A few days back, the old boy in Room H took a look at these shots before his operation, and he says, 'Ah, now I can die happy!'"

I laughed. I found him a more welcome visitor today than the relatives who tiptoe through hospital-room doors with pained looks on their faces. When he had finished his cigarette, he stuck another behind his ear and left the room.

For some reason I felt in high spirits. This peddler had come instead of the priest. Bringing pornographic pictures in place of the *fumie*. Today should have been a day for me to think about many things, to put various affairs in order. Tomorrow's operation would be unlike my first two; the doctors anticipated massive hemorrhaging and danger because my pleurae had fused together. The risk was so great they had left it up to me whether or not to go through with surgery. Today I had intended to put on a face so bland it would seem that cellophane had been stretched over it, but that porn peddler had nipped that plan in the bud. And yet, in their own way, those murky photographs with their sallow images were proof of God's existence.

When the officers of the feudal domain raided Takashima, the villagers were reciting their evening prayers. They naturally had lookouts posted, but the police were already storming into the farmhouse chapel when the sentries rang the warning bell.

In the light of the moon that night, ten men—including two leaders of the peasant association—were hurriedly transported to Urakami. Among them, for good or ill, was Tōgorō. From the outset his comrades had the uneasy foreboding that Tōgorō would apostatize. He had been such an irksome anomaly in this village of fervent faith. Despite his massive stature, Tōgorō was a coward.

On past occasions Tōgorō had been lured into quarrels by the young men of neighboring villages. Though he was twice the size of an average man, there were times when he skulked back to Takashima clad only in his loincloth, having been thrown to the ground and stripped of all he had. Fear of his opponents rather than a Christian resolve to turn the other cheek prevented him from offering any resistance at such times. It was not long before the villagers of Takashima came to despise him. For that reason, although he was already thirty years old, he was the only young man of his age without a bride. He lived alone with his mother.

Of the ten prisoners, Kashichi held the highest position in the village. He was a man of principle, and the evening before the interrogations began at Urakami, he offered special words of encouragement to Tōgorō. "Deus and Santa Maria will surely grant us strength and courage. Those who suffer in this world are guaranteed a place in heaven," Kashichi reassured him. Tōgorō studied the others with the terrified eyes of a stray dog, but at their urging he joined in the chanting of the Credo and Pater Noster.

Early in the morning on the following day, the interrogations began at the office of the Urakami magistrate. The prisoners were bound and dragged out one by one to the cold, gravel-floored interrogation room, where the officers brought out the *fumie*. Those who would not recant their faith were beaten severely with an archer's bow. But before the bow had even been raised over Tōgorō, he ground his soiled foot into the face of Christ in the image. With sad, animal-like eyes Tōgorō darted a glance toward his comrades, who were disheveled and covered with blood. The officers then drove him out of the magistrate's headquarters.

"We're going to shave you and get a blood sample now." This time a nurse came into my room, carrying a metal tray and a hypodermic. Her job was to shave the fine hairs from the area targeted for surgery tomorrow and to determine my blood type for transfusions.

When she removed my pyjama top the chilly air cut into my skin. I raised my left arm and did my best not to giggle as she moved the razor along my armpit.

"That tickles!"

"When you bathe, be sure to wash really well back here. It's all red."

"I can't wash there. It's been very sensitive since my last operation. I can't scrub it."

There is a large scar on my back, cut at a slant across my shoulder. The area is swollen, since an incision was made twice in the same place. Again tomorrow the cold scalpel would race across that spot. And my body would be soaked with blood.

After Tōgorō's desertion the remaining nine men stubbornly refused to apostatize. They were placed for a time in a Nagasaki prison, and the following year—1868—they were loaded into a boat and sent to Tsuyama, near Onomichi. Rain fell that evening and drenched the open boat, and the prisoners, having only the clothes they were wearing, huddled together to ward off the cold. As the boat pulled away from Nagasaki, one of the prisoners, Bunji, noticed a man dressed like a dockworker standing at the edge of the water.

"Look! Isn't that Tōgorō?"

From far in the distance, Tōgorō was peering toward them with the same sad, appealing eyes they had seen when he apostatized. The men lowered their eyes as though they had gazed upon something filthy, and no one uttered another word.

The prison for these nine men lay in the mountains some twenty-four miles from Tsuyama. From their cell they could see the officers' hut and a small pond. At first there was little harassment, and the officers were lenient. Even the food they received twice a day was something for which these impoverished farmers could be thankful. The officers laughed gently and told them that they could eat better food and be given warmer clothes if they would merely cast off their burdensome religion.

In the autumn of that year, fourteen or fifteen new prisoners arrived unexpectedly. They were children from Takashima. The men were surprised at this strange move by the officials, yet pleased to be able to see some of their family after so long a time. But soon they were forced into the realization that this move was part of a psychological torture they came to refer to as "child abuse."

Occasionally the prisoners heard weeping from the adjoining cell, where their children were incarcerated. One afternoon a prisoner named Fujifusa pressed his face to the tiny window of the children's cell and saw two emaciated boys catching dragonflies and stuffing them into their mouths. It was obvious that the children were being given scarcely anything that could be called food. The other men listened to this report and wept.

They begged the officers to take even half of their own "good" food and share it with the children, but this was not allowed. They were told, however, that all they had to do was reject their troublesome religion, and they and their children would go back to their dear village pleasingly plump.

"There. All done."

The nurse pulled out the hypodermic, and as I rubbed the spot where the needle had entered, she held the vial filled with blood up to the light at eye level.

"Your blood is dark, isn't it?"

"Does it mean something's wrong if it's dark?"

"Oh, no. I was just commenting on how dark it is."

As she went out, a young doctor I had not seen before came in. I tried to sit up in bed.

"No, no. As you were. I'm Okuyama, Department of Anesthesia."

Okuyama turned out to be the anesthetist who would assist at my operation the next day. He went through the formality of placing a stethoscope on my chest.

"In your previous operations, did you awaken quickly from the anesthesia?"

In my most recent operation, the doctors had cut away five of my ribs. I remembered that the anesthesia had worn off just as the operation ended. The pain I experienced then was like a pair of scissors jabbing through my chest. I described the agony for Okuyama.

"This time, please keep me knocked out for at least half a day. That was terribly painful."

The young doctor smiled broadly. "We'll aim for that, then."

When it became clear that the men were still not going to apostatize, the tortures began. The nine men were separated and placed in small boxes, in which they were unable to move from a seated position. Holes were bored near their heads to allow them to breathe. They were not permitted to leave the boxes except to relieve themselves.

Winter drew near. The prisoners began to weaken from cold and exhaustion. In compensation, however, they began to hear laughter from the adjoining cell. The officers, being fathers themselves, had given food to the children. The nine men in their individual boxes listened silently to the laughing voices.

At the end of the eleventh month a prisoner named Kumekichi died. The oldest of the nine, he had been unable to endure the cold and the fatigue. Kashichi had had great respect for the old man and always asked his advice whenever something happened in the prison. He was therefore deeply affected by his death. Peering out through the hole bored in his box, Kashichi reflected on how weak his own will had become. And for the first time he hated the traitor Tōgorō.

Again the door opened softly. Father? No. Once again it was the porn peddler.

"Captain!"

"What? You!"

"Actually . . . I've brought you a good luck charm. . ."

"I told you I wouldn't buy any."

"Not pictures. I'm giving you this for free. Then if your operation's a success, you can thank me by purchasing the pictures and books I bring around." He lowered his voice to a whisper. "Captain, I can get you a woman. It's strictly 'no trespassing' around here. You can lock the door. You've got a bed. Nobody'll know!"

"Yes, yes."

He was clutching an object in his hand. Before he left he set it on the table beside my bed. I glanced over and discovered a tiny wooden doll, grimy from the sweat and soil of the peddler's hands.

They were taken from their boxes when winter came, but the mornings and nights continued cold. From the mountain to the rear they heard sounds like something splitting open. It was the sound of branches cracking from the cold. Thin ice stretched across the tiny pond between the prison and the officers' hut.

One day near evening, the officers came and took two prisoners, Seiichi and Tatsugorō, from the cell. They cast the two into the frozen pond and beat them with poles each time their heads bobbed above the surface of the water. When they lost consciousness from the painful torture, Seiichi and Tatsugorō were carried back to the prison in the arms of the officers. The six remaining men joined their voices with Kashichi's and recited the Ave Maria over and over again. But many were choked with sobs during the final benediction, "Holy Mary, Mother of God, pray for us sinners now and at the hour of our death."

Just then, through the cell window Kashichi caught sight of a tall, thin man glancing about him restlessly like a beggar. The man, whose hair and beard grew wantonly like an exile's, turned toward him, and Kashichi involuntarily shouted, "It's Tōgorō!"

An officer came out to drive the intruder away, but Tōgorō shook his head and seemed to be making some sort of fervent plea. Eventually the first officer summoned another, and the two spoke together for a few moments. Finally they took Tōgorō to the only empty cell in the prison.

"He's one of you," the officers announced, confusion written on their faces. When they were gone, the eight prisoners sat in silence and listened to the sound of Tōgorō shuffling about in the dark.

"Why did you come?" At last Kashichi asked the question in all their minds. He felt vaguely uneasy. It had occurred to him that Tōgorō might be a spy for the officers. Even if he weren't a spy, his presence might further dampen the already weakened spirits of the others. Kashichi had heard from the dead Kumekichi that the officers employed such cunning devices.

Tōgorō's reply was unexpected. In a soft voice, he told them that he had come here and surrendered on his own.

"You?! . . ."

When the men jeered at him, Tōgorō tried to stammer out a defense. Kashichi silenced them.

"Do you realize that you'll be tortured here? If you're going to make it harder for the rest of us, you'd better go back home."

Tōgorō remained silent.

"Aren't you afraid?"

"I'm afraid," Tōgorō muttered.

Then he blurted out something very strange. He had come here because he had heard a voice. He had most certainly heard a voice. It had instructed him to go just once more to be with the others. "Go to them in Tsuyama. And if you fear the tortures, you can run away again. Go to Tsuyama," the tearful, pleading voice had said.

That night the only noise that broke the stillness outside was the sound of branches splitting on the mountain. The prisoners listened intently to Tōgorō's story. One grumbled, "A nice convenient tale for him to tell, isn't it?" To him, the story sounded like something Tōgorō had made up so that his friends and fellow villagers would forgive him for his betrayal two years earlier. "If you fear the tortures, you can run away again." It seemed just another handy way of talking himself out of difficulty.

Kashichi was half inclined to agree, but another part of him refused to believe that Tōgorō's story was a hoax. Unable to sleep that night, he listened thoughtfully to Tōgorō's body stirring in the darkness.

The following day Tōgorō was taken out by the officers and hurled into the pond. The other prisoners joined Kashichi in reciting the Credo as Tōgorō's childlike screams filled their ears. They prayed that God would grant strength to this weakling. But in the end the voice they heard nullified their entreaties. Tōgorō renounced his faith to the officers and was pulled from the pond.

Still, Kashichi was relieved to know that his suspicions about Tōgorō being a spy had been mistaken. "It's all right. It's all right," he thought.

No one knows what happened to Tōgorō after the officers set him free. In 1871, the eight prisoners were released by the new government.

Father Inoue arrived. He opened the door softly and came in, just as the porn peddler had done. Though it was cold outside, a thin layer of perspiration coated his pale face. We had been friends in our school days, and together we had gone to France, sleeping in the hold of a cargo ship among coolies and soldiers.

"I owe you an apology."

"You couldn't get the *fumie?*"

"No." Someone higher up in the church hierarchy had ordered another priest to take the *fumie* from Nagasaki to the Christian Archives at J University.

Inoue had a deep red birthmark on his forehead. He was a curate in a small church in downtown Tokyo. The overcoat he wore had frayed sleeves and his black trousers were worn at the knees. Just as I had imagined, his figure somehow resembled that of the man in the mountaineering cap. But I told him nothing of that encounter.

Inoue told me that he had seen the *fumie*. The wooden frame was rotting away. The copperplate figure of Christ, covered with a greenish patina, had probably been fashioned by a country laborer in Urakami. The face resembled a child's scribble, and the eyes and nose had been worn away until they were no longer distinguishable. The *fumie* had been lying neglected in a storehouse at Mr. Fukae's home in Daimyō.

Puffing on our cigarettes, we changed the topic of discussion. I asked Father Inoue about the Last Supper scene in the Gospel of St. John. This was a passage that had troubled me for some time. I could not understand the remark Christ made when he handed the sop to the traitor Judas.

"And when he had dipped the sop, he gave it to Judas Iscariot, the son of Simon. . . Then said Jesus unto him 'That thou doest, do quickly. . .'"

That thou doest, do quickly. Obviously referring to Judas' betrayal of him. But why didn't Christ restrain Judas? Had Jesus really cast the traitor off with such obvious callousness? That was what I wanted to know.

Father Inoue said that these words revealed the human side of Christ. He loved Judas, but with a traitor seated at the same table, he could not suppress his hatred. Inoue believed that this feeling resembled the complex mixture of love and hate a man feels when he is betrayed by the woman he loves. But I disagreed.

"Jesus isn't issuing a command here. Maybe the translation from the original has been gradually corrupted. It's like he's saying, 'You're going to do this anyway. I can't stop you, so go ahead and do it.' Isn't that what he meant when he said, 'My cross is for that purpose,' and spoke of the cross he had to bear? Christ knew all the desperate acts of men."

The choir practice on the roof seemed to have ended. Afternoons at the hospital were quiet. Sticking to my rather heretical views in spite of Father Inoue's objections, I thought about the *fumie* I had not seen. I had wanted to see it before my operation, but if I couldn't, I would just have to accept it. Father Inoue had reported that the copperplate image of Christ, set in a rotting wooden frame, had been worn away. The feet of the men who had trampled on it had disfigured and gradually rubbed out the face of Christ. But more than that copper image of Christ was disfigured. I think I understood the sort of pain Tōgorō felt in his foot as he trod on it. The pain of many such men was transmitted to the copperplate Christ. And he, unable to endure the sufferings of men, was overwhelmed with compassion and whispered, "That thou doest, do quickly." He whose face was trodden upon and he who trod upon it were still alive today, in the same juxtaposition.

Still vaguely in my mind were thoughts of the small, yellow-edged photographs the peddler had brought in earlier. Just as the shadowy bodies of the man and woman moaned and embraced in those pictures, the face of the copperplate Christ and the flesh of men come into contact with one another. The two strangely resemble one another. This relationship is described in the catechisms that children study on Sunday afternoons with nuns in the rear gardens of churches that smell of boiling jam. For many years I scoffed at those catechisms. And yet, after some thirty years, this is the only thing I can say I have learned.

After Father Inoue left, I snuggled down into my bed and waited for my wife to come. Occasionally the feeble sunlight shone into my room from between the gray clouds. Steam rose from a medicinal jar on an electric heater. There was a bump as something fell to the floor. I opened my eyes and looked down. It was the good luck charm the peddler had given me. That tiny wooden doll, as grimy as life itself.

FRIENDS

Abe Akira

Translated by Virginia Marcus

Abe Akira was born in Hiroshima in 1934, but he has lived in Kugenuma, not far from Tokyo, most of his life. As a student at Tokyo University, he majored in French literature, focusing on the works of Stendhal, and actively participated in university theatrical productions. After college he worked for a Tokyo broadcasting company as a producer of both television and radio programs. In 1971, however, he left that profession to devote himself to his writing, which had already received favorable attention in literary circles.

Most of Abe's stories belong to that distinctive genre of Japanese literature known as the "I-novel," in which the author makes explicit his use of personal experience. He made his debut in 1962 with "Kodomobeya" (The Child's Room), a short story about a young boy and his retarded older brother. Abe turned to the broadcasting studio for his inspiration in such stories as "Tokyo no haru" (Spring in Tokyo, 1967) and "Hibi no tomo" (Friends, 1970). Haunted by the pathetic figure of his unsuccessful father, a veteran of the Second World War and a living symbol of a defeated nation, Abe wrote several stories and a novel, Shirei no kyūka *(The Commander's Furlough, 1970), that deal with the final years of his father's life and his own feelings of humiliation and shame.*

Although Abe's stories touch upon such ponderous themes as insanity, suicide, and shame, the author chooses to focus on everyday events and seemingly insignificant details. He does not dwell on the mysteries of life and death, nor does he indulge in sentimentality. Yet, by weaving together the details of ordinary lives, Abe achieves a work of psychological depth and creates a world that speaks of a larger humanity.

*   *   *

One day Urashima dropped into my office.

"Hatori's in bad shape," he said. "I understand he hasn't been to work for some time."

"So he's back in again?" Seated at my desk, I let out an involuntary laugh. "Hatori's illness" had become a kind of password between Urashima and me.

"This time it looks pretty bad."

"Have a seat," I said. Urashima pulled up a chair. How many times had we already discussed it? I chuckled, though I didn't mean to laugh at my friend's misfortune. We tried to help Hatori, and often talked about his problem, but it was always painful. "So he's back in again?" The words echoed. It made me sad to realize that I was now capable of such an indifferent remark.

Some time ago I had seen Hatori in good spirits, though even then he had seemed a little out of sorts. He sat next to us that night, sipping a beer as we drank our whiskey. I remember that every so often he would take out some pills the doctor had given him and gulp them down.

Hatori himself was aware of his problem. "I get so nervous," he had said, "I can't talk to anyone. I listen without responding. I don't use words—I just blink. People talk to me, but I can't answer and say how I feel. Instead I stare at things. I keep to myself all the time."

No one had to tell him to go to the hospital. He went on his own. For at least a month, and sometimes for as long as three or four, he wouldn't show up at work. His disappearances came as no surprise—everyone knew about his "vacations." No doubt the other cameramen welcomed his absence, for when he was himself Hatori was considered the best cameraman at the studio.

When the three of us worked together or went drinking, Urashima and I would find ourselves bothered by Hatori's sudden silences. As his symptoms grew worse, he didn't even blink any more. He stared at us with his eyes wide open like a baby, oblivious to everything. He fixed his swollen, bloodshot eyes on one spot, as if he were a statue. We blamed ourselves, in part, for what happened. As soon as he started to withdraw, we should have let him rest; instead, we ignored his illness and took him around with us every night as we always had.

When he did come to work, we could see that he was growing more and more withdrawn. Once when we were working with him on a documentary, he started taking pictures of strange objects. He had gradually lost interest in the people we were sent to film. With the utmost care he shot one roll after another, focusing his camera on everything but the subject at hand—the hollow of a gnarled, rotting tree, a broken drainpipe, a child's old, abandoned tricycle, leaves fluttering in the wind.

Some of us expressed sympathy for him, but no one had much hope for his recovery. Those who once envied Hatori's reputation and skill were now given the chance to succeed him. His illness provided them with the perfect opportunity. Gradually he was taken off the important shows. "He's not himself," they reasoned, giving him insignificant jobs more suited to a novice. Veteran cameraman that he was, Hatori had trouble accepting his demotion. We could see that humiliation and anxiety were slowly eating away at him.

Although he had no special assignments, he would leave for the office early in the morning and spend precisely eight hours at his desk. He sat there staring off into space as he puffed away on a cigarette. His face had become swollen. He hardly uttered a word to anyone. There wasn't so much as a single sheet of paper on his desk—not a speck of dust. He would return from his "vacations" before he should have, without fully recovering, and forcing himself in this way only made matters worse. At first, he went to the hospital once a year. Then two or three times a year. The space between visits grew shorter and shorter, and the number of his days off increased.

Before Urashima came by, he had called Hatori's wife to see how he was doing. I asked him what she had said.

He hesitated. "I guess she doesn't want us to visit him."

"Oh?"

"His eyes are swollen from the medicine." Urashima put his hand to his face. "It seems his face has changed, too. She said the medicine doesn't work any more." It irked me that Urashima had instinctively lowered his voice, as if he were afraid of being overheard.

"Don't you think he'd be glad to see us?" I asked.

"Maybe so." He seemed reluctant to answer and sounded dissatisfied.

In the end we didn't go to the hospital. To tell the truth, I didn't want to see Hatori's face in that condition. Besides, we had been there once before. One afternoon we had slipped away early from the office to visit him. When we left him in the evening, we decided to go out for a drink. Nothing was said, but we both knew we couldn't go straight home after seeing him like that. He had been fond of his drink, and since this was now denied him, I suppose we thought we would drink his share for him. We kept telling ourselves how depressing it had been, but even so we had a good time together.

"Do you think we've had too much?" I asked Urashima. "He'll be an invalid soon, and we'll still be here drowning our sorrows."

What could we do for him? I had no solutions. To Urashima it may have sounded as if I didn't think Hatori would ever get well. He was more optimistic than I, and he seemed free from guilt. He wanted Hatori to recover so that he could work with him again. His work wasn't quite up to par when Hatori was away.

In spite of how we felt, we both sensed that Hatori's wife did not appreciate our concern for her husband; rather, she seemed to resent us. From her point of view, we belonged to the company that had made her husband sick. As if her situation weren't difficult enough, she also had two children still in elementary school to look after. Hatori often talked about his wife to us. She seemed to be an ordinary housewife.

"It's so crowded where we live," he had once told me. "No breathing space at all. When we built the house after we got married, it was out in the middle of nowhere. One night my wife was taking a bath, and somebody peeked in the window. She screamed, and I ran outside, but he'd already gone. . . She'd tell me how lonely she got, especially during the day. The studio was new then, remember? It meant everything to us. We worked day and night. Our wives had to bring clean shirts and underwear to the office—we were never home. The first year of our marriage I traveled all the time. Who had time for a honeymoon? Before long our first boy was born. One night when I did get home, I came out of the station, and there was my wife, standing at the gate with our baby in her arms, crying. That's how bad things were. . . Anyway, you ought to come over sometime. It'd make my wife happy."

Once, on my day off, I did go to visit them. Though small in stature, Hatori's wife seemed a reliable sort of person. Looking at her, it was hard to imagine her as the young woman sobbing at the gate with the baby in her arms. I realized that Hatori had someone he could depend on, and I felt that some of the burden had fallen from my shoulders.

The moment she saw me she said, "What a fuss he's been making, ever since this morning! 'We'd better clean up the bathroom for Inoue,' he'd say, and then he'd hurry off and clean it himself. He scrubbed the hallway. He hung around the kitchen and kept asking me, 'Did you buy this? Did you buy that?' Finally I said to him, 'Just what kind of person is this Mr. Inoue?'"

She was hospitable enough, but she stared at me, looking troubled by something. Perhaps I was mistaken, but initially I detected a derisive tone in her voice, as if she envied the closeness we men had shared.

"He's always been like this. He gets wrapped up in whatever he does—his work, his friends. It almost frightens me." She sounded like an older sister talking about her sickly brother.

That night Hatori and I sat up talking by the brazier with a bottle of saké at our side. I can remember warming it in the kettle on the heater behind us. The two cats his wife had taken in loitered around us as we drank. Hatori called to them, as if he had suddenly remembered their names, and threw them a piece of dried fish. His face was flushed and he talked freely.

"You know when I first got sick? It was when we were on assignment up in a fishing village near Sendai. Yamaya was there—he's still in my section, you know. We had to shoot a story about a shipwreck, and we were staying at an inn nearby. Let's see, when was that? . . . One day after work we went back to the inn together, took our evening bath, and had a drink. The others kept on drinking, but for some reason I was preoccupied with the next day's shooting. I went down to the beach by myself to have another look at the location. I couldn't see much, though; it was night. Come to think of it, I was already starting to act strangely.

"I looked over the harbor in the dark and started back to the inn. It was more like a cheap lodging house than an inn, actually, but it did have a small garden. You could go straight to the beach from there. Just as I came into the garden, I heard Yamaya and Iwama, the lighting man, talking in the shadow of a tree. 'He doesn't work for his money! He can't even do a decent job, and he has the nerve to think he's a hotshot. He can drop dead, for all I care.' It was Yamaya. I stood there frozen, I couldn't move. I had worked hard on the beach that day. I'd worked until I thought I'd drop. My jacket and pants were soaking wet, but I'd lugged that camera around all day. And when I got back to the inn, all I could think about was the next day's work. There was no reason at all for him to say what he did. I had trusted Yamaya. I'd always done exactly as he told me, only to have him turn around and lie about me. It would've been another story if he'd said it right to my face, but he cornered someone when I wasn't there and tore into me. I was disgusted! I was miserable. I didn't want to think that Yamaya was that kind of person. Standing in that pitch-dark garden, I wished I had misheard him. But I hadn't. If only I'd come back a minute later, or a little earlier, I wouldn't have heard him say it. . . I hid in the shadow of a tree until Yamaya and Iwama left the garden. Then I crept up to my room and went to bed before anybody else." Hatori broke off at this point. He had trouble breathing, and his flushed face grew even redder.

"The next day we went to the house where the drowned fisherman had lived. We were filming his widow. Holding an infant to her breast, she clung to her husband's coffin. Suddenly I felt like it was all my fault, and I got down on my knees and apologized. I begged her forgiveness, I had to, or I couldn't have lived with myself. On my knees, I apologized over and over again.

"The tears streamed down my face, and the woman cried for me. I began to imagine that I had killed her husband at sea and that she and I were having an affair. I was so ashamed that I finally took my camera and ran out of the house in my bare feet. Apparently, I went back to the inn. After that, I can't remember. . . I think Yamaya canceled the shooting session and cabled Tokyo to arrange for our return. As I recall, he kept saying 'Hatori, don't worry. We'll be back soon. Don't worry.'"

The rest was a blank. On his way home from Sendai, apparently, he staggered off the train at Utsunomiya, lay down on the platform, and pleaded with Yamaya to set him free. The company informed Hatori's wife about this bizarre behavior, and when she saw for herself how disturbed he was, she burst into tears.

The news about Hatori spread quickly throughout the company. His "breakdown" was the butt of jokes whenever we went drinking. No doubt, Yamaya and Iwama were responsible for telling everyone what had occurred.

But was it really Yamaya who had attacked Hatori behind his back? It had happened in the darkness of a garden, and there was no way of knowing. Yamaya was considered a shifty individual, but we were all schemers to some extent. It would be unfair to presume that Yamaya was the one who pushed Hatori to the edge. It seems closer to the truth to say that the team of Yamaya and Hatori was ill-fated from the start.

The employees all had different theories about Hatori's illness. Some thought he had filmed too many tragedies. The wounded children, the distraught mothers, the helpless cripples had finally overwhelmed him. Hatori had been told what to shoot, and he earned a living at it, but the fact remained that he had seen too much unhappiness. His heart went out to the victims, and he blamed himself for their suffering. Some thought he was too sensitive for his line of work. Others wrote it off as a sign of fatigue.

But what kind of man was Yamaya? I once worked for him temporarily, and remember being five minutes late for a field trip. Yamaya knew he could count on me, so I thought he would wait. But he left without me, taking another crew member instead. He didn't give me a minute's leeway. I hurried after them only to find that, for all the rush, he hadn't even bothered to start work yet. There he sat, lounging in the sun, smoking a cigarette with the others. He was waiting for me.

When I apologized, he said, "It's okay. Don't worry." He smiled and sounded as if he meant it. But then he took me aside so that no one else could hear. "Listen, the boss came by and asked about you. I kept things under wraps." He sounded reassuring, as if it was all taken care of. And yet I found out afterward that before leaving the studio that morning he had made a point of telling the supervisor that I was late.

What a strange man, I thought—a real opportunist. What did he have to gain? Clearly Hatori was in a bad way, but Yamaya also had his problems. He kept a tight rein on his crew, but he often took days off himself. Whenever one of his own productions was broadcast, he failed to show up the next morning. Who knows, he may have felt some obscure sense of shame that prevented him from facing his colleagues.

Only a few days ago Yamaya was made section chief.

As I listened to Hatori that evening, I began to feel nervous. I knew it wasn't easy for him to restrain himself. His wife and children had gone to bed, but I remembered the look of uncertainty and caution in his wife's eyes that afternoon. She must have been afraid that her husband would spend the night talking to me.

Hatori was surprisingly calm when he finished telling me about the incident with Yamaya. He asked if I would like some soup. "The soup I make is better than my wife's," he said as he went into the kitchen. When he stood up, the two cats he had been holding were thrown from his lap. They stretched and followed him with their long tails raised high. I could hear him opening and shutting the refrigerator and chopping some scallions. I wondered if he had invited me so that he could confide in someone about Yamaya.

His youngest son's desk stood in the corner of the room, and a crayon drawing of a monster was pasted on the wall. "Dinosaur: Terasaurus; Height: 200 feet." The handwriting appeared to be the boy's. Later, when we talked about his son, Hatori opened the desk drawer and took out a piece of paper to show me. The teacher had marked the upper right-hand corner with three red circles to indicate an A. "He wrote about me at school," Hatori said. The title of the composition was "My Father."

> My father is a TV cameraman. My father and I do not see each other very much. He goes on a lot of business trips. When he comes home, he always says he is tired. When I try to ride on him piggyback, he says, "Get out of here!" But I still like my father, even though he says such things. Do you know why?

Hatori's son Kōji had innocently asked his classmates, "Do you know why?" I only had to read it once, however, to see what lay behind it. Ever since Hatori became ill, the company had tried to avoid sending him on location. Hatori's wife probably didn't want her first-grade son to know about his father's visits to the hospital. She must have told the boy that he was away on business.

When I was applying for my job at the studio, I had to take an entrance exam. I also needed a recommendation from someone who worked there. There was no one I could ask directly, but I used some connections and was introduced to a man called Hiramatsu. At that time he was serving as acting manager for the department that made commercials.

I remember the day in autumn when I went to meet Hiramatsu. I had dragged out my school uniform to wear, and as I climbed the hill to his office, I was depressed by the smell of my own perspiration. I found Hiramatsu in the annex. There were no windows in the room, and when I opened the door the air reeked of acetone from the film-splicing glue. It smelled vaguely like apples. A sixteen-millimeter camera and an editing table strewn with empty film cans filled the center of the room. A filthy couch, probably crawling with bedbugs, stood near the wall. If my memory serves me correctly, Hiramatsu was flirting that afternoon with a woman on the couch. I may be exaggerating somewhat, but, in any case, he sat sprawled out in his shirt-sleeves with a young woman beside him. The girl was heavily made up and presumably had a part in his commercials.

Speaking with a thick Kansai accent, Hiramatsu introduced me to her. "This is Inoue—top of his class at college." He didn't say anything about her. She barely acknowledged my presence, but finally said something like "Oh, is that so?" She then added in a singsong voice, "I don't like smart men." She looked at me and tried to make amends. "Oh, I'm sorry. The truth slipped out."

"That's 'cause you're not too bright," teased Hiramatsu. The woman, embarrassingly familiar with him, seemed to enjoy being Hiramatsu's plaything and began running her hands all over him. Such was my introduction to the world of television.

Hiramatsu gladly gave me a recommendation, but as I was leaving he warned me that I should reconsider. "A guy like you doesn't belong in a place like this. You won't fit in if you haven't had two or three wives, like me."

More than ten years have passed since then. Somewhere along the line I married. I have lived with my wife ever since. Hiramatsu left the studio a long time ago. He said that he didn't like working for other people. He started a business of his own, supposedly, but I don't really know what he's been doing. Several men at the studio followed his example and divorced their wives without a second thought. One even seduced a colleague's wife.

I have a feeling that an incident involving a young man named Kudō was behind Hiramatsu's resignation. Kudō took the examination and joined the company at the same time as Urashima and I, over ten years ago. He was one of about forty who started working for the studio that year. After Kudō finished the three-month training course, he was assigned to the commercial department under Hiramatsu. The summer of the following year he committed suicide.

I met Kudō for the first time on the morning of the company induction ceremony. It seemed odd that we hadn't met before. After our group interview we had been called together on many occasions for private interviews, a physical examination, and a series of training lectures that went on for a month. You would think we would have run into each other earlier, but I was sure that we were meeting for the first time.

That morning I was held up for some reason on the way in and had to hurry to the studio. Another new employee had also come late and was talking with the guard at the reception desk when I arrived. He was a hulking man with closely cropped hair and metal-rimmed glasses. He had a hearty laugh, though it was sometimes difficult to say just what he was laughing about. I had hurried to the studio because I was ashamed to be late for the induction ceremony; Kudō, on the other hand, didn't seem bothered in the least. He struck me as a disagreeable sort.

The guard directed us to a rented hall nearby, where the ceremony was being held. Kudō and I left the office together, but it was only I who seemed to feel a sense of urgency. Kudō made no effort to quicken his pace. He sauntered! He swung his shoulders and held his head tipped slightly back—perhaps to keep his glasses from falling off. He didn't utter one word to me on the way to the hall.

Yet my friendship with Kudō began that morning. He became my first friend at the studio. We had been assigned to different sections, but we would often go out to lunch together. Our comradeship was based solely on the fact that we were the only two who had arrived late for that function.

At first I found Kudō offensive. I thought that he was patronizing and I sensed a certain aloofness in his boisterous laughter. He seemed a good deal older than the rest of us who joined. He told me that after graduating from college he had taken some part-time jobs and had worked as a day laborer. He had also held a job as boiler man for the maintenance department on a U.S. Army base.

Once when I caught a cold Kudō advised me to take some salt for it. As we walked along, he explained that somehow salt thickens the blood, and that he always used it to cure his own ailments. After he died, it was our talk about salt that I remembered most about him.

Whenever we had lunch together we would go to a nearby restaurant that served fried pork. The place was run by a woman about thirty years old who had been in the business only a short time. "I'll take you to a good place," he had told me the first time we went out. I wondered why he thought so highly of it. Not so much as a sign hung outside the shack tucked away at the end of the street. It looked like a storage shed. We had to eat at a counter just large enough to seat three people. I had never seen such an awful place. The woman, who had an infant strapped on her back, was deep-frying the meat while a pale little boy played at her feet. The sullen look on her face suggested the miserable life she led. Perhaps she had lost her husband.

Even for that neighborhood, the restaurant was conspicuously inelegant, and the portions too generous. When the baby wasn't screaming beside us as we ate, the mother was giving the other child a scolding right under our noses. But how could you demand atmosphere or service when the prices were so low? And yet she had a hard time attracting customers to this filthy place. She simply didn't have enough experience to make a profit; and it wasn't long before it closed, reverting to a storage shed. Now and then I would remember and walk by to see what had become of it.

Kudō had gone to the shed every day while it remained open. He must have held out until the end as her most faithful customer. Every time we stopped there to eat he would say, "Isn't she nice?" Perhaps he was secretly drawn to this unfortunate woman who eked out a meager existence by running a tiny restaurant. He seemed to be attracted to the air of misery that enveloped her. In the whole time that I knew him, it was only when he talked about this woman that he would let down his guard and reveal the hidden desires and sorrows that his boasting belied.

Three days before Kudō committed suicide he had told Hiramatsu about his plan. Hiramatsu unexpectedly came by my office one afternoon. He didn't seem to have anything particular on his mind, he was just grumbling the way he did when someone slipped up on the job.

"He's going to do it, no matter what. I told him he's crazy—he's out of his mind. But it's no use. 'Don't stop me. Let me at least die the way I want to,' he said. I don't know what to do about him."

"Huh? What's he want to kill himself for?" I asked, letting out a laugh. But the question was ridiculous, and I realize now just how idiotic it was.

"Who knows? He didn't give me any details," Hiramatsu replied. "I have no idea what's wrong. When we go out drinking together, he's always good for a few laughs. And he does a hell of a lot better with women than I do. . ." Hiramatsu sounded as if he were annoyed with a disobedient younger brother. But it was clear to me that he was, in fact, very upset. It wasn't easy for him to accept the idea that Kudō might commit suicide—his outlook on life wouldn't allow it. I realized then that Kudō was fortunate to have Hiramatsu as a boss.

"Where is he now?" I asked.

"He's in the studio working on a commercial. Do me a favor. Go and see him."

After Hiramatsu left the room, I went downstairs. I made my way slowly to the studio where Kudō was working and poked my head in nonchalantly, as if I had dropped by merely to observe. Four or five people—probably actors or agents—were standing around the tiny set in the corner of the studio. Kudō was nowhere to be seen. When I looked up, though, I saw him in the control booth. He was sitting in the director's chair, resting his chin on his hands. He gazed down with a vacant look on his face. I couldn't tell if he saw me or not, and I left the studio without talking to him. I wondered if this would be his last assignment. Did he really plan to kill himself tonight? I stood there helpless. I was not at all proud of myself.

I don't remember what the product had been that day: one of those phony cure-alls, maybe, or a new brand of instant soup. All I know is that the day Kudō died he was working at the studio as usual.

Hiramatsu had tried his best to make Kudō change his mind. That night he took him out drinking. He must have thought that Kudō would have a few drinks, relax, and then reconsider. It was naive of him to think the plan would work, but I couldn't have thought of a more effective one.

From one bar to the next Hiramatsu fed Kudō drinks. "Please don't go through with it—for my sake," Hiramatsu begged. No doubt Kudō thought it was a ludicrous request, but he was nevertheless moved by these emotional pleas. Finally, he said haltingly, "Well, if that's how you feel, I'll think it over." Hiramatsu breathed a sigh of relief. He could let down his guard. He had been determined to follow Kudō around all night, never leaving his side. Now he was able to relax. By the time they parted on a street corner in the middle of the night, Hiramatsu felt thoroughly at ease. In fact he had fallen all too quickly into a drunken stupor, while Kudō, being younger, had kept a clear head.

In the end Kudō had outsmarted Hiramatsu. He knew that he had to go with Hiramatsu that evening. If he didn't, his boss would come barging into his room during the night and ruin his plan. Kudō went drinking with him and timed things so that Hiramatsu wouldn't learn about his death until at least noon the next day. As he must have planned all along, Kudō returned to his room during the night and crushed some sleeping pills in a mortar. Apparently he swallowed the powder in separate doses so that he wouldn't vomit and fail in his attempt. A few miscellaneous books lay beside his bed. One of them was a lengthy novel by a postwar writer, a controversial figure when we were in college. He had probably bought it at a secondhand bookstore. The covers had been torn off and the pages were frayed.

Hiramatsu had had too much to drink that night, and the following day he came to the office later than usual. He assumed that Kudō's absence meant only that he was sleeping it off. But when he hadn't shown up by noon, Hiramatsu realized his mistake. It was too late. He ran to Kudō's room. Kudō was still alive, and Hiramatsu rushed him to a hospital. I was told that he regained consciousness briefly and, with a pained expression on his face, whispered to Hiramatsu, "Why don't you leave me alone?"

When I heard about Kudō's death, my throat suddenly became very dry. I imagined the scene: a dimly lit room in the middle of the night, Kudō pushing back the metal-rimmed glasses that slid down his nose as he carefully crushed the sleeping pills. But more important, I couldn't forget the novel that Hiramatsu had told me Kudō had left at his bedside. It had never been among my favorites. At some point I may have flipped through the book, but I hadn't read it. Not a single line deserved serious attention—such was my prejudice against that particular novelist. What's more, I even disliked people who openly professed an admiration for him. My friendship with Kudō had not been a very close one, and yet I felt that in dying with that novel at his side he had somehow rejected me. He could have found an opportunity to discuss literature with me, but he never once mentioned the subject.

Can someone die for a book? The very idea seemed threatening—almost violently so. I have never owned a book that was worth dying for, least of all a novel. Could a novel bring about someone's death? It had never crossed my mind before. But wasn't I jumping to conclusions? Dying for a novel was a ridiculous notion. Kudō did not die for that book; the book did not tell him to commit suicide. All I know for certain is that he left the novel at his bedside. He didn't care that others would think he had been fond of it. In fact, he probably hadn't given it much thought. But to an observer, the tattered book lying next to the cold, lifeless body began to take on greater significance.

Kudō left no suicide note behind. Instead, on a scrap of paper he had scribbled "Don't touch me. I'll haunt you." As if enclosing instructions, he had placed the message next to what would become his own corpse, the disposal of which would present problems. But the words bore no resemblance to a suicide note. The piece of paper together with the body somehow formed a unit; the one served no purpose without the other.

I hadn't intended to write about this at all. I don't feel one way or another about Kudō. As a matter of fact, after his death no one showed too much concern. When they heard his name mentioned, few people could recall what kind of man he was—or even what he had looked like. What did make an impression on me was the way he had rushed to his death. It seems to me that when people choose to die so hastily, they make fools of those who are left behind. Their death forces us to realize how senseless it is to go on living, jotting down our muddled thoughts. To Kudō, no doubt, we appeared as niggling critics who constantly misjudged one another.

I remember the day we were told about his death. Late that afternoon, the fools all took turns visiting the department he had belonged to. When they heard the story, they walked out of the room in disbelief. But then, with renewed courage they would reconsider: "Kudō's dead? Then he won't be working any more. I guess that's one way to retire. But I'm alive—and still in good shape." I could accept this kind of unpretentious thinking: a manly attitude, I thought.

Others, however, lingered by Kudō's desk with blank expressions on their faces, smoking their cigarettes and wondering why he had done it. They pried every little detail out of a distant associate of Kudō's who had gone to his room to see the body. "How awful!" they would exclaim, and light another cigarette. Did they really mean it? Were they genuinely upset? I don't think they felt an ounce of regret. They put on a show of concern, but it was just a façade. When a colleague dies, do we go numb? Are we paralyzed by another's death? No, we aren't to blame. The deceased is at fault. It's he who makes a mockery of us all.

I was a fool too, in my own way. I thought I was different from the others. I thought I knew something they didn't know, and I held them all in contempt. How stupid they were! I wanted to scream at the top of my lungs, "Now you're upset? I knew three days ago that he would die!" I wanted to tell them as they stood there idly, "Stop it! That's enough! Go home!"

After Hatori's illness had begun, Urashima and I were assigned to different departments. Since Hatori remained in the same job, we felt as if we had deserted him. One afternoon I went for tea with Tsutsumi, a woman who had worked for the studio part-time. I was surprised when she told me that she had been to see him. I didn't think a young woman would go to that kind of hospital by herself, but I was even more amazed at my own thoughtlessness. I had forgotten to visit Hatori. As Tsutsumi spoke, she seemed to imply that Urashima and I should have been the first to visit him, but, since we hadn't, she had gone in our place.

"Hatori was so happy to see me," she said. "He says his wife hardly ever comes. He showed me his room. 'Here's where I stay. We're all friends here,' he told me when a strange group of patients came over. One wanted to show me the pictures he had drawn. Another asked if I would read a poem of his. I didn't know what to do. There was a funny smell about them. . . Hatori and I talked outside on the lawn until it got dark. At one point he took out his harmonica and played for me. He was very good at it, and I didn't mind—until he asked me to sing. He said he'd accompany me if I'd sing 'The King' by Murata Hideo. I didn't know the words but he insisted on teaching me. I hummed the tune while he taught me the lyrics. It sounded so sad I couldn't bear it. I decided to leave. It was dark and Hatori showed me to the road. Then he asked me to visit him again. Once was all right, but I'd feel awkward going again. After all, I'm not his wife—I'm nothing to Hatori. It'd be strange for me to visit him all the time, don't you think?" Tsutsumi smiled weakly.

Tsutsumi had in fact been close to Hatori. He had helped her at the studio and taken an interest in her personal life as well. Hatori treated her as his protégée and even attempted to arrange a marriage interview for her. He had spent an inordinate amount of time on the photograph for the marriage portfolio. When I went to visit him at home one day, he happened to show it to me. Hatori was a professional photographer and he had taken a fine photo, but Tsutsumi was not especially attractive and somehow she had a slightly forlorn look about her.

"Pretty good, don't you think?" he said as he showed me one splendid photo after another. He had obviously taken great care with the background and the composition.

"You did a fine job," I replied.

"She's a nice woman," Hatori added.

Of course I didn't disagree with him. Tsutsumi was a kind, straightforward young woman, though occasionally she would make a mistake at work and show very little concern over it. Urashima had once told me that she wrote in a peculiar way; for instance, she wrote the character for "shoes" backward.

Hatori's wife opposed the arrangements for the marriage interview. "It's no good—not with that girl. Absolutely no chance of a successful match." I had listened to their conversation. She seemed to feel that the young man under consideration possessed all sorts of fine qualities and that he would have no trouble finding a wife. Her voice was filled with spite and made me feel ill at ease.

"Do you think so?" Hatori asked his wife. Putting the photos away, he added, "I don't know; she's a nice woman. You don't think they'd make a good couple?"

Hatori didn't want to hurt Tsutsumi's feelings. Without mentioning the marriage interview, he had asked her to work as a model for him. She knew nothing about the complications with Hatori's wife.

I was glad that Tsutsumi had visited Hatori and that she had sung at least one song for him. When he was at work, he used to take her out for lunch or tea. After he became ill I would sometimes see Tsutsumi walking by herself. She was still unmarried. She seemed worn out. I wondered if she felt that her chance of marrying had slipped away. Perhaps she had given up any hope of finding a husband. When I bumped into her one day in the hall, I noticed dark rings under her eyes. She looked gaunt, and I asked her how she was feeling. She gave a vague reply, then added as an afterthought: "I don't know why, but I'm so tired lately."

Urashima and I got out of the taxi in front of the university hospital. As we turned to look at the white building, Hatori appeared out of nowhere. We were startled to find him standing right in front of us. The atmosphere of the place had also taken us by surprise.

A few months had passed since we had last seen him. The swelling had gone down, and at first glance he seemed to be doing well. But his hair looked a bit odd—a hospital employee had given him an unusually short crew cut—and although there wasn't a cloud in the sky, he was wearing rubber boots. He talked normally, however, and told us that he felt fine.

Hatori had phoned me one afternoon at the studio when I wasn't at my desk. Someone gave me the message: "You had a call from a fellow named Hatori. It sounded as though he'd been drinking. He was probably calling from a bar." But Hatori had phoned from the hospital. The medicine made his tongue heavy, and to a stranger it seemed as if he'd had too much to drink. When I told him this, he laughed and asked excitedly, "Really? That's what he thought?"

It was around three o'clock when we met him, and since he was convalescing satisfactorily, he had been given permission to go out. So the three of us walked around the streets near the hospital and stopped at a coffee shop to talk. Though Urashima and I had never been to the hospital before, we learned that Hatori was in a ward on the fifth or sixth floor.

As soon as we saw him he began talking nonstop. "There's someone from the university in my room. He goes around telling everyone that he's the son of a famous professor. No one knows if he's telling the truth or not. He was active in some student movement, but then he started to lose his grip. So he ended up here eventually. And now all he does is moan and groan. He says he wants to die, he can't take it any more. I'm not the only one he complains to, either—he corners just about everybody. Sits and whines all day.

"Finally I lost my temper and told him to stop acting like a baby. I even threatened him. I rolled up a newspaper and lit it with a lighter. Then I held it up to his face and yelled, 'What do you think of this, you idiot!' Then I took a razor blade and cut deep into my finger and showed him the blood. 'Take a look at this,' I screamed. 'Now don't give me any more of your whimpering!' He was trembling, but since then there's been no more wailing when I'm around."

Hatori stared at us with his eyes wide open. A bandage was wrapped around one finger. He showed us the palm of his hand. A large mark in the shape of a swastika had been drawn on it with red ink. We let him ramble on without uttering a word ourselves. As I listened to his impassioned talk, I was overcome with sadness. He had attacked a weaker patient by setting fire to a newspaper and slashing his own finger. Hatori had somehow thought he was helping him. I wondered how he had managed to get a lighter and a razor blade into the hospital ward.

"Since I've been here," he continued, "three people have committed suicide. All of them hanged themselves." Then he changed the topic again. "I became very friendly with a wonderful woman down the hall. She's older—maybe around fifty—and she's not like other women at all. She's a saint, she's so good. She recovered completely and they released her, but I want to see her again when I get out, so I asked her to write down her name and address. You should see her handwriting. It's beautiful. . . Oh, her address. I forget the number of the house. Shimorenjaku, Mitaka City. Anyway, her name is Nakamura Yaeko."

He talked on and on. Finally, he added, "I'm really much better, but I still get nervous. It's not good for me. I have to learn to relax." He had worked himself up, and he seemed to realize he should take his medicine. He took some pills from his shirt pocket and gulped them down with a glass of water.

"It must be shining," I said. But it was a bad joke. I shouldn't have been so flippant.

"Yes, it's shining—like a sword," Hatori grinned. He laughed a nervous, unpleasant laugh, and his face flushed with embarrassment.

I had been referring to an offhand remark he'd once made. He had told me there was a sword inside his head, and it either gleamed or grew dull according to his mood. I don't remember the circumstances, but I know that his face had turned red that day, just as it had now. The sword must have been shining. "I'm ready for anyone," he'd said. "Bring on your bows and arrows. I'll slash down any enemy with this sword of mine."

I realized that the weapon inside him should have been put to use. He should have pulled it from its sheath, as he'd threatened, and brandished it about. He should have lashed out at Yamaya and the others. If only he had lunged his sword at them, he wouldn't be confined like

315

this today. But Hatori couldn't bring himself to draw the sword against anyone. He wasn't that kind of man.

It was already six o'clock, Hatori's curfew. Urashima and I were ready to leave, but Hatori didn't seem to want to go. "Please stay a little longer. It's no problem for me," he said as he stood up. He went over to the cash register to make a phone call. We heard him talking excitedly. He told them he would be having dinner out. We ate a simple meal at the coffee shop, and when we were finished Hatori began to search his pockets for money. All he had was small change—not enough to cover the bill—but we had no intention of letting him pay anyway. We left the restaurant and walked back to where he'd met us. There we shook hands and said our good-byes.

"Which one is yours?" I asked Hatori as I looked up at the white building.

"On the fifth floor—over there." He pointed to a room. The sky had already grown dark and the lights shone in the rows of windows on each floor. Actually, I never did know which room he was pointing to. Hatori did not seem at all reluctant to return to the ward.

Although he had given us detailed directions to the bus stop, we took a taxi. On the way home, as we discussed Hatori, we found ourselves wondering where we could go for a drink.

RIPPLES

Shibaki Yoshiko

Translated by Michael C. Brownstein

Shibaki Yoshiko was born in Tokyo in 1914, the eldest daughter of a dry goods store owner. She studied English at Surugadai Women's College, but went to work for Mitsubishi to support her mother and two younger sisters after her father died. In the meantime, her first stories began appearing in several minor literary magazines. In 1937 she joined the circle of writers associated with the magazine Bungei shuto; *and four years later she was awarded the prestigious Akutagawa Prize for* "Seika no ichi" (The Fruit and Vegetable Market). *That same year she married an economist, Ōshima Kiyoshi.*

Shibaki is perhaps best known for her series of stories depicting the lives of Tokyo's bar girls and prostitutes, beginning with "Susaki paradaisu" (Susaki Paradise) *in 1954. Her next triumph was the historical trilogy tracing the lives of women in a single family from the beginning of the Meiji period to the present day. The first two parts,* "Yuba" (Dried Tōfu) *and* "Sumidagawa" (The River Sumida), *appeared in 1961. The third part was the autobiographical* "Marunouchi hachigōkan" (No. 8 Marunouchi), *which came out in 1962. This was followed in 1963 by* "Kashoku" (Gay Lamplight) *and* "Konjō" (This Life), *forming a trilogy within the trilogy.*

In 1972, Shibaki was awarded the eleventh annual Women's Literary Prize for her most recent collection of short stories, Seiji kinuta (The Porcelain Fulling Block). "Hamon" (Ripples, 1970) *is taken from this collection.*

One Sunday, a short man dressed in a black suit suddenly turned up at Takako's house. If he had been a salesman, the man would have gone to the house next door, then come to Takako's and left immediately, but he had come on business. She could not tell how old he was, but from the excited look on his face Takako sensed that he brought good news even before she looked at the business card he produced. This was just the sort of extraordinary event she had been vaguely expecting; no matter what this is, she thought, she must welcome it if it would help her break through the impasse she had reached. She went to summon her mother, who was often in bed with rheumatism.

The man asked if there were only two in the family. Takako lived with her mother and worked at a university library. Her two older brothers and older sister had left home when they married, and only Takako remained. Her brothers rarely visited their mother; her sister lived in another prefecture and never even wrote. Their mother, Ritsu, said she couldn't help thinking that her children were lost to her once they married. She would look coldly at Takako, as if to ask when she too would abandon her. Since the death of her husband at an early age, Ritsu had tried her best to hang on to the family assets until her children were settled, but before she knew it, she had become a penniless old woman. She was robbed of the pleasure of giving her grandchildren everything she wished, and so was reluctant even to have them over. Her daughters-in-law came to visit now and then, but they never brought the children and usually went home early. Her oldest son lived in a public housing complex and it put him in a bad mood when she asked him for money. And when his wife sent the money, he didn't even include a note with it. Her youngest son worked with his wife and lived with her family.

Ritsu was always saying that if she had the money she would go to a nice retirement home, but Takako refused to consider it. On days when she felt well enough, Ritsu made delicious suppers, but when the sky threatened rain, she lay in bed with her eyes fixed in a gloomy expression, fretting over her daughter's late return from work.

"I can't help it; it's my job. There's no reason to get upset just because supper will be an hour late."

"No one knows what it feels like for an old woman to lie in bed alone. If I could go to a rest home—a nice one with a lawn—I'd have friends, and I'd feel so much better."

"If we ever get some money you're more than welcome to go!" Takako realized that her own peevishness was mounting. As long as she lived with her mother, it seemed, she herself would never enjoy any happiness.

Lately she had fallen into the habit of dreaming the impossible whenever she felt overwhelmed by life or by her ties to other people. In the morning, for instance, when she opened her eyes and parted the curtains, she imagined that she was living on the third floor of a large, comfortable apartment building with flowers on a sunlit terrace. Turning around, she would see a man still asleep in the dark inner bedroom: that had to be Tamura. "How wonderful," she would think, "I'm married!" She never used to eat a good breakfast before leaving for work, but now she would heat up the beet soup she'd made the night before, and sit combing her hair until the aroma of the soup awakened him. It was important to her that living above the ground floor prevented any chance intrusion. But then, she did not think her brothers, her sister, or even her mother took her marriage prospects seriously.

Only the night before, when she was with Tamura, Takako had felt awkward about evading him when he said he wanted to move to a new apartment. He asked her what she thought of "life" and told her they were too old to be meeting on the streets—and besides, it was tiresome. With a faint smile, Takako said it didn't bother her.

"You're always missing the point, aren't you? I've had it with the way things are—do you think there's a future if we continue like this?"

Tamura had become testy. He worked in a research lab and was thinking about studying in Germany, but he was beginning to feel weighed down by her. They used to meet every Saturday, but now the relationship would probably collapse if she didn't phone him. Not that Tamura would break off with her. Once he had invited her to an art exhibit, not so much to look at pictures with her, shoulder to shoulder, but because he had tickets and it was better to go with someone than no one at all. Looking at paintings by Turner, both agreed they found in them a moving, dreamlike quality, and she did, after all, enjoy herself at the time; but that was hardly enough to satisfy her. She and Tamura exchanged intellectual-sounding theories about art, but their conversation never had the intimacy that a man and a woman standing close together might have reached. Still, she had no one else but him, so she could only be evasive when he talked about the future.

As they started home after spending that Saturday evening together, Tamura let slip that his older sister was urging him to marry into a family as an adopted son and heir. If he were to do this, Takako started to say, his sister could spend her twilight years in peace, but she swallowed her words. Once that much was said, their relationship would be finished. His sister worked in a globe-fish restaurant and spent the two days each month when it was closed resting at his apartment. With her help he had graduated from college, and the only family they had was each other. He told Takako he did not want a home where his sister would be uncomfortable. Tamura's circumstances touched Takako deeply, for she herself was stuck with her mother in a life of constant quarreling. Fettered by family ties, she and Tamura shared the same fate. Even so, she was wounded by the ambivalent expression on his face when he spoke of marrying into another family.

Takako rarely went to Tamura's apartment, afraid that people would talk. Gossip was somehow quick to reach his sister's ears, and he detested that. The possibility of marrying into another family became the trump card in a relationship that had already been played out. Takako walked along in stubborn silence. Although she was annoyed that their three-year affair had reached an impasse, she did not know who was at fault or what had gone wrong. When they reached the station, Tamura bought the tickets and watched her expression as he handed her one. She dropped the ticket. "Don't be so careless!" he snapped, picking it up. Takako couldn't bear fond farewells; they were only a ruse to get away from someone as smoothly as possible. She clutched her ticket as she climbed the stairs to the platform. The train arrived before they could reach an understanding, and she got on. She gazed at him through the window as the train started moving and bit her lip: she could not, she thought, just back out of the affair as matters stood.

Few visitors came to the house where Takako lived with her ailing mother. She showed the man in the black suit into the parlor and saw that, up close, he was middle-aged—much older than she first thought. The name on his business card read "Commercial Promotions, Inc.," and his errand had something to do with Miki Seiichirō. Miki was Takako's father, who had died twelve years before. Takako had no idea what sort of business Commercial Promotions was engaged in.

"Our company develops land and sells it in lots. Right now we're developing Karuizawa and Nasu." The man produced an old newspaper clipping and showed them one of his company's advertisements. Takako's father, he announced, owned almost half an acre in Karuizawa adjacent to the property being developed by Commercial Promotions, and they wanted to know whether Miki had left any instructions concerning it.

"My husband died. . . ," Ritsu stammered in confusion as she searched her memory. "Did he have any such property? It's nice to find out that he owned land in Karuizawa, but I'll have to give it some thought."

Seiichirō, a geologist, went to Manchuria during the war, and after the surrender worked at a university in Kyushu while his wife and children remained in Tokyo. His work often took him hiking into the mountains. Though he had little contact with his family, he was a decent man who would never have purposely kept them in the dark about land he had purchased. According to the real-estate agent, the land was registered in 1942, almost thirty years earlier. The area, he told them, was not called Karuizawa then. When she heard the old name, Ritsu was faintly reminded of something.

"Now that you mention it, my husband once loaned money to someone during the war, and I remember him asking what I thought about getting some land as security, but I'm not sure what happened after that. My husband went to Manchuria. Then his acquaintance passed away, so perhaps he even forgot where he got the land from. The value of money changed when the war ended, and the money he had loaned didn't seem worth its face value. . ." Ritsu told her story just as she remembered it.

"I see. In its present state, the land slopes sharply and there are no houses on it. I heard that during the war one square yard was worth less than a pack of cigarettes. Our company decided to develop the bluff and sell it off in lots. That's when we discovered you owned the property. We'd like to discuss the matter, but . . . excuse me for being so blunt— do you have the title?"

"Hmm . . . I wonder where he put it?" Ritsu was going to say she had never come across anything like that, but stopped herself. Even so, now that her husband was dead and they had moved, she still couldn't fully believe such unexpected news.

"I might add," he said courteously but with added emphasis, "it has taken me more than three months to find you."

The owner of the land, he had learned, was not living at the address recorded in the land registry. He inquired at the ward office, but their building had burned down during the war, so they had no official documents to consult. He checked into one thing and another, but all clues to the owner's whereabouts had vanished in the war. The agent learned that the previous owner had also died, but his family reported that he had sold it to someone connected with the Investigation Bureau of the Manchurian Railway.

The Manchurian Railway Company was dissolved after the war; there was no way to find out where its former employees had scattered. The real-estate agent had been ordered by his superiors to find Mr. Miki Sei-ichirō. He spent day after day searching through railway company archives and, in the end, all he had to go on was the names of several men who had compiled data for the company. One had died, but another who was still alive, an old man living in retirement in Zushi, provided the name of yet another man who had once been with the Investigation Bureau. On his way to see this third man at his present company, the agent told himself: "Now I'll find out what happened to Miki."

This man told the agent that he had worked for the Investigation Bureau in Harbin. When asked about Miki, he had no distinct recollection of him, but he didn't think there were too many sections within the bureau. The path cleared again when the man came up with the names of two or three others he had worked with in Manchuria, and the agent was spurred on at the thought that this time he would unearth something definite. He interviewed several other people connected with the railway before he found out that Miki Seiichirō had not been an employee of the Manchurian Railway at all, but a scholar commissioned by them to conduct geological surveys. He was understandably excited when he first heard the words "I knew Miki." But it meant nothing to have found someone who had known Miki in the past if the man could provide no clues to his present whereabouts. The man who had known Miki, however, telephoned an old acquaintance as the agent stood by, and learned that Miki had passed away.

Elated and disappointed by turns, the real-estate agent one day heard that Miki had been living in Seijō when he died. But it was getting dark, so he returned home, looking forward to the next day. When he joined his wife and son at the dinner table, his wife laughed: "Since when did you become a private detective?" And she teased him, saying, "Look out . . . there's someone behind you!"

At first he had been angered by this tiresome, pointless assignment: it really had nothing to do with his job at the company. But now he had set his sights on locating Miki's heirs and had thrown himself into the task. Finding Miki's family had become a mission. Unlike the mundane uncertainties of buying and selling land, where only one deal in a hundred was ever finalized, he felt the excitement of the chase, of moving at full tilt. Tenaciously he pursued his quarry, and at the end of a day of wasted effort he would think to himself: "Tomorrow for sure." Soon the elusive Mr. Miki seemed to beckon to him from up ahead. He found the old rented house the Miki family had moved to from Seijō. Walking himself stiff for three months had paid off; and when he checked the nameplate on the doorpost, he smiled with relief rather than professional satisfaction. Until Takako answered the door, he all but forgot that he had come to strike a deal. "Are you the daughter of Mr. Miki Seiichirō?" At her reply he muttered to himself: "At last!"

" . . . You went to all that trouble?" Ritsu, who had moved from house to house over the years and now had nothing in the bank, sighed and glanced at her daughter. Takako was amazed at the man's persistence and the intricate trail he had sniffed out, for he spoke as if he had done nothing remarkable. She doubted that the land could be worth much if her father had forgotten all about it.

"We'd be very grateful if you would sell us the land for development."

"How much do you think it's worth?"

"Well, it's a bluff, so it can't be used for anything in its present state. I imagine it's worth about five hundred yen per square yard."

Takako's eyes lit up when she calculated that their half acre was worth about a million yen. "I'd love to see it! I've never been to Karuizawa."

"It's a difficult place to find your way around in. And Karuizawa is cold now, though it's nice once summer begins. If you're willing to sell, we could pay you a million two hundred thousand yen. It's a good price."

"Even if we don't have the deed?"

"We'll be able to work something out, I'm sure."

Ritsu fidgeted happily and replied that, though she herself had no objections, she would have to get the consent of her children. Once again the man's face assumed the businesslike expression of a real-estate agent and he made a date to visit them again. As he got up to leave, he paused a moment and asked if, on his next visit, they might show him a photograph of Mr. Miki, if they had one. He wanted to see the face of the person who had kept him going for three months. Feeling kindly toward the man, Takako escorted him to the door and watched him leave.

Ritsu's health seemed to improve the more money she had on hand, and now took a turn for the better: the pain in her elbows and knees abated and she cheered up. She was buoyant even in her daughter's company, and they began to laugh together for no apparent reason. The sudden news promised an unbelievable amount of money, and Takako wondered if she could put her mother in a pretty rest home, one that had lawns and flower beds. It would be a gift from a father who had been indifferent to money. Takako hoped that her mother could then live out her years in peace.

Her oldest brother, Hideichi, and Yasuo, her other brother, hurried over to the house as soon as they heard the news. What surprised Takako was that even Namiko, her older sister who lived in distant Hirosaki, showed up. Though the seasons came and went, Namiko never sent so much as an apple, but now she left her seven-year-old child behind and raced to her mother's house. Takako didn't think she would have come so quickly even if she had been told her mother was seriously ill. Since none of them had ever heard about the land their father purchased thirty years before, they listened to Ritsu's tale in utter disbelief.

"He got the land as security for a loan and then forgot about it in the confusion after the war, is that it? I suppose it was because, like everyone else, he was in a state of shock for those two or three years."

"I guess it was something like that."

Hideichi had never spoken at leisure with his father, either when he was going back and forth to Manchuria, or later, when he went hiking in the mountains. Even when he died suddenly of a heart attack, Hideichi had not been at his bedside. Having pinned all his hopes on the Chinese continent, his father doubtless cared little about what happened to a half acre of poor ground in Karuizawa.

"It was a coup, even for Father, wasn't it?" Namiko's face broke into a smile.

"The real-estate agent certainly worked hard to find us. I hear there are unscrupulous businessmen who, given the chance, would put an unregistered deed in someone else's name." Hideichi felt grateful to the agent and savored the realization that the family owned land. "Even Mother used to complain about Father, but I'm sure she thinks better of him now."

"You know, I do believe your father did something right, after all," Ritsu said rather self-consciously, and made them all laugh.

Enjoying the lighthearted atmosphere, Takako felt closer to her family than she had in a long time. "If we do get a million two hundred thousand," she said, "it would last Mother a long time. How about going to a rest home?"

Takako's words somehow disturbed them. They all fidgeted in silence for a moment. Then Hideichi spoke: "Do you think you can put Mother in a private rest home for a million yen or so?"

Namiko, sitting next to Hideichi, took a different tack: "I gather the value of land in Karuizawa has skyrocketed. . . Shouldn't we look into it?"

The man had mentioned Karuizawa, but he told Takako that the bluff was outside Komoro and that the company was just beginning to clear the land. She didn't know whether the figure he had quoted was a suitable price for half an acre or not, but she thought perhaps they should go along with the man's offer because of all the trouble he'd gone to in locating them. It was a windfall they hadn't expected in the first place.

"Takako—did he say it was definitely a half acre that had been registered? If we have it surveyed it may turn out to be even more." Hideichi had become serious. Namiko immediately adopted the same tone as her brother:

"It might be more valuable than we think; it's no ordinary thing for a real-estate company to seek out the owner so eagerly."

"I agree with Namiko," Yasuo added. "We might take a loss if we go along with what he says and dispose of the land for the price they're offering." Yasuo had heard from his wife's family that property in Karuizawa was worth at least twelve hundred yen per square yard. Someone would have to go there and investigate.

Takako looked at her brothers. The joy of discovering that the Miki family owned land had been swept from their faces and greed had taken over. Expecting that something like this would happen, Takako had made the first move by suggesting that they use the money for their mother's living expenses or to send her to a retirement home. If they were not going to look after their mother themselves, then this windfall had to be used to support her for the rest of her life.

Takako did not mention that the real-estate agent seemed reluctant to show them the property. They decided that the brothers should negotiate on behalf of the whole family, no matter how things turned out. Hideichi and Yasuo wanted someone to examine the property before they met with the agent, and after all their wrangling decided that the slow, timid Hideichi should go. Yasuo, who by nature usually bustled about in a confident way, regretted that he had to go to Osaka on business. As they chatted about the land under development, their half acre seemed to grow larger and larger, swelling into a preposterously big plot.

"The minute I heard it was half an acre," Namiko said, "I knew it couldn't be worth less than three million yen. You've got to keep your eyes open so we don't get swindled by the real-estate company." Looking at the happy faces of her mother, brothers, and sister, Namiko added that, if it turned out to be that much money, she too wouldn't mind a small share. Then she began to complain about the daily pressures of scratching out a meager living as a clerk in a distant prefecture; her daughter's studies; the cruel fate that kept her from returning to her company's main office after their move; her daughter's talent for the piano and the cost of her lessons—on and on she rattled, mixing self-pity with self-praise.

"We all have problems," Hideichi said, turning away from her. Her brother, he pointed out, had found life rough as well. Yasuo felt constrained living with his in-laws, and joked that he couldn't go home again unless he got his share; that very morning he had left the house with a look of self-assurance on his face. The discussion took another turn when someone suggested that their father's legacy should be divided up in the legal way.

"In other words," Hideichi said, "Mother should take one-third, and we four should get one-sixth each."

Only Takako objected: "A million yen is a lot of money, but if we split it up it won't come to much. Think about that!"

"You say that because you don't know what a burden a family can be."

"In short," Yasuo said, "we'll hope for three million yen; then Mother's share would come to a million."

"Then how much would we get?" Namiko asked. "Half a million? Is that right?"

Rebuffed by her brothers and sister as they rambled on, Takako's lips trembled: she wanted to insist that their mother had a right to the entire three million. This was her mother's last opportunity to go to a rest home. And that would mean freedom for Takako as well. She could no longer keep still, knowing she was on the verge of losing Tamura. Takako looked at her mother, who seemed smaller as she sat amidst her sons and daughters with a confused look, rubbing the painful joints of her fingers.

Though her children did not come right out and demand a share of the money, Ritsu could tell what they had in mind; and though she wanted to be generous toward them all in true motherly fashion, her parental pride was wounded when they started talking in terms of sixths or thirds of the money. If they divided it up, she wondered uneasily, wasn't it likely that this great sum would spark off a family quarrel? She also understood Takako's feelings quite clearly: she was now intent on packing her mother off to a rest home. Her children were tossing around numbers in the millions, and she was concerned that the important thing—the initial offer—would be lost in the void of human avarice. Like Takako, Ritsu preferred to sell the property, with no strings attached, to the man in the black suit for his efforts. But she was hemmed in by lively talk of what half a million yen could buy.

Karuizawa is about two hours and ten minutes by express train from Ueno Station. Takako invited Tamura along, and they left from Ueno. The season for fall excursions was almost over. Several days earlier, Hideichi had gone to Karuizawa and had been able to verify the land in his father's name at the registration office; but even though he had wandered around looking for the property using the office's topographical map, he had not found it. He had returned exhausted, having only walked around an area close to what seemed to be their property. He asked Takako to go, and they decided that she should have the man from the real-estate company guide her. She spoke to Tamura, who showed some interest and joined her on the trip.

"You come from a good family," Tamura said. "A repatriate like me has no relatives to consult with, not to mention any land." He felt a little resentful toward Takako, who now had property in her dead father's name, but he nonetheless decided to go and see what sort of land it was.

"Come from a good family?" Takako mused, and took it sarcastically. She wished he had seen how her brothers and sister had wrangled over the distribution of the money. As her sister was leaving to go back to Hirosaki, she all but stuck out her hand and demanded, "When do I come back for the money?" Her brother Yasuo remarked that, if it all turned out well, he would like to travel abroad. Each of them probably wished he could have the money all to himself. Takako was happy to be going to see the property but was reluctant to face the man in the plain black suit from the real-estate company: she thought he could probably see right through them.

"How much will your brothers sell the land for?" Tamura asked.

"They seem to be thinking of two or three times as much as the man offered. Before people settle on an actual price, they like to dream about all the money they can—enough to build a house or take a trip. Out loud I say that I want to give it all to Mother, but in fact I've been thinking about you and me going to Guam. Why Guam, I don't know. . ." Takako suddenly remembered that Guam was where couples went for a honeymoon. With the promise of coming into some money, she was dreaming of being happily married.

"Guam!" Tamura said scornfully. To have a taste of a foreign country for five or six days—was that the best she could do? Whenever he got fed up with his dead-end job at the research lab, or with life on his meager salary, Tamura thought about being free and pursuing a pleasant career—as a restaurant manager, perhaps, or a bathhouse cashier. Living abroad as a vagabond was another of his daydreams. Reassuring images floated before his eyes no matter what his dream entailed; marrying into another family was one more potential avenue of escape. Of course these fantasies would all evaporate if things started going well at his present job, and Takako's money fulfilled his dreams to some extent. But just hearing about the windfall no doubt made his unfortunate sister envy or resent Takako.

It was almost noon when they reached Karuizawa. The sky was clear but a cold breeze was blowing on the heights. Tourists who had come to see the late autumn leaves had boarded their buses. Following the agent's directions, Takako and Tamura went to the branch office of Commercial Promotions. Takako felt nervous, knowing that the man would not be very happy to have them come. He had said that he worked in the Karuizawa office half a month at a time in order to show clients from Tokyo around. Fliers announcing property tours were taped up on the glass door of the narrow office, which fronted on the street. Only one employee was there, talking to another customer. He told Takako that the other agent would be back any moment. A kerosene heater was burning in the center of the room, and the other customer, a fat man who seemed to be a local, was talking to the agent about the new development.

"That mountain is a long way off," he said as the agent listened impassively, "but the view is good once you get up to the top, so I suppose the property will sell." Takako and Tamura looked at a wall map show-ing the post-development subdivisions. Then the fat man got up and left, and Tamura followed him out to buy some cigarettes.

Even the towns around summer resorts become deserted during the off-season. Tamura was back by the time the man in the black suit re-turned to the office. Small in stature, he seemed to have aged since Ta-kako had last seen him. He greeted them cordially, but his face betrayed no emotion to these clients who had turned down his original offer on the property and traveled all the way up here to view their holding. Only when he learned that Tamura was not a member of Miki's fami-ly did he look closely at their faces.

A car finally arrived and he took them to the property. They raced down the highway, and when they had gone some distance from the town of Karuizawa, Mt. Asama appeared on their right. The first snow had fallen about five days before, the man told them, but it had soon melted. "I suppose it's what you'd call a 'light dusting,' perhaps? The mountain was pretty with just a touch of white on it. . . We say that sales slow to a halt once the first snow can be seen on Asama."

The car went through Naka-Karuizawa, around the base of Mt. Asama, then turned onto a road going back in the other direction. As they made their way up the mountain road, moving farther and farther away from Karuizawa Heights, Takako realized that the area at best was only on the outskirts of a summer resort, and that they had been wrong to ob-ject to the price. She felt ashamed of having behaved in such a self-important way in front of Tamura too. The mountain road was covered with the red leaves of late autumn, and golden foliage still clung to the branches of the trees.

They were heading up an incline when the partly developed property suddenly came into view. Workers were moving boulders and tree stumps; apparently they were going to level off a small hill with a bulldozer. A few trees were left untouched. The Miki property was a grove of small trees on the opposite side. They got out of the car and had started toward the hillside when Takako gasped. The slope was bright with sunlight and a wonderful view greeted them: directly opposite and beyond the highway below, the whole of Mt. Asama stood revealed. Tamura too had never seen the entire mountain so close, and he stood motionless beside Takako.

The agent pointed: "There's nothing quite so beautiful as Asama from this angle. The view is my treat for you. The trouble is, it's a little far away."

"I had no idea it was such an exhilarating spot," Takako said. The man smiled uncomfortably. Takako and Tamura walked through the grove of trees from one end of the property to the other as the agent pointed out its boundaries. A half acre was not as big as they thought, and being on an incline it seemed rather hazardous. But whenever they glanced up, there was the view of the mountain. When the man left them to talk with the workmen, Takako and Tamura sat down on a tree stump. The sun was warm, but with the cold breeze, they could feel the coming of winter on their ears and the tips of their noses.

"It's wonderful, isn't it," Tamura said. "It's as if someone had dragged that huge mountain right into our own yard. I've never known such luxury."

"It would be a shame to sell it."

"I'd buy it myself if I had the money. I'd build a little house and spend the whole day watching the smoke rise from the mountain—that's how lazy I am."

Takako imagined the always listless Tamura idly stretched out. She thought of having a cottage here in the mountains. Squirrels probably scampered through the trees during the summer, and she pictured pure white laundry hanging out to dry on a line between two of the trunks. Now and then Tamura would bicycle down to the bottom of the hill to buy some French bread. Her visions of happiness were always modest and sentimental. Couldn't they leave me even a tenth of an acre? she wondered. She had a right to something, however small it was.

The bulldozer started moving, turning up the black soil. Roused from its slumber, the earth grumbled as it undulated. Doubtless they would soon knock down the trees and terrace the slope where Tamura and Takako were sitting.

"This place is worth more than a million," Tamura said. "You have to admire the shrewdness of a businessman who'd try to get you to sell it sight unseen. That guy looks honest and gentle, but he's a go-getter, that's for sure. He looks stubborn too, like he wouldn't budge an inch. You were almost had."

"I'm glad we came. But how am I going to bargain with him?"

"I'd tell him 'no sale.'"

The man walked back toward them. As they watched him stagger up the hill, he looked smaller and more agile; his pants were obviously too short.

"Aren't you cold?" he asked. "There's a strong breeze."

"We were talking about building a house and living here," Takako said. "But if we sell it, then it's all over!"

"It would be difficult to bring water up here," the man explained gently. "Our company owns the water rights to this entire mountain, so it's impractical for an individual to try to build a house."

Takako fell silent with disappointment, so Tamura continued for her: "I suppose the lots will be worth a fair amount, considering the location."

"We'll price the lots when they're finished. The land is almost worthless before it's developed; it's just the side of a hill. Mr. Miki's property wasn't worth anything until we laid out the subdivisions."

No doubt that was true, but it was also a fact that this land belonged to the Miki family. Now that they had seen it, the terms under which they would let it go would have to change. The man spoke in a low voice as he pulled up some dead weeds; once it was leveled by the bulldozer, he said, the Miki land would also become expensive resort property, but it would be foolish to miss this opportunity. There was a resonance in his voice Takako had not heard before, an urgency that made her uneasy. He had been so lively, and his face had seemed so human that first day at her home; perhaps that had been his real face, peering out from the shadows of this other side.

The white smoke billowing from Mt. Asama became a single cloud that shaded the mountain. The man's face would probably not reveal any sign of distress even if she flatly refused to sell the property. His expression was determined; he was used to bargaining and would not budge. If he did, his three months of searching would lose all meaning. Takako had been led astray by her own estimation of a man who, though basically good, could turn nasty. When he urged them to start back, the cloud was beginning to shroud the mountain, leaving only a view of the valley.

The mountain road, buried under fallen leaves, had turned dusky enough that it seemed a rabbit or a fox might run out. At the bottom of the mountain, the car turned onto the main highway and headed back toward Karuizawa. Anxiously Takako realized that her brothers would probably be furious if she failed to sell the property. Tamura was silent too and gazed out the back window.

The man led them to a coffee shop by Karuizawa Station. After taking a soothing sip of her hot drink, Takako's mood also softened. The real-estate agent started telling Tamura how business on the heights slackened off with the first snow, and how his work then switched to Tokyo. As they talked, the conversation again turned to haggling over the price. The man said they would give a million and a half yen for the property, but that was their best offer. The figure seemed too low, Tamura answered; a half acre in that area would go for six million yen, but he would settle for half that. Tamura grew more and more aggressive, promising to go back to Tokyo and persuade the Miki family to agree— this despite the fact he had never even met Takako's brothers! The agent answered curtly: Their price was out of the question. He made no move to eat the sandwiches that had been brought to their table.

When the man finally announced that he could make no better offer, Takako suddenly felt that her resolve was far weaker than all of Tamura's calculations. It was easy for him to talk recklessly about someone else's property. Takako finally asked, in view of the differences between the two men, if the agent could try once more to raise his price a little. "Isn't this half acre going to bring you quite a bit of money once you develop it?" Tamura argued, but the man would not agree to a higher figure because, he said, he would lose his profit margin. For the first time he scowled. His changing expressions caught Takako's eye.

On the train back to Tokyo, Tamura was in an eager mood as he drank some beer. "The man is stubborn, but one more try should do it," he said, as if he were talking about a horse race. "Two and a half million yen for the half acre is a bit too much, but it's certainly worth four million an acre, so we'll hold firm at half that amount." He chattered on, spurred by his own enthusiasm. "How much of that would you get?" he asked. Counting on his fingers, Tamura worked out Takako's share, insisting that he had a right to join in the bargaining. "It's less than I thought, but then you've got a lot of people in your family, haven't you!" Still, there was enough for a deposit on a two-bedroom apartment, with money left over for a short trip abroad as well. Takako had never seen him so excited, but looking at him, she felt a sort of sediment collect in her heart as they laughed together. Would they split up? Would he marry into another family? Such concerns vanished in the face of a little money. She turned away from him, but his giddy talk made her feel empty: even she no longer had the heart to give up her share for her mother's sake.

Takako sometimes wondered what hopes sustained the real-estate agent. He seemed honest and gentle, but in certain respects he was as solid as a rock, and he knew how to intimidate. He led Hideichi and Yasuo by the nose into a compromise, though they put up a fuss. Even when the talks snarled, he never once suggested they owed him some consideration for the trouble he'd gone to in finding the Miki family. No doubt he lived by suppressing such human, self-centered feelings.

Namiko, who came back to collect her share of the money and returned home cheerfully, sent a chopstick box of Tsugaru lacquerware to her mother. Subsequently, a letter came asking if her mother would lend her the money to buy a small apartment, and assuring her that she would pay her back with interest. Ritsu crumpled up the letter and threw it into the wastebasket. Takako, pretending not to notice, went for a walk. While she was out, Hideichi dropped by and suggested that they build a cottage in the garden of his mother's rented house, and that his family should live with her.

"Who would live in the new addition?"

"Well, the children," Hideichi answered and blushed slightly. He said he couldn't abandon her, bedridden as she was with rheumatism. Besides, if they all lived together, she'd have no more worries. Ritsu replied that she would think it over, but realized that the six hundred thousand yen she had set aside had brought her only momentary happiness. She did not mention Hideichi's proposal when Takako came back from her walk.

A cold wind now blew through the streets of Tokyo as well. Takako exchanged a gift coupon at a department store on her way home from work on Saturday and then went to an office in an unfamiliar part of town. Commercial Promotions was located in a small office building, and when she pushed open the door, she saw a number of men sitting at desks crowded one right next to the other. She told the receptionist the name of the man she had come to see. He stood up from a desk at the back and walked over to her. Unlike the shabby-looking figure she had seen at the office in Karuizawa, here he was neatly dressed. He seemed free for the moment, so they left the office and he guided her to a near-by coffee shop.

"Is there something I can do for you in regard to the property?" He looked sincere, in an effort perhaps to give the impression that he could be relied on.

"Thanks to you, the sale of the property is settled. I'd be happier if we discovered some more land that my father had forgotten about." The man smiled vaguely, unsure of the reason for her visit. The family had sold the land for a million eight hundred thousand yen.

"Have you finished grading the land on the hill?"

"It started to snow when we were about half done. You went at a good time."

"I don't think I'll go there again, but the view of Mt. Asama was beautiful. The bank of trees was nice too; I enjoyed spending the day there. It's strange to think my father never saw it."

"You'll go again, I'm sure. Why don't the two of you go next year, for a vacation?"

Wondering what Tamura would say to that, Takako drew her parcel closer. Ever since the agent had located her family, she had been completely absorbed in selling the land, but now, finally, she was able to come and thank him. The gift was only a symbol of the gratitude that she alone seemed to feel. A look of surprise flitted across the man's face. Searching for someone for three months had been a remarkable experience, but he'd never expected any of them to make a courtesy call afterward. He gazed at the department-store package that Takako handed over.

"It was only my job."

"I think what you did was extraordinary."

"I do a lot of investigating—locating people, character references—but Mr. Miki's case was like grabbing at a cloud. I took an interest in it right from the start. I imagined that anyone willing to buy land like that would be rather indifferent to money; I thought we'd reach an agreement as soon as I found him."

He had tried coming to grips with the task of finding Miki, but hadn't known where to look. Then, just when he had reached a dead end, the name "Manchurian Railway" had turned up. "I've got it now!" he'd thought, and went to see one person after another. But the men who had worked together in the Investigation Bureau had gone their separate ways. A vague image of the man he was looking for took shape in his mind. The slender thread of clues he followed between his regular duties formed a path that, little by little, began to clear ahead, and he felt encouraged. Facing head-on the challenge of ferreting out the Miki family, he put all he had into the task. Whenever he worked himself up, telling himself "Today's the day," his son would say admiringly how tough Dad was. After doing business for more than fifteen years, with all the pressures of profit and loss, of haggling over prices, his face had become dead, inelastic, a patched-up mask that, though still a face, had ceased to be his own. The search for Miki Seiichirō had enabled him to reclaim what he had forgotten. He told Takako that it was he who should thank her for allowing him such a rewarding experience.

"I'm sure my dead father is also happy that you found us." Takao listened happily to his story. She had put a photograph of her father in her handbag, but felt it would seem too theatrical to take it out.

"It's been business as usual since I found you." The man took a cigarette from a blue pack of Patto's and lit it. This was the first time she had seen him smoke.

"Those are odd cigarettes, aren't they?"

"I've smoked Patto's for a long time. They're low in nicotine. I go to the tobacco shop in front of the Employment Security Office and buy thirty packs at a time." His features relaxed as the tension left his face. It was the most natural of his faces Takako had seen. Though thinking it was bad to keep a man away from his work, she decided to stay for a few more minutes. She would never see him again, and for her as for him, this moment seemed very precious.

THE PALE FOX

Ōba Minako

Translated by Stephen W. Kohl

Ōba Minako began her literary career in 1968 with the publication of her prize-winning short story "Sambiki no kani" (The Three Crabs, tr. 1978), which, like many of her stories, is set in a coastal town in North America. To some extent this recurrent setting is based on the author's experience of having lived for twelve years in Sitka, Alaska. In a broader and more literary sense, however, it is a setting appropriate to the themes of many of Ōba's stories, such as Kiri no tabi (Journey through Mist, 1976). Her fog-shrouded coasts are places where people live their lives seeing things only imperfectly, drifting through random encounters with figures that emerge and disappear in the mist.

Fog and mist are metaphors for loneliness and the need for freedom, themes that are depicted in other ways as well. Garakuta hakubutsukan (The Junk Museum, 1975) presents an international cast of characters who have no common language, customs, or social background. Ōba's characters are routinely isolated in alien cultures, but are nevertheless tough enough to find freedom, often through creative use of memory and imagination. Her novel Urashimasō (Urashima Grasses, 1977) develops similar themes in greater detail and complexity.

Other concerns complicate Ōba's misty world. Science and technology, intruding randomly and yet inevitably on the lives of modern men and women, require new kinds of human relationships and new concepts of identity. And while doing away with traditional patterns of life, these same technologies threaten the destruction of life itself. But Ōba does not shun this development. Rather, she sees it as opening new avenues of behavior for those who have the imagination and the strength to embrace this new world.

The author sometimes uses straightforward narrative but more often prefers a montage technique, especially in works of fantasy like "Higusa" (Fireweed, 1968) and "Aoi kitsune" (The Pale Fox, 1973). Both are stories of love and death full of vivid imagery that is sometimes beautiful, often grotesque. Ōba's subtle and complex literary world provides no answers, but casts a fresh and occasionally disturbing light on the human condition.

*   *   *

"It's been a long time," said the Pale Fox.

Seven years ago, when they were lovers, a melancholy look in the man's downcast face had reminded her of a fox. Sometimes, in the pale light of the moon, or washed perhaps by the light of a neon sign, his face took on a bluish cast, and since that time she had referred to him in her mind as the Pale Fox. His sharp, narrow chin resembled a fox—a fox pausing in a moonlit forest, head cocked toward the moon.

"These white flowers smell nice," said the Pale Fox, "but the thistles, roses, and nettles are a nuisance."

Turning away from the light, the Fox's eyes shone amber, like glowing charcoal or Christmas tree lights.

"It's been seven years, hasn't it?"

The Pale Fox was like a priest who performed the ritual with faultless precision. The priest's eyes were too far apart for a fox, and each drifted independently. For some reason she enjoyed running the tip of her finger down between his eyebrows to the bridge of his nose.

"That's a vulnerable spot. It gives me the shivers when you do that; it makes me feel I'm about to be stabbed by an assassin." The Pale Fox disliked her doing this, but was reluctant to brush the woman's finger away.

The Fox's nose was moist in the moonlight.

The woman thought: I wonder why Father says this is the grave where

338

Mother is buried? It is such a splendid and majestic tomb. It might have been the grave of some venerable priest clothed in rich, brocaded vestments, or a great warrior in full armor and helmet, or a grand minister of state with drooping moustaches.

The funeral must surely have been splendid, too, with much fanfare and a service carried out in the glare of footlights, attended by joyous throngs of celebrities. The choreographer of this spectacle would have been called the Priest of Heaven, and would have led the reading of the scriptures and the voluptuous sobbing of the mourners. Yes, this was the funeral it must have been.

By now, of course, the grave was encrusted with moss and lichen, and it was impossible to read the inscription carved on it. All she could make out was a single Chinese character that seemed to be the word for "great." Yet once it had been a glittering and elaborate tomb.

Though the flesh in the casket had decayed and putrefied, beautiful women had gathered in attendance. Ladies who had flinched at the smell of corruption had risked being thrown into prison. It was a grave of writhing anguish.

This was a grave that wielded power, that threw back its shoulders in pride; this was a grave that laughed arrogantly with cold eyes and a thin smile. But this was all vanity now, for the corpse had rotted and the tomb was crumbling.

The forest was heavy with gloom. When the black birds started up with a mournful cry, cold drops fell from the trees and she looked up. Far away, between the overlapping leaves, was the violet sky.

The path was slippery with mud, and fungi that reminded her of withered and broken oranges grew from the fallen tree trunks. There were others with plump, fleshy umbrellas that spread wide like patches of snow.

Each time her father stumbled, he clutched at her. His hands were cold, and the daughter felt that a corpse was touching her. Still, she was curious about this landscape of death being shown her by a corpse, and she appreciated each stop they made.

"I found Mother's grave. I looked for it everywhere and couldn't find it, but then all of a sudden I saw it, thanks to the way the light was shining."

It was like the abalone clinging to the rocks. Somewhere down among the forest of gently waving sea tangle there comes the glitter of a fish's belly, and suddenly you see it, the tight, tender flesh of the abalone enclosed in its shell, deep within the lush growth of moss.

Her father was delighted. From his youth he had been happiest gathering abalone and edible fungi. He was a metal craftsman by trade who had brought his workshop to the rocky shore of this island and devoted the greater part of each year to making metal objects. Toward the end of the year, he would take everything he had made to the city to sell; but apart from that one annual journey, he remained on the island. The children enjoyed spending several months there with their father during the summer. Stretching out like a backdrop behind the rocky shore was a pine forest where all sorts of fungi flourished.

His eyes were as sharp as an animal's when he probed for abalone trembling beneath the surface of the sea, or the thin, white stalks of fungi hidden in the forest under fallen leaves. He would find each mollusc among the seaweed and pull its living flesh from the rocks where it clung fast. The woman imagined the old man's twisted jaw and superimposed the image on the sharp jaw of the Pale Fox.

"It was a place like this, your mother's grave."

Her father had discovered the grave deep in the inner recesses of an ancient temple on the edge of the pine forest. At the back of the tomb he had found a small door leading to the crypt. He had tried to open it, but it was choked with moss and would not move. Some grass with small, white flowers grew in a crack in the stone that marked the door to the crypt. There were also ferns.

"Your mother is sitting in there. I could see her knee," said her father. "The swelling in her shins seems to have subsided. The color of her earlobes isn't good, though."

Mother had to have her ears pierced to wear the earrings that Father made for her. The daughter remembered from her childhood that when Mother's ears had been pierced, Father had disinfected them so they would not fester.

The shells of the abalone were hidden by sea moss; the tomb was covered with forest moss. When she bent to examine the moss more closely, the beauty of a microcosmic world spread out before her. The stone tomb beneath it became an illusion; the vision of elegance vanished.

Clutching his cane of polished rose root, her father resembled a gaunt, white cat. He smiled and his eyes gleamed with a small, blue flame.

"Shall we burn a cigarette instead of incense?"

Searching in her handbag, she found two cigarettes; they were all she had left. She lit one and put it on the moss. The white paper absorbed some moisture and she watched it go out, leaving only a wisp of smoke. She lit the remaining cigarette and inhaled, turning aside to keep the smoke from getting in her eyes. Then, as though her mother were a patient lying on the tombstone, she held the cigarette out between her fingers so that the sick woman could take it in her mouth. She stayed like that for a while, waiting for the ash to lengthen and fall off.

After all, it was tobacco that had killed her mother, and now that she was dead, her father frequently offered cigarettes at the family altar.

She felt as though she were playing house with her father. It was as though they had joined hands and were dancing around some ancient tomb, playing a children's game. In the shadow of the tombstone, a toad sat watching.

For seven years she had heard no news at all, then suddenly, one day, a man came to see her and it was the Fox. His arrival was totally unexpected, like waking in the morning to find a single leaf by her pillow.

The Pale Fox was smoother than the polished rose root. He believed he had a very beautiful body; he liked to stand straight and walk slowly. She realized he was probably waiting for some word of praise, but felt it was too much trouble to try and find a compliment to satisfy his vanity. At the same time, she was ashamed of her own indifference.

The Pale Fox told her that during the seven years they had been apart, he had married, lived with his wife for four years, and then left her.

"She was like one of those dolls that can shed tears. Whenever I came home, I would find her sitting in the same place, in the same position. In the end she became like a moth, the large sort that crawl around on walls."

"First you say she's a crying doll, and then she's just a dried-up moth stuck to the wall."

"Finally that's all she was, just a spot on the wall. She was the sort of woman who dreams of finding happiness in ordinary family life. She had done nothing wrong, that's why it was such a shame. I even changed my mind after we had separated, and we tried meeting several times, but we never talked about anything. We slept together each time we met, but we couldn't talk about things. I'd leave again as soon as our lovemaking was done. At that point she changed from a moth into a butterfly sitting with its wings folded. As she sat, dust would rise from her wings and make me wheeze."

He paused, then tried to explain his own silence by saying, "Some people talk a lot. I think they lose something when they talk too much."

The woman gazed with admiration at the Pale Fox, who spoke as little as possible in order not to lose anything.

He was, however, the sort of man who could never suit his actions to his words, or his deeds to his thoughts, and so he always ended up talking when the woman remained silent. Nevertheless, he apparently felt obliged to explain what he had done during those seven years.

"I was exhausted the whole time we were married. The constant weariness made my bones ache as though I was carrying a load with straps cutting into my shoulders. I always do what I want, and yet while my own life-style was selfish, I felt some responsibility toward my thoroughly unselfish partner. At the bottom of my heart I suppose what I really want is a woman who'll be a slave to me."

"I'm sure there are women in the world who'd be happy to be your slave. But if you ever encountered one, you'd start dreaming of a woman you could treat as an equal. You really would. Haven't you learned yet that the tyrant is always bound by the tyrant's debt? In your case, the only way to free yourself is to free the other person as well."

"But women all renounce their freedom; it's a way of binding their men to them." Somewhere in his heart the Pale Fox dreamed of having a slave, but in reality he could never manipulate women in that way.

Seven years ago he had asked her to marry him, saying that he intended to be a good husband. The expression on his face had revealed the pathetic determination of someone who was throwing his own freedom away. This frightened the woman and she recoiled from him.

She could imagine him saying the same thing to his former wife before their marriage, and she pitied him. To make unrealistic promises, to make promises he could not keep, could only lead to hopelessness in the long run.

It was when he was completely beaten that he dreamed of possessing a slave. If a woman chooses to be a slave, presumably the man's guilt is resolved and this allows him to behave as he pleases. The woman understood this man's fantasy very well; he wanted her to fall on her knees and embrace him, but she felt it was too much bother. Again she felt ashamed of her indifference.

"You are too fond of women. That's why it's impossible either to pledge yourself to one single woman or to treat us simply as objects. But, you know, you're probably fond of women because women are fond of men. If women were not allowed to know men, if the person you married were not allowed to know any man but yourself, she still wouldn't necessarily become the sort of woman you want. A woman can't be treated as a woman if she's lost whatever makes her one. The sort of marriage you had in mind depends too much on someone who's lost her identity as a woman."

In an encounter like this, mood is more important than logic. And so, solemnly, tenderly, they proceeded with their ritual, devoting themselves to it wholeheartedly, and when the ceremony had reached its climax and ended, they were left clinging to the altar like a pair of bats, physically and emotionally drained. Once the ceremony was over, her earlier indifference returned, and she became embarrassed by her lack of enthusiasm. In the end she compromised by telling herself that different people just have different ideas, and that it does no good to ignore other ways of thinking.

The Pale Fox dozed. His arms, twined around her waist, went limp. She could see one ugly, swollen wart on a stubby finger; it reminded her of the skin near the ears of lizards she had seen the previous day at the botanical gardens. They had kissed for the first time in seven years standing in front of a pair of lizards locked in a motionless sexual embrace. The immobile lizards looked like stuffed animals in a specimen case.

His warty finger also appeared to be stuffed. The wart seemed to spread and grow until it resembled a crater. Countless white fungus stalks grew out of this crater.

Her father called again from the island. He had called twice while she was out. Praying Mantis, the man she was living with, passed on the information that he had phoned, but she did not feel like returning his call, and left again.

Her father was in the habit of ringing his seven children one after the other, making the same call to each. The woman was usually the last to be called. She was, after all, the youngest child. Apparently he had said the rocks on the island were covered with abalone, but that was long ago, and now the rocks were covered only by moss. Whatever phase the moon was in, there was only moss that may have looked like abalone shells clinging to the rocks.

"I told her you called, but she left again in a hurry," explained Praying Mantis when her father phoned yet again. The following day, before she had decided whether or not to return his call, there was a fourth phone call from the island, and when she picked up the receiver, she heard her father's hoarse voice.

"We're having lovely weather here on the island. Why don't you come for a visit? The place is full of abalone. There's a new moon now and there are always plenty of them around then."

Unable to endure this senile fantasy, she said, "As usual, the Mantis has a guest here just now."

"I see. A guest is it? I remember in the old days your mother and I used to think up all sorts of excuses for declining our parents' invitations to visit, because we wanted to meet each other instead. . . I'll go to your mother's grave again and offer a cigarette from you. It occurs to me that you're the only one of the children who knows where that grave is, so I want you to remember how to find it." Her father hung up the phone.

Her mother had borne seven children, and not one of them had provided a monument for her grave. In her will the mother had requested that her ashes be scattered over the sea. The children had some notion that the surging waves would transform her into various shapes. But the father was disappointed by the children's devotion to their mother's will.

Soon the Pale Fox awoke. He drew the woman to him, but it was clear he did so only because he felt obliged to. Even while he longed for a woman slave, the Fox continued to treat women with respect. Understanding this pathetic dream, the woman playfully scratched his beautiful body all over and tugged at his hair.

Like a child on a visit somewhere who wants to go home, the woman longed to return to Praying Mantis. He was a strange man, devoted to that form of ecstasy peculiar to the mantis in which the male is killed and devoured by the female. He enjoyed hearing women talk about other men they had known. He was curious about women only if they displayed curiosity about men. Searching now for words that would flatter the Pale Fox, she moved about the room making gestures, throwing glances that might appeal to him. She did not have the patience for anything more; all she wanted now was to sleep, to sleep next to the Mantis with her leg thrown over his stomach. (The woman could not sleep unless her legs were slightly elevated.)

It would not do to stay with the Pale Fox until morning, and she realized that this feeling confirmed once again the reason she had recoiled from living with him seven years ago.

If he were a real fox, she could put a collar on him and fasten it to the bedpost. Yet, even then, in the morning she might find that he had disappeared, leaving only the collar lying on the bed, the chain still attached. The Pale Fox, it seemed, was always changing into something else. The woman was indifferent to the gallant youth he sometimes became; what captivated her was his true form, a fox sniffing out his prey. She liked his beautiful blue fur, his erect ears, sharp jaw, moist nose, his surprisingly long, pink tongue, bushy tail, and glittering, golden eyes. But the Fox in his true form always eluded her, escaping to the forest; she only caught glimpses of him.

Just as she was getting dressed, the Fox, too, felt a longing for his home in the forest. "We should probably be going now," he said. "I'm leaving town tomorrow," he added, "so it would be better if I went back to my own hotel tonight. I have to pack my things."

As he got up, the Pale Fox said, "Shall we go out for something to eat?" He was looking at the key that lay on the bedside table. They no longer had any use for it, since they would not be coming back to this room.

They locked the door as they went out, leaving the key behind. Outside a warm, muggy wind blew; and the large, red sun perched on the horizon directly in front of them, wrapped in a cloak of gray smog. Groups of people hurried along in the gullies through forests of tall buildings. From the expressions on their faces, they seemed to have forgotten what a dreary business it is to be faithful. In the stores where the stench of the city was blown away by air conditioners, people kept their sullen, bloated faces downturned, and shuffled aimlessly like caged animals.

The man and the woman carried on an absurd conversation. They spoke of buying a villa together on the island. Neither of them had any money, of course, and even as they talked of buying a villa, both were thinking how impossible it would be for them to live there together. As they talked, each fantasized about imaginary slaves.

While they ate their meal of raw, spiced meat, the woman saw a reflection of herself in a wall mirror. It showed a cruel, voracious insect that only slightly resembled her elderly father. The insect appeared covered with a veil of spider web, while the Fox had transformed himself into a beetle. Their wings tangled together and their conversation was meaningless.

Mother's earlobes, she remembered, had been discolored and unhealthy-looking. Had it been her sister who retrieved Mother's earrings from the ashes after the body had been cremated?

When she arrived home, the Mantis said, "There was a phone call from your sister. Something about your father. It seems something has happened. She said he was taken into protective custody yesterday by the island police. Did he seem normal the last time you saw him?"

"I didn't notice anything wrong," said the woman.

"Your sister says he should be put in an institution."

"Oh."

The father had seven children. None of those seven children was opposed to the idea of putting their father in an institution. What they had in mind was a mental hospital located on top of a hill on the island.

In its advertising, the hospital used pictures of the surrounding fields in spring, clothed in a haze of yellow blossoms. Crested white butterflies fluttered over the yellow fields, and there in the midst of them stood a white building, rising like some fantastic castle. It seemed to float above the ground; a white-clad ghost without feet.

When she awoke the next morning the woman realized she had left behind at the hotel an ornamental hairpin her father had made when he was young. Her mother had given it to her as a keepsake. It was not yet check-out time, so she hurriedly caught a taxi and set off for the hotel. When she explained to the desk clerk that she had left the key in the room and locked herself out, he rang for the bellboy, but then, remembering, said, "Oh, wait a minute. Your husband came back a little while ago. I gave the key to him."

The woman was heading for the elevator when it occurred to her that he should be at his hotel packing and that he hadn't originally planned to come back. She went to the house phone and dialed.

Soft and light as a feather, the voice at the other end was clearly the Fox's. He was not a beetle now.

"Hello, it's me. I left my hairpin there, on the shelf in the bathroom. It's silver and shaped like a fish; the eyes are inlaid bits of black coral. It's a keepsake from my mother. Could you bring it to me before you check out? Or send it by registered mail."

The woman listened carefully, straining for any sign that he had another woman in the room with him, but she heard nothing. Without a word in reply the Pale Fox put down the receiver.

Two or three days later the hairpin arrived safely in a small, registered envelope. There was not even a note to go with it.

IRON FISH

Kōno Taeko
Translated by Yukiko Tanaka

Modern Japanese fiction, particularly by women writers, is filled with descriptions of small incidents or glimpses of everyday life, the accumulation of which forms our reality. Kōno Taeko (1926–), however, does not concentrate on details in order to create an illusion of reality. A closer look at her stories reveals the fact that the various parts of her detailed descriptions do not necessarily match one another. The result is a sense of incongruity. What Kōno tries to suggest is the precarious relationship between the real and the imagined, or the objective and the subjective.

The shocking motifs of her early stories, centering around sadomasochistic fantasies, have become less obvious in her more recent works, and a new theme has emerged: the awakening of freedom. Under circumstances where the main character finds herself both physically and metaphysically imprisoned, the meaning of reality is reevaluated. The woman in "Tetsu no uo" (Iron Fish, 1976) tries to recapture the extraordinary experience of her first husband who was killed while serving as a "human torpedo": his last moments in the ultimate confinement of an underwater grave seem to hold for her a key to understanding her own life and reality, her past as well as her present.

During World War II the Japanese Imperial Navy made large torpedoes that carried a man inside, an aquatic version of the kamikaze pilot. Though these "human torpedoes" had very little impact militarily, they are a grimly effective reminder of the tragedy of war. "Iron Fish" is told from the point of view of a woman who was left behind by one of these men.

Kōno's stories have been included in anthologies of World War II fiction. Hers is the generation whose youth was spent in factories rather than schools. With the end of the war, Kōno has stated, a new sense of freedom came to her; it urged her to write. It took a little over a decade, however, before she was recognized in the Japanese literary world. With her novel Kaiten-tobira (Revolving Door, 1970), *her position was firmly established as one of Japan's most important contemporary writers, and she continues to venture into new realms of fiction writing. Recently she has also gained a reputation as a literary critic. Kōno lives with her artist husband in Tokyo.*

*   *   *

We were the last to leave the room. As we both slowly descended the stairs, stopping in front of the exhibit on the wall and at the display case on the landing, an attendant came down right behind us. Hardly any visitors could be seen in the rooms downstairs, and another attendant was picking up the signboard to bring inside.

"Are you closing? Is it too late to look around?" asked a person who had just come in.

"We close at four," answered the attendant.

The clock on the wall showed that it was not quite four. A few people had come into the front lobby, unaware of the closing time. Soon the two attendants, who had already changed their clothes to go home, came back to close the large front doors, leaving one door ajar as they departed.

"They're closed," a voice remarked outside the doors.

Stragglers inside began leaving one by one from the now darkened lobby. We were also walking toward the door.

"Would you excuse me for a moment?" she suddenly said to me.

"Let me hold that for you," I said, indicating her umbrella; like most women, we did things like that for each other. She seemed puzzled for a moment, then looked at what she had in her hand.

"It's not raining now, is it?" she said to herself, and handed me the umbrella. "Why don't you go on ahead. I'll join you soon." She returned the way we had come.

I left the building, trying not to look back to see where she was going. I thought I understood why she wanted to return; it had not been necessary, then, to offer to hold her umbrella. The reason we had stayed until closing time in the first place was her obvious reluctance to leave, which didn't seem unreasonable. It must have been the front lobby that she couldn't resist seeing again. She wanted to be there, to look at the place once more without my company.

When we had arrived, the rain had almost stopped; now the sky above the trees was faintly colored by an autumn sunset. I went down the stone steps to the drive, still trying not to look back the way I had come, and slowly walked along the gravel in the front garden. The narrow garden was met by a walkway. I took the walkway, turned, and continued until I came to an arrow pointing toward the building I had just left. I stopped there and neatly folded both umbrellas. The ground was covered with fallen leaves. I played with the leaves, poking them with the umbrellas, remembering that there were several pressed leaves and flowers among the various articles that had belonged to those men. They looked quite incongruous beside the rougher, more disturbing items in the display case. Their color had faded against the paper underneath, which was also discolored. In the same case I had seen several photos of young women, or perhaps I should call them girls. One of these young victims must have pressed those leaves and flowers. The paper strips cut in irregular sizes, and the manner in which the leaves and stems had been taped here and there, told of the awkward hand of a girl who used scissors to make tape in the days before the invention of cellophane tape. A few of the leaves had retained their original bright color. I too had pressed pretty leaves and cut paper tape when I was a girl. The pressed leaves I had made were consumed in that gigantic fire ignited by remote control at the end of the war. There were several years' difference between the girls in the photos and myself, which is why I had escaped the tragic death that overtook them. Their deaths seemed so extraordinary because they were caused by something controlled from a distant location: the very nature of remote control made the whole thing difficult to understand.

I heard footsteps and turned around. It was an old woman in a worker's uniform. I walked back a little way to a spot where I could see the front of the building. Both doors were closed, with the two small round handles side by side. I had not yet started to worry. I assumed that she would appear at any moment from behind a tree or the pedestal of some statue, smiling awkwardly as she put away the handkerchief with which she had just dried her tears. I looked at the side of the building, where I saw a metal door. I went to see if it would open, but it didn't move. Its resistance filled me with a sudden apprehension: I realized that the front doors must also be locked.

The two ring-shaped handles turned out to be ornamental: underneath was another more ordinary handle with double keyholes. This wouldn't turn either. I went around to the other side of the building to make sure she was not there, then returned to the main door and started pushing and pulling the handle.

"They close so early, don't they? We thought it'd still be open, too." I turned and saw an elderly couple on the steps. They must have thought I had also come too late: they sounded sympathetic.

"Yes. It's still early," I agreed absentmindedly. I pretended to be looking at the building while I waited for them to leave. Then I went back to the door. Hoping no one would come, I pulled and twisted the handle unsuccessfully and then banged on the door. Next I tried pulling the handle while I pushed on the other door, hoping to make a small crack through which I could talk. Before long I noticed that the lower keyhole was one of those old-fashioned, mushroom-shaped fixtures that are larger than a keyhole of more recent design.

On a small piece of paper I wrote both her name and mine, and pushed it through the keyhole with a matchstick. I heard a tiny flutter as the paper dropped to the floor on the other side, then realized that I had no way of telling if she had picked it up. I wrote another note and this time pushed it halfway through the keyhole.

I was certain the paper would disappear from the hole, but when it actually did, I felt as if I had witnessed the strangest thing in the world. I lowered my head and brought my eye to the keyhole. It was dark on the other side, and I couldn't see anything. Then suddenly a voice was talking to my eye.

"I'm all right. Don't worry. . . I want you to go."

"What do you mean?"

"I want you to go home."

"Then what?"

There was no answer. I banged at the crack where the two doors met.

"Please leave me to do what I want. Pretend that you don't know anything. I'll be angry if you don't. . ."

I had been afraid that she was in trouble, but now I detected something ominous and probably illicit about her behavior.

"What in the world are you. . . ?" I raised my voice. I was not sure whether I was concerned for her or simply curious as to why she was doing something clearly forbidden.

"Someday you will understand."

"Don't be ridiculous," I snapped at her.

"I'll tell you sometime, if I can. But don't do anything that will make me angry. Please. You simply have to let me do this."

I shuddered. She sounded as if there was no chance that she would tell me why she was doing this. Her words echoed deep in my ears, like the ringing of a gong struck by a monk about to undergo some particularly arduous discipline. When I realized after a time that she was not going to answer me any more, I felt dizzy; I saw the glittering blades of those swords on display, the brownish circles of bloodstains on the clothes, and the characters in the many letters written by those men in their final days—all swirling up into the air.

The rays of the sun were fast dying away, a fact I must have noticed for my own benefit. I stared at the closed door, thinking about the pink telephone I had seen inside the building. There must be a black public phone as well, I thought. She had made a call on the way here, so she had that little black address book with her; she must have looked up my number in the same book when she called me yesterday from the station. Perhaps she would weaken and change her mind; she might try to call me out of desperation. If so, I must be at home. Resolutely I turned my back on the door.

Three different images haunted me throughout that night—images of the monk and the rigors of his trial; of a criminal; and of an accident victim (I couldn't rule out the possibility that she had met with some mishap). I felt the same awful tension that people must have experienced as they prepared to lift the giant bell of Dōjōji, which Princess

Kiyo had hidden inside. The anxiety was so real my stomach actually began aching. It was not that she had broken in, I tried rationalizing; if she simply remains inside and does nothing, it isn't a crime. But if she steals an item or two that she feels she must have, I must let her know that I won't betray her. I'm not afraid of being arrested for it. As I went over all this in my mind, I realized that I ought to try and rest; I would need all my strength on the following day. It would obviously be busy.

That was four years ago. She told me later what she did that night, which I spent without sleep. The following is what I have put together from the story she told, with a few assumptions of my own.

Sometime, somewhere, her first husband had bade a last farewell to several of his close friends and had entered the belly of an iron fish before putting to sea. His wife knew nothing about this. The iron fish had destroyed itself against another great fish—or was it a small iron island, whose upper half lay flat on some distant ocean? Her husband died, destroyed with the iron fish. His flesh was torn into many pieces that drifted down to the bottom of the sea, where they must have attracted the real fish feeding there.

She had heard that her husband had been enshrined along with innumerable other men and some women who had died extraordinary deaths, though each death was different in the manner and degree of its tragedy.

She had not been to the place where her husband was said to be enshrined. They had been married less than a year when he left her to serve his country. He came back to her only twice after that to spend a night with her. Both times he neither told her where he had been nor where he was going. One hundred and sixty-two days after his second overnight visit, she was informed that her husband was no longer of this world. By counting the days she realized that she had been unaware of his death for one hundred and twenty-one or twenty-two days. Her married life had lasted less than two years.

When it was confirmed that her husband was indeed among the enshrined, she did not go to visit the spot. It was not that she was skeptical about the act of enshrinement: rather she simply did not feel like going to a place that must be horribly gloomy. Whenever people asked her why she hadn't been, or more directly told her that she ought to go, she responded that she would go someday. Inwardly, however, she had a very different feeling; it was an attitude that could only be explained with an expression she had never used before: "The hell with it."

When she thought about her reluctance to visit her husband's shrine, she realized that the gloominess of the place was only one of her reasons after all. The main reason was that it was not yet time. She wanted to experience her husband's death all by herself, to feel the loss personally. She did not think she could do so yet. Excessive public reaction was partially responsible for her attitude, but then, for many more years after the public had ceased to pay much attention to the matter, she still couldn't have his death all to herself.

The time came when she was able to feel her husband's death personally, and by then her image of the shrine was even drearier than ever. Her reluctance had now changed to rejection, and she saw no meaning in such a visit. She knew that a time would come when she would associate morbidness with the place; she also knew that she would then go there just to make sure she was right about it. Meanwhile, whenever she thought about the visit, she was somehow certain that she wouldn't be able to explore the shrine alone and at leisure; its meaning for her was greater than its association with her husband. It was something she could possess all to herself, doing whatever she wanted there.

Time went by and she remarried. Seven years had passed since her first husband's death, but it hardly felt that long. She was still only twenty-seven, however, and that at least seemed real to her. Her first marriage, the loss of her husband, and her second marriage all seemed to have come rather quickly. After the second marriage, she began referring to her late spouse as "my first husband," even to herself.

It was not only out of consideration and politeness toward her second husband that she refrained for so long from visiting her first husband's shrine. And she was reassured somehow, knowing that she would go there someday just to see for herself what a grim place it was. She was also reassured by the thought that she had not been kept from making the visit and neglected her first husband out of consideration for her second; neither had she tried to slip away to pay her respects and thereby ignored the feelings of her new spouse. It helped her decision seem more natural when she and her husband moved to a city a long way from the shrine. When she decided to visit the place on an impulse while she was away from home, with me as a companion, nearly a quarter of a century had passed since the loss of her first husband.

It was an autumn day and, unfortunately, raining. In spite of that, the site was remarkably airy and light. This surprised her, since she had always thought it would be gloomy. There were broad gravel walkways, lanes lined with large trees, areas that looked like small parks, and open spaces adorned with young trees here and there. The place was filled with a cheerful brightness which spread to every edge and corner of the vast expanse, and the autumn rain and falling leaves seemed even to enhance its lightness.

"I'm so glad," she said to herself repeatedly. If it had been as gloomy as she had imagined, she would have felt remiss in her duties to both her first and second husbands: remiss in not having visited sooner for the first and in coming after all in spite of the second. She might even have regretted coming. Things were very different from what she had expected, however, and she felt free to think whatever she wanted.

The spot where her first husband was enshrined along with many other men and some women was a building made of natural rocks, wood, and metal. There must be places he would rather have gone to stay, she thought. She wondered whether he had seen this shrine before he died. But he must have known when he entered the iron fish that he would come here after his death. He might have quite liked this cheerful place; in fact, it was the sort of spot his spirit might have wanted to revisit now and then, though not, perhaps, on this particular day.

The ornaments on the building's exterior were not inappropriate. She saw the words "Pray for the dead" hanging from the branches of a tree. On another placard was the phrase "Rest in peace." Quite a few people who knew him were still alive, so she doubted somehow that his repose was all that peaceful.

There were a few annex buildings on the vast grounds, and it was into one of these that she locked herself.

The voice from the other side of the iron doors stopped when she refused to respond. So she went straight to the iron fish in the lobby and placed her hands on the side of its body. The surface was very rusty, and her hands felt as if they were rubbing against scales. She then stepped under the wooden rail to get even closer to the thing, and lay down so that she could embrace its body with both arms. The fish was too large for her arms—it looked as if she were clinging to it. As she held it, her body was filled with the sense that she had a right and duty to be there.

Altogether over a hundred iron fish had sunk one after another. Each had been ripped apart and scattered on the bottom of the sea. Years later, one of the fish was discovered with most of its body somehow intact. It was this salvaged body that she now embraced.

Earlier in the day, when she had first seen that long tapered cylinder in the center of the lobby facing the door, she hadn't known what it was. "This is what he rode in," she'd muttered to herself as she read the explanation on the plate. "He must have entered from this hole here," she said, noticing a round opening on top that had lost its lid. She reached her arm out to touch it. Then she came back to the plate. "So it was forty-six feet long," she noted with some surprise. She could see that it was very narrow, only four feet in diameter, and to herself she acknowledged that her husband must have found it suffocating. Since one opening faced the main door through which light still shone in, she could see halfway through the empty cylinder, which was sliced in two. The light, however, did not reach all the way to the other end. She could imagine how claustrophobic her husband must have felt.

As she moved on, looking at other exhibits, she forgot about the cylinder, but it was not because she found something else that strongly drew her attention. When she remarried, she had divided most of her first husband's belongings among a few of his acquaintances. For herself she kept some pictures and a set of badges, which she knew were at the bottom of her velveteen-covered jewelry box. The exhibits in the display cases did not seem particularly valuable or significant in her eyes. She saw me walking away from one case with a sudden awkward motion: in it was a document which read at the end, "Neither debt nor guilt nor any tie to women need I feel." She noticed me turn my face away and wipe my eyes. Someone of our generation, who has lived through and yet not personally experienced the war's most tragic moments, tends to react more strongly to such relics, she thought. She looked at the exhibits, taking more time than she needed, because I was examining them carefully.

When she came back down to the main floor and stood in front of the fish-shaped cylinder, she again thought of the claustrophobia. That sensation was intensified after one of the building's front doors was closed, darkening the lobby. When she made me leave by myself, however, she had intended to follow me right away, as she had said she would. She merely wanted to be inside the cylinder in slightly darkened surroundings. She wanted a chance to experience the feeling of being in there alone, while one door of the building was still open.

Before that chance had come, it was already almost four. In two minutes the other door would be closed. She felt as if it was going to close and trap her husband in that suffocating cylinder. If she wished, she could do exactly as he had done and lock herself in. And in that attempt she had almost succeeded. Her heart began to pound.

She was still standing in the semidarkness of the lobby when the last visitor left. The way to the stairs was blocked by a metal bar, which the attendants had locked a few minutes earlier as they were leaving. While she had been waiting for the place to become totally deserted, she had pretended to be looking at some of the exhibits by the wall near the entrance, like a late visitor reluctant to leave. Now she moved slowly, checking the two doors that she had not seen the attendant lock; she found they too had been secured. At the end of the lobby was a wall of frosted glass; beyond it was a conference room with wooden desks and benches. The light coming from the small room in the back went out at four. She hid herself when she saw an old cleaning woman locking the door to that room.

It was still not very dark in the building when the old woman latched the large front door, thereby shutting her in. The ceiling of the conference room was glass, and light came into the lobby through the frosted pane. There must have been some windows by the staircase, too: some light reached down from that direction as well.

It seemed as if the iron fish were now deep in water. She noticed a very dim light rising from the bottom of the ocean.

Part of the cylinder rested on some tiny white pebbles spread in a rectangular wooden frame. The light at the bottom of the sea was the reflection of those white pebbles faintly gleaming in the darkness. It was not yet completely dark—there was enough light to tell where the pebbles lay.

At the bottom of the deep sea she touched the white pebbles; she held them in her palm, then scooped them up in both hands. Earlier in the day she had seen a child doing the same thing. As she held the pebbles, she became convinced that the flesh of her husband's dead body on the ocean floor had not been consumed by fish and become part of their bodies; he had been dispersed and scattered about like these little stones.

Her husband had been a young, fastidious man. Perhaps she thought of him in that way because she herself had been young then. He had probably seemed fastidious because he was immature, even awkward; but she, being clumsy and even less mature, couldn't think of ways to help him relax.

"We must get a move on," he often used to say. That was the only habit of his that she could remember. No doubt the prevailing mood of the times made him use the phrase, but he also seemed to have employed it as an expression of hope that they would soon become open and intimate with one another. And perhaps he was also implying that, though young, they were a married couple and must remember to behave appropriately so that others would treat them as such. Once he even used the phrase in their marriage bed. It was much later, however, that she was able to reflect on this rather comic habit of speech: at the time she had merely listened to him with the seriousness of a student being given a lecture.

There was one more expression, come to think of it: "I'd like. . ." He would say, "I'd like you to consult me in advance," or "I'd like you not to do things like this," or "If there's a movie that you want to go and see, I'd like to know." Was he trying to convey a sense of urgency in this expression, too?

"What was it that you wanted me to do, dear?" she said. Her smile suddenly turned into a sob, and she covered her mouth with her hands. "What do you want me to do now?" she asked, overwhelmed by a surge of gentle affection for him. "I'd like you to refrain from such pointless remarks," she thought her husband would have said.

She explored the slightly curved bottom of the cylinder with her hands, then climbed into the iron fish. Once inside, she slowly straightened up, but her head bumped the ceiling before she could stand straight. Her husband, who had been taller than she, would have had to bend over even more, she thought, and she stooped down a little further. Then she took a few steps, feeling the side wall. She realized that there were rings, one or two inches in diameter, set along the wall. There must have been another curved board set on the rings, she thought, and she stooped down even more. She remained in that position for a while.

"Have you thought of anything you'd like me to do for you?" she said, squatting and rubbing the bottom part of the cylinder near her feet. Her hands touched hard, fine, sharp pieces of flesh. Again she remembered seeing a child doing just what she was doing.

Had he not wanted to see the brightness of the sun again, to breathe the fragrant air, to stretch his arms toward the sky? But he wouldn't respond to her questions and tell her what he would have liked. Her husband would not speak, and she didn't know how to help him say it. She felt the two of them had not changed since those days. A fastidious person he had been, her first husband.

Her first marriage had been so very short, and soon she had spent more years with her second husband. Over the many years of her second marriage, when she thought about her first husband, she felt that his share of her life had been unfairly small. Somehow it seemed to be her own doing, but she couldn't understand why she felt that way.

Whether because of the moon, the stars, or simply cloud, the sky seen through the glass ceiling of the conference room was not completely black. She could judge the height of the ceiling, but the floor was in total darkness. She sat on a stool, which she had brought from the conference room and placed next to the iron fish, and leaned against a wooden rail behind her.

She felt that she had remarried too soon; her second husband had been only two years older than him, though it was seven years since his death. But perhaps that thought simply allowed her to feel more freedom in her present relationship. Perhaps she wanted to feel free.

Her second husband did not want to talk about his first wife; he almost never referred to her first husband, either. Once when the conversation naturally touched on him, he said, "That's because he was on his way to the front." And simultaneously the words "departure" and "war"—words she had seen so frequently in those days—loomed before her. She saw the image of her first husband superimposed on the phrase "a man on his way to the front," and it revived his memory with double intensity. That was the first and last time her second husband mentioned him, although he didn't purposely avoid the subject. "You must have been awfully good in your previous life, being picked by a man as nice as me to start marriage all over again. Although I'm not sure I picked the best sort for retraining." His joke gently implied that she need not feel uneasy about being remarried. She had never felt more grateful to him than at that time. It was for those words, spoken very early in their marriage, that she had stayed with him, she thought. There were times, however, when she felt she had been deceived by them. And it was then she felt like doing something to find out if she had in fact been led astray.

She tried to discover what sort of disillusionment or what sense of attachment her first husband might have felt toward her when he shut himself up inside the iron fish. Had they been a specific kind of emotion? Perhaps. She couldn't help regretting that more time from her life had not been spared for him.

As she thought about these things, leaning against the wooden rail in the deep darkness, she realized that the emotions she was now experiencing for her first husband had been fostered by her life with her second, and that her first marriage had made her react with keen appreciation to the comment that her current companion had made soon after their remarriage. Was there someone, somewhere, telling her this? She thought she might be able to answer this if she could see the brightness of the sun again.

PLATONIC LOVE

Kanai Mieko

Translated by Amy Vladeck Heinrich

Kanai Mieko (1947–) was born and educated in Takasaki, and published her first collection of fiction, Ai no seikatsu *(Love Life), at the age of nineteen in 1968. In the same year she was awarded a prize for her poetry, although her first book of poems,* Madamu Juju no ie *(The House of Madam Juju, tr. 1977), was not published until 1971. She has continued to write both poetry and fiction—novels as well as short stories—since. Ibuse Masuji noted, of her first collection of stories, that her fiction creates an impression similar to the feelings one has looking at an abstract painting, and her work continues to demand an active participation from her readers. In the afterword to the collection* Puraton-teki ren'ai *(Platonic Love, 1979), she wrote: "Since it happens that the people who read a work of literature delete portions as they skim over them, read into some parts words that weren't written there, and so add to the work, the person called 'the author' is not the only one who writes a work of literature." In the title story, the narrator recounts her strange relationship with the "real author" of her stories, examining the sources of creativity and exploring the dangerous shoals of self-discovery and self-definition.*

*   *   *

If I ever have to prove to her that I am "the author," I suppose I would have to do it by writing an essay or a book. I became acquainted with her . . . well, in this case I don't know that "acquainted" is exactly the right word . . . at any rate, our strange relationship began when I wrote my first story. I received a letter that started: "I am the person who wrote the story published under your name." Letters with the same opening sentence began to accumulate, equal in number to the things I wrote, and while I kept trying to ignore them, the truth is I found myself completely unable to do so. As long as I continued to write these stories, she was always with me. But there was no name or address on the letters, so I had no way of communicating with this "real author." The relationship between the "real author" and myself was completely one-sided. Of course, it was only "one-sided" from my point of view; if you looked at it from hers, you might not think of it that way. But still, I didn't even know if it was really a "she" who wrote the letters.

The envelopes of the earliest letters have already yellowed. They were a variety of square white envelopes of different sizes and textures, and at various times the color of the ink was green or sepia or purple. Green and sepia and purple inks have a Taishō flavor to them, and I hate them. The handwriting had practically no individuality. As with nearly everyone after the war, the handwriting was nothing like the sort of calligraphy you would write with a brush; the characters were the kind you learn when you use a printed book as a model, and could hardly even be called clumsy. In all honesty, they were just like the characters I write —reflecting an undisciplined quality that carelessly says, if it's legible you can't complain.

Perhaps the letters were from someone who had tried to write a similar story—one could easily imagine it happening. Or some young poet my own age, speaking about my first effort, might have said, "I could write something like that in a single night," and duly caught me by surprise. Just about anyone who has read one or two things that might pass as stories could do the same sort of work. On the face of it, it did seem feasible, I suppose.

Leaving aside the unthinkable case of a story with exactly the same contents, it certainly wasn't impossible that someone had written something very similar. Aren't all "literary works" essentially the same? On reading her first letter—I remember the rustling, tactile sound when I opened the neatly folded, thick foreign paper—I admit I couldn't suppress an uncomfortable feeling that must have been some lingering sense of pride, and yet I felt it really didn't matter who the author was. The conceit of "I wrote that" became repellent all the more quickly if I was, in fact, the one who wrote it. Why shouldn't I cede the "authorship" of that story to an unknown person, and become the "author" of a different story? Yes, I would declare myself the "author" of an entirely different work. . .

Every time I published a story, a letter was invariably delivered to me, and I couldn't help getting a little fed up. Still, she was undoubtedly my most ardent and essential reader, though it was authorship she claimed, and chance might even prove it true. In any event, I first came to realize that one particular story had been written (by her? by me?) as a result of a letter from her. I kept this secret for quite a while because I didn't know how to explain it, and because for some unknown reason I felt reluctant to tell anyone about her.

Yet whatever I wrote, she would doubtless insist that she had written it herself. I might ask, "When could I possibly have read what you wrote?" and with a little smile—unconsciously I was inclined to imagine her smile as beautiful—she would say, "Don't you even remember that?" Naturally I couldn't even try to ask her questions, but simply read what she wrote, as if it were a privilege I'd been singled out for. Our relationship was concerned exclusively with the writing of stories.

In a sense I was made to suffer because of her, but gradually a curiosity about her made me wish that I knew what kind of person she was, what kind of life she led, what sort of things she was attached to, what experiences she had had, what on earth she thought about. I tried to give her a body. But I was filled with doubts, including, in fact, the question of whether she was a man or a woman. Frankly, I despised my own body, and it was painful to think of the "real author's" body as something beautiful. I sang to myself like a poet in love. You have a body!—oh, the wonder of it! Suspended in my (our) dreams. . . I even thought that if she and not I had written those few slight, inadequate works (and wasn't the description itself a means of scorning her existence?), then I would have the satisfaction of knowing I had nothing to do with them. But it was my hand that had formed those characters, or remained locked in my inability to write them. I even thought of asking other writers if they had ever received letters from someone who called herself the "real author." I might have discovered that I was not the only victim of a person who played malicious, complicated, and even fairly sophisticated pranks. There was no evidence that this wasn't a vicious and persistent piece of mischief.

I don't mean to suggest, of course, that she bothered me twenty-four hours a day. I had my own life, and I was perfectly able to enjoy it. It was a commonplace, ordinary life; I was bored occasionally, but not so often that the boredom gnawed at me, and I had no interest in the experiences that seem to make reality precious only as misfortune makes it tangible. In short, I had probably grown used to getting by without the pathetic confusion to which younger, more innocent sensibilities are so susceptible; the feelings that result from encounters with a too precise and lucidly contoured world. When I feel constrained by an overbearing world in which I cannot write, am I not already trying to start to write? So, as must be the case with any writer, rather than read my own stories (but she doesn't say that: she says the stories *I wrote*), I preferred the many works of other writers I enjoyed. And this in spite of the jealousy that goes with reading them.

I decided to go to Yugawara and take along the notes for a new story I had to get started on, together with some pieces I wanted to revise for a collection; I also took several books I hadn't yet read, and a manuscript which some strange temptation had made me commit myself to write on "Discussing My Own Work." Of course there was some doubt about how qualified I was to comment on "my own work" but, leaving that aside, I had enough money from my royalties to be able to stay at a hot spring for a while. And I must admit I was drawn to the tradition of writers staying at hot spring resorts to work.

Why is it that, try as we might to avoid discussing our own work, or the work we plan to write, in the end we wind up telling all? In spite of being enjoined to silence, words emerge. . . We start with the desire to discuss the truth, and in practice we go on to speak in terms that veil the truth. What is required and anticipated in the act we call "discussing one's own work"? Perhaps it is a form of confession. And within that act that pretends to be confession, I dream of a form in which, concealed, lie books that have ingeniously turned into illusions.

In the end, I had nothing to confess. It was just that in reading my own stories I felt a curious passion. Just supposing that the story were really something she had written, it might have been exactly because I was already her reader that I felt so strong a passion. Still, I had no more than a title for the story I planned to write: "Platonic Love." And who on earth would write it? She or I?

As I expected, "Platonic Love" didn't progress a single line; there wasn't a word written in my notebook, and I spent five days just walking during the day and reading or drinking alone at night. I tried to focus "Discussing My Own Work" on some short pieces I had written three years earlier, but the words turned out to be all hers, all taken from her letters. In an effort to resist her, I tried writing about the rabbit's pelt that was nailed to the grayish brown wooden door of a grocery store in Hanamaki (exposing the skin where the spilled blood had turned to glue), or about the dream of rabbits I'd had in the berth of a train on the way to Iwate. I tried to remember the winter sky smothering the town of Hanamaki and the rows of streets, the translucent white and bloodless sky over those arteries of gray and brown and pale blue in an ordinary, characterless, provincial town. But as I feared, I wasn't sure if I had actually been there. The requisites for life, the liveliness that embodies a town, at times even the confusion, were quite removed from the Hanamaki I seemed to know, and the town disappeared in the labyrinths of my memory. The town where "the soul of the silent city made me choose the road" had lost its form, and even the untanned rabbit's pelt, which I surely must have seen, had disappeared completely. Weren't they things I had read about once in some story? It wasn't I who saw or wrote about them. No, that pelt, with the brown, red, and purple gluelike blood and fat adhering to it, was nailed up in a story I had read, wasn't it?

It was so quiet in the setting sun in that very seedy, amateurishly run inn that there seemed to be no other guests, and the mountains that used to form the view from the west windows were blocked from sight by the gray concrete building of a large tourist hotel, so of course the guest rates were cheap enough to allow quite a long stay. A clumsy picture of a crane with a sly expression was painted on the sliding door, yellowed over the years by the late afternoon sun, and a scroll with a poem about the pathos of an egret in the snow was hanging in the alcove. A small black-and-white television right in front of it, an old low wooden table, stained all over with rings from beer glasses, with a tea set on it, a mirror stand draped with a faded length of printed silk, and a clothes rack with three hangers were all the furnishings in the room. Every day I had a bath a dusk, then sadly drank alone in silence, eating the home-style cooking prepared by the landlady: sweet-and-sour pork, sashimi, and salad with store-bought mayonnaise. And if I had to say what the great virtue of eating alone is, it would simply be that if you read a book while eating, no one is offended. Shadowing me on this trip (and how many little trips have I taken alone!) was the constant recollection that I had brought along the notes for my story. I would remember to try and listen for the voice calling me to start the story I had been as yet unable to write, and in the middle of the bath, where the surface of the water shone like pink metal in the setting sun, I would be moved to tears. I would think that the absent "he" or "she" who had withdrawn from the protagonist was really the unwritten story itself, and I cried as my feelings were exposed. My body melted into the large bath, and it was already not a body, nor was it hot water that weighed upon and enveloped it, wrapping it in warm gentleness, but something other than me floating in the water that united and merged me with all existence. In the rose-colored sunlight trembling in the milk-white mist of steam and silence and stillness, time was stretched out, and the bath would begin to expand as though in a dream within a dream, and I would not be the one dreaming, but she would be the one dreaming and I just a character in that dream; and then that eerie vision would melt into the water again. Suspended in my (our) dreams. . .

After lunch one day, when I was walking along a road by a mountain stream that flowed through the park, a woman I didn't know spoke to me. In spite of her hesitant manner, she began speaking with a certain obtrusiveness. She spoke as if she knew all about me, and intuitively I realized that this very woman was the "real author." The image I had secretly cherished of her reflected an unconscious vanity and hope, and, as I wrote earlier, was associated with the word "beautiful"; but it was rude to the "real author" to look so crestfallen when I realized that it wasn't really appropriate. (Not only is it simply not my style to explain in detail how it was inappropriate, but it would be discourteous.) And then she asked me to join her for lunch since she hadn't eaten, and, unable to resist, I answered that I had eaten but would keep her company with a cup of tea or something. We sat opposite each other at a window table in a coffee shop near the park entrance, where she ordered the most expensive roast beef sandwich, and crabmeat salad and coffee; I ordered just a cup of coffee. I actually don't remember most of what we talked about, except that she discussed the as-yet-unwritten story "Platonic Love," accompanied by the crunching sound of lettuce and celery being chewed. Yes, the "real author" discussed "Platonic Love," pausing to lick off her fingers any juice that dropped from her roast beef sandwich. Not only did I miss my chance to ask her what her motives were in sending me those letters, I also had to pay the bill for her sandwich, salad, and three cups of coffee. It was about three o'clock when I returned to the inn.

I know I should have written my "Platonic Love," but now I feel no great desire nor any great need to do so.

When I got back home, there was a letter from the "real author," as I expected, but it contained no particular thank-you for the lunch; it was the manuscript of "Platonic Love" that she had spoken about then.

I've tried and tried to convince myself that I should be able to get by without reading it. It would be extremely simple to throw it in the garbage or burn it without reading it. It would be easy to stretch out my hand to the letter on my desk, with my name written in that awful handwriting (which looks exactly as if I had written it myself), and dispose of it so completely that I would never have to think it had ever existed. I could take the letters (all the letters she's sent) out into the garden, douse them with kerosene, and strike a match. I would have to fill a bucket with water and be careful to control the fire. In a very short time, flames would lick at those letters and swallow them up, sending up a pale purple smoke; and only a light pile of crumbling black ashes would remain, to be drenched with water and trampled into the ground. But I sink into my chair with the hopeless feeling that nothing would have been destroyed. In the end I will probably publish "Platonic Love." And I will probably say it is my work.

THE CRUSHED PELLET

Kaikō Takeshi

Translated by Cecilia Segawa Seigle

Kaikō Takeshi was born in Osaka in 1930. His keen sympathy for the human condition has its origins in his own suffering and starvation in postwar Japan and the pressure of having to feed his mother and sisters at the age of fourteen after his father's death. But it was also those physically and spiritually deprived years that laid the ground for his development as a tough, vigorous, and sensitive writer.

Although he barely attended Osaka City College, taking one odd job after another, he did manage to get a law degree before joining the Suntory Whiskey Company and setting up its advertising department almost single-handedly. After receiving the Akutagawa Prize in 1958 for his Hadaka no ōsama *(The Naked King, tr. 1977), he left his job and concentrated on writing short stories and novels on large-scale sociological themes. In early works such as* Rubōki *(The Runaway, 1959; tr. 1977),* Nihon sanmon opera *(A Japanese Threepenny Opera, 1959), and* Robinson no matsuei *(The Descendants of Robinson Crusoe, 1960), he deliberately avoided an auto-biographical approach both in terms of material and emotional involvement, achieving an objectivity that resembled that of a social historian. Kaikō was sent by one of Japan's leading papers to Israel to cover the Eichmann trial as a special correspondent, but it was his participation in the Vietnam War in 1964–65, a veritable purgatory for him, that proved a turning point and provided new material he could treat with passion. For virtually the first time, he was moved to reveal himself in his work, and in* Kagayakeru yami *(Into a Black Sun, 1968; tr. 1980) and* Natsu no yami

(Darkness in Summer, 1969; tr. 1973), both prize-winning novels, his involvement with his subject matter is sharply personal. The first is a brilliant exposition of corrupt Saigon and its ordinary people caught between "the devil and the deep blue sea" and patiently coping with the difficulties of daily life—a journey culminating in the novelist's shattering experience of the battle front. The other is about a writer who, devastated by his Vietnam experience, escapes to Europe. Reviving his affair with a former girlfriend, another Japanese exile, he slowly heals and recharges himself only to return to Vietnam. Kaikō is a master of the word picture employing all the sensory elements—smell, taste, sound, touch—to evoke an intense and accurate atmosphere. This uncommon skill and the power of his compassionate observation have won him several prizes in the field of reportage alone.

The present story, Tama kudakeru (The Crushed Pellet, 1978), delves into the question of artistic freedom in a dictatorship, and was awarded the first Kawabata Yasunari Prize in 1979. It shows Kaikō's ability to embrace human beings as they are, and his sensitive reaction to a great writer's death and to a friend's grief over it. The curious title is symbolic. The character for tama (ball or pellet) in Chinese (yü) also stands for jade, or something precious. The two characters in the title together form a compound word suggesting a heroic, crushing death, a term familiar to Japanese of the war generation. The fact that the ball in this case is only human skin seems to hint at the fragility of the human being.

*   *   *

Late one morning, I awoke in the capital of a certain country and found myself—not changed overnight into a large brown beetle, nor feeling exactly on top of the world—merely ready to go home. For about an hour I remained between the sheets, wriggling, pondering, and scrutinizing my decision from all angles until it became clear that my mind was made up. Then I slipped out of bed. I walked down a boulevard where the aroma of freshly baked bread drifted from glimmering shop windows, and went into the first airline office I encountered to make a reservation on a flight to Tokyo via the southern route. Since I wanted to spend a day or two in Hong Kong, it had to be the southern route. Once I had reserved a seat and pushed through the glass door to the street, I felt as though a period had been written at the end of a long, convoluted paragraph. It was time for a new paragraph to begin and a story to unroll, but I had no idea where it would lead. I felt no exhilaration in thoughts of the future. When I left Japan, there had been fresh, if anxious, expectations moving vividly through the vague unknown. But going home was no more than bringing a sentence to a close, and opening a paragraph. I had no idea what lay ahead, but it aroused no apprehension or sense of promise. Until a few years ago, I had felt excitement— fading rapidly, perhaps, but there nonetheless—about changing paragraphs. But as I grew older, I found myself feeling less and less of anything. Where once there had been a deep pool of water, mysterious and cool, I now saw a bone-dry riverbed.

I returned to the hotel and began to pack, feeling the familiar fungus starting to form on my back and shoulders. I took the elevator to the lobby, settled my account, and deposited my body and suitcase on the shuttle bus to the airport. I tried to be as active as I could, but the fungus had already begun to spread. On my shoulders, chest, belly, and legs the invisible mold proliferated, consuming me inwardly but leaving my outer form untouched. The closer I came to Tokyo, the faster it would grow, and dreary apathy would gradually take hold.

Imprisoned in the giant aluminum cylinder, speeding through a sea of cotton clouds, I thought over the past several months spent drifting here and there. I already felt nostalgia for those months, as though they had occurred a decade ago instead of ending only yesterday. Reluctantly, I was heading home to a place whose familiarity I had hated, and therefore fled. I went home crestfallen, like a soldier whose army has surrendered before fighting any battle. Each repetition of this same old process was merely adding yet another link to a chain of follies. Unnerved by this thought, I remained rigid, strapped to my narrow seat. I would probably forget these feelings briefly in the hubbub of customs at Haneda Airport. But the moment I opened the glass door to the outside world, that swarming fungus would surround me. Within a month or two, I would turn into a snowman covered with a fuzzy blue-gray mold. I knew this would happen, yet I had no choice but to go home, for I had found no cure elsewhere. I was being catapulted back to my starting point because I had failed to escape.

I entered a small hotel on the Kowloon Peninsula and turned the pages of my tattered memo book to find the telephone number of Chang Li-jen. I always gave him a call when I was there; if he was out, I would leave my name and the name of the hotel, since my Chinese was barely good enough to order food at restaurants. Then I would telephone again at nine or ten in the morning, and Chang's lively, fluent Japanese would burst into my ear. We would decide to meet in a few hours at the corner of Nathan Road, or at the pier of the Star Ferry, or sometimes at the entrance to the monstrous Tiger Balm Garden. Chang was a prematurely wizened man in his fifties, who always walked with his head down; when he approached a friend, he would suddenly lift his head and break into a big, toothy smile, his eyes and mouth gaping all at once. When he laughed, his mouth seemed to crack up to his ears. I found it somehow warm and reassuring each time I saw those large stained teeth, and felt the intervening years drop away. As soon as he smiled and began to chatter about everything, the fungus seemed to retreat a little. But it would never disappear, and the moment I was the least bit off guard, it would revive and batten on me. While I talked with Chang, though, it was usually subdued, waiting like a dog. I would walk shoulder to shoulder with him, telling him about the fighting in Africa, the Near East, Southeast Asia, or whatever I had just seen. Chang almost bounded along, listening to my words, clicking his tongue and exclaiming. And when my story was over, he would tell me about the conditions in China, citing the editorials of the left- and right-wing papers and often quoting Lu Hsün.

I had met Chang some years back through a Japanese newspaperman. The journalist had gone home soon afterward, but I had made a point of seeing Chang every time I had an occasion to visit Hong Kong. I knew his telephone number but had never been invited to his home, and I knew scarcely anything about his job or his past. Since he had graduated from a Japanese university, his Japanese was flawless, and I was aware that he had an extraordinary knowledge of Japanese literature; and yet, beyond the fact that he worked in a small trading company and occasionally wrote articles for various newspapers to earn some pocket money, I knew nothing about his life.

He would lead me through the hustle of Nathan Road, commenting, if he spotted a sign on a Swiss watch shop saying "King of Ocean Mark," that it meant an Omega Seamaster; or stopping at a small bookstore to pick up a pamphlet with crude illustrations of tangled bodies and show me the caption, "Putting oneself straight forward," explaining that it meant the missionary position. He also taught me that the Chinese called hotels "wine shops" and restaurants "wine houses," though no one knew the reason why.

For the last several years, one particular question had come up whenever we saw each other, but we had never found an answer to it. In Tokyo one would have laughed it off as nonsense, but here it was a serious issue. If you were forced to choose between black and white, right and left, all and nothing—to choose a side or risk being killed— what would you do? If you didn't want to choose either side, but silence meant death, what would you do? How would you escape? There are two chairs and you can sit in either one, but you can't remain standing between them. You know, moreover, that though you're free to make your choice, you are expected to sit in one particular chair; make the wrong choice, and the result is certain: "Kill!" they'll shout—"Attack!" "Exterminate!" In the circumstances, what kind of answer can you give to avoid sitting in either chair, and yet satisfy their leader, at least for the time being? Does history provide a precedent? China's beleaguered history, its several thousand years of troubled rise and fall, must surely have fostered and crystallized some sort of wisdom on the subject. Wasn't there some example, some ingenious answer there?

I was the one who had originally brought up this question. We were in a small dim sum restaurant on a back street. I had asked it quite casually, posing a riddle as it were, but Chang's shoulders fidgeted and his eyes turned away in confusion. He pushed the dim sum dishes aside and, pulling out a cigarette, stroked it several times with fingers thin as chicken bones. He lit it carefully and inhaled deeply and slowly; he then blew out the smoke and murmured:

"'Neither a horse nor a tiger'—it's the same old story. In old China, there was a phrase, 'Ma-ma, hu-hu,' that meant a noncommittal 'neither one thing nor the other.' The characters were horse-horse, tiger-tiger. It's a clever expression, and the attitude was called Ma-huism. But they'd probably kill you if you gave an answer like that today. It sounds vague, but actually you're making the ambiguity of your feelings known. It wouldn't work. They'd kill you on the spot. So, how to answer . . . you've raised a difficult question, haven't you?"

I asked him to think it over until I saw him next time. Chang had become pensive, motionless, as though shocked into deep thought. He left his dumplings untouched, and when I called this to his attention, he smiled crookedly and scratched something on a piece of paper. He handed it to me and said, "You should remember this when you're eating with a friend." He had written *"Mo t'an kuo shih,"* which means roughly "Don't discuss politics." I apologized profusely for my thoughtlessness.

Since then, I have stopped in Hong Kong and seen Chang at intervals of one year, sometimes two. After going for a walk or having a meal (I made sure we had finished eating) I always asked him the same question. He would cock his head thoughtfully or smile ruefully and ask me to wait a little longer. On my part, I could only pose the question, because I had no wisdom to impart; so the riddle stayed unsolved for many years, its cruel face still turned toward us. In point of fact, if there were a clever way of solving the riddle, everyone would have used it—and a new situation requiring a new answer would have arisen, perpetuating the dilemma. A shrewd answer would lose its sting in no time, and the question would remain unanswered. On occasion, however—for instance when Chang told me about Laoshê—I came very close to discerning an answer.

Many years ago, Laoshê visited Japan as leader of a literary group and stopped in Hong Kong on his way back to China. Chang had been given an assignment to interview him for a newspaper and went to the hotel where Laoshê was staying. Laoshê kept his appointment but said nothing that could be turned into an article, and when Chang kept asking how the intellectuals had fared in post-revolutionary China, the question was always evaded. When this had happened several times, Chang began to think that Laoshê's power as a writer had probably waned. Then Laoshê began talking about country cooking, and continued for three solid hours. Eloquently and colorfully he described an old restaurant somewhere in Szechwan, probably Chungking or Chengtu, where a gigantic cauldron had simmered for several centuries over a fire that had never gone out. Scallions, Chinese lettuce, potatoes, heads of cows, pigs' feet—just about anything and everything was thrown into the pot. Customers sat around the cauldron and ladled the stew into soup bowls; and the charge was determined by adding up the number of empty bowls each person had beside him. This was the sole subject that Laoshê discussed for three hours, in minute and vivid detail—what was cooked, how the froth rose in the pot, what the stew tasted like, how many bowls one could eat. When he finished talking he disappeared.

"He left so suddenly there was no way to stop him," said Chang. "He was magnificent. . . Among Laoshê's works, I prefer *Rickshaw Boy* to *Four Generations Under One Roof*. When Laoshê spoke, I felt as though I had just reread *Rickshaw Boy* after many years. His poignant satire, the humor and sharp observation in that book—that's what I recognized in him. I felt tremendously happy and moved when I left the hotel. When I got home, I was afraid I might forget the experience if I slept, so I had a stiff drink and went over the story, savoring every word."

"You didn't write an article?"

"Oh, yes, I wrote something, but I just strung together some fancy-sounding words, that's all. I wouldn't swear to it, but he seemed to trust me when he talked like that. And the story was really too delicious for the newspaper."

Chang's craggy face broke into a great wrinkled smile. I felt as though I had seen the flash of a sword, a brief glimpse of pain, grief, and fury. I could do nothing but look down in silence. Evidently there was a narrow path, something akin to an escape route between the chairs, but its danger was immeasurable. Didn't the English call this kind of situation "between the devil and the deep blue sea?"

Late in the afternoon of the day before my departure for Tokyo, Chang and I were strolling along when we came to a sign that read "Heavenly Bath Hall." Chang stopped and explained.

"This is a *tsao t'ang*, a bathhouse. It's not just a soak in a bath, though; you can have the dirt scraped off your body, get a good massage, have the calluses removed from your feet and your nails clipped. All you have to do is take off your clothes and lie down. If you feel sleepy, you just doze off and sleep as long as you like. Obviously some are better than others, but this one is famous for the thorough service you get. And when you leave, they'll give you the ball of dirt they scraped off you; it's a good souvenir. How would you like to try it? They use three kinds of cloth, rough, medium, and soft. They wrap them around their hands and rub you down. A surprising amount of dead skin will come off, you know, enough to make a ball of it. It's fun."

I nodded my consent, and he led me inside the door and talked to the man at the counter. The man put down his newspaper, listened to Chang, and with a smile gestured to me to come in. Chang said he had some errands to do, but would come to the airport the next day to see me off. He left me at the bathhouse.

When the bathkeeper stood up I found he was tall, with muscular shoulders and hips. He beckoned, and I followed him down a dim corridor with shabby walls, then into a cubicle with two simple beds. One was occupied by a client wrapped in a white towel and stretched out on his stomach, while a nail-cutter held his leg, paring skin off his heel as though fitting a horseshoe. The bathkeeper gestured to me, and I emptied my pockets and gave him my billfold, passport, and watch. He took them and put them in the drawer of a night table, then locked it with a sturdy, old-fashioned padlock. The key was chained to his waist with a soiled cord. He smiled and slapped his hip a couple of times as though to reassure me before going out. I took off all my clothes. A small, good-looking boy in a white robe, with a head like an arrowhead bulb, came in and wrapped my hips from behind with a towel and slung another over my shoulder. I followed the boy into the dark corridor, slippers on my feet. Another boy was waiting in the room leading to the bath, and quickly peeled off my towel before pushing the door open onto a gritty concrete floor. A large rusty nozzle on the wall splashed hot water over me, and I washed my body.

The bathtub was a vast, heavy rectangle of marble with a three-foot ledge. A client just out of the tub was sprawled face down on a towel, like a basking seal. A naked assistant was rubbing the man's buttocks with a cloth wrapped around his hand. Timidly, I stepped into the water and found it not hot, nor cool, but soft and smooth, oiled by the bodies of many men. There was none of the stinging heat of the Japanese public bath. It was a thick heat and heavy, slow-moving. Two washers, a big muscular man and a thin one, stood by the wall, quite naked except for their bundled hands, waiting for me to come out. The large man's penis looked like a snail, while the other's was long, plump, and purple, with all the appearance of debauchery. It hung with the weight and languor of a man with a long track record, making me wonder how many thousands of polishings it would take to look like that. It was a masterpiece that inspired admiration rather than envy, appended to a figure that might have stepped from the Buddhist hell of starvation. But his face showed no pride or conceit; he was simply and absentmindedly waiting for me to get out of the tub. I covered myself with my hands and stepped out of the warm water. He spread a bath towel quickly and instructed me to lie down.

As Chang had told me, there were three kinds of rubbing cloths. The coarse, hempen one was for the arms, buttocks, back, and legs. Another cotton cloth, softer than the first, was for the sides and underarms. The softest was gauzy and used on the soles of the feet, the crotch, and other sensitive areas. He changed the cloth according to the area, tightly wrapping it around his hand like a bandage before rubbing my skin. He took one hand or leg at a time, shifted me around, turned me over, then over again, always with an expert, slightly rough touch which remained essentially gentle and considerate. After a while, he seemed to sigh and I heard him murmuring "Aiya. . ." under his breath. I half opened my eyes and found my arms, my belly, my entire body covered with a scale of gray dead skin like that produced by a schoolboy's eraser. The man seemed to sense a challenge and began to apply more strength. It was less a matter of rubbing than of peeling off a layer of skin without resorting to surgery, the patient task of removing a layer of dirt closely adhering to the body. Talking to himself in amusement, he moved toward my head, then my legs, absorbed in his meticulous work. I had ceased to be embarrassed and, dropping my hands to my sides, I placed my whole body at his disposal. I let him take my right hand or left hand as he worked. Once I had surrendered my body to him the whole operation was extremely relaxing, like wallowing in warm mud. Soap was applied, then washed off with warm water; I was told to soak in the tub, and when I came out, again warm water was poured over me several times. Then he wiped me thoroughly with a steamed towel as hot as a lump of coal.

Finally—smiling, as though to say "Here you are!"—he placed a pellet of skin on my palm. It was like a gray ball of tofu mash. The moist, tightly squeezed sphere was the size of a smallish plover's egg. With so many dead cells removed, my skin had become as tender as a baby's, clear and fresh, and all my cells, replenished with new serum, rejoiced aloud.

I returned to the dressing room and tumbled into bed. The good-looking boy brought me a cup of hot jasmine tea. I drank it lying in bed, and with each mouthful felt as though a spurt of perspiration had shot from my body. With a fresh towel, the boy gently dried me. The nail-cutter entered and clipped my toes and fingernails, trimmed the thick skin off my heels, and shaved my corns, changing his instruments each time. When the work was completed, he left the room in silence. In his place, a masseur entered and began to work without a word. Strong, sensitive fingers and palms crept over my body, searching and finding the nests and roots of strained muscles, pressing, rubbing, pinching, patting, and untangling the knots. Every one of these employees was scrupulous in delivering his services. They concentrated on the work, unstinting of time and energy, their solemn delicacy incomparable. Their skill made me think of a heavyweight fighter skipping rope with the lightness of a feather. A cool mist emanated from the masseur's strong fingers. My weight melted away and I dissolved into a sweet sleep.

"My shirt."

Chang looked at me quizzically.

"That's the shirt I was wearing until yesterday."

When Chang came to my hotel room the next day, I pointed out the dirty pellet on the table. For some reason, only a twisted smile appeared on his face. He took out a packet of tea, enough for one pot, and said that he had bought me the very best tea in Hong Kong; I was to drink it in Tokyo. Then he fell silent, staring blankly. I told him about the washer, the nail-clipper, the boys, the tea, the sleep. I described everything in detail and reveled in my praise of these men, who knew one's body and one's needs so thoroughly, and were devoted to their work. One might have called them anarchists without bombs. Chang nodded only sporadically and smiled at whatever I said, but soon fell to gazing darkly at the wall. His preoccupation was so obvious that I was forced to stop talking and begin packing my suitcase. I had been completely atomized in the dressing room of the bathhouse. Even when I had revived and walked out of the door there seemed to be some space between my clothing and my flesh. I had felt chilly, and staggered at every sound and smell, every gust of air. But one night's sleep restored my bones and muscles to their proper position, and a thin but opaque coating covered my skin, shrouding the insecurity of stark nakedness. Dried up and shriveled, the ball of dirt looked as if it might crumble at the lightest touch of a finger, so I carefully wrapped it in layers of tissue and put it in my pocket.

We arrived at the airport, where I checked in and took care of all the usual details. When only the parting handshake remained before I left, Chang suddenly broke his silence. A friend in the press had called him last night. Laoshê had died in Peking. It was rumored that he was beaten to death, surrounded by the children of the Red Guard. There was another rumor that he had escaped this ignominy by jumping from the second-floor window of his home. Another source reported that he had jumped into a river. The circumstances were not at all clear, but it seemed a certainty that Laoshê had died an unnatural death. The fact seemed inescapable.

"Why?" I asked.

"I don't know."

"What did he do to be denounced?"

"I don't know."

"What sort of things was he writing recently?"

"I haven't read them. I don't know."

I looked at Chang, almost trembling myself. Tears were about to brim from his eyes; he held his narrow shoulders rigid. He had lost his usual calm, his gaiety, humor, all, but without anger or rancor; he just stood there like a child filled with fear and despair. This man, who must have withstood the most relentless of hardships, was helpless, his head hanging, his eyes red, like a child astray in a crowd.

"It's time for you to go," he said. "Please come again."

I was silent.

"Take care of yourself," Chang said and held out his hand timidly; he shook mine lightly. Then he turned around, his head still downcast, and slowly disappeared into the crowd.

I boarded the plane and found my seat. When I had fastened the seat belt, a vision from long ago suddenly returned to me. I had once visited Laoshê at his home in Peking. I now saw the lean, sinewy old writer rise amid a profusion of potted crysanthemums and turn his silent, penetrating gaze upon me. Only his eyes and the cluster of flowers were visible, distant and clear. Distracted, I took the wrapping from my pocket and opened it. The gray pellet, now quite dried up, had crumbled into dusty powder.

THE CLEVER RAIN TREE

Ōe Kenzaburō

Translated by Brett de Bary
and Carolyn Haynes

There are surely few readers of this volume for whom "The Clever Rain Tree" (Atama no ii rein tsurii, 1980) will prove a first encounter with the distinctive fictional world of Ōe Kenzaburō. Published more than two decades after Ōe's youthful "Shiiku" (The Catch, 1958; tr. 1959) won him the coveted Akutagawa Prize at the age of twenty-three, "The Clever Rain Tree" represents the mature style of a writer whose prolific output has gained him recognition, both at home and abroad, as one of Japan's leading postwar novelists.

Ōe, the third son in a family of seven, was born on January 31, 1935, in the village in rural Shikoku that appears, in various mythologized forms, as a recurrent motif in his fiction. Ōe was six at the start of the Pacific War, lost his father and grandmother at the age of nine, and, as a ten-year-old, learned of the atomic bombing of Hiroshima and Japan's unconditional surrender. He has since traced his perceptions of a "void behind the print"— that awareness of the tenuous link between writing and reality which infuses his work—to his childhood in this isolated village from which the world was knowable only through printed words or the occasional, threatening appearance of enemy warplanes.

Ōe's adolescent years overlapped with those of the American Occupation and the abrupt "reversal of values" (kachi tenkan, as Japanese historians phrase it) experienced by Japanese during the recovery from the war. Ōe entered Tokyo University in 1954, completing a major in French literature and a thesis on the fiction of Jean-Paul Sartre in 1959, as the

*country became enveloped in the political turmoil surrounding the renewal
of the U.S.-Japan Security Treaty. In 1960, Ōe married Yukari, daughter
of the well-known writer Itami Mansaku. His fiction from this early period
was acclaimed (and sometimes deprecated) for its unusual combination of
sensuous lyricism, sexual farce, and philosophical inquiry incorporating such
Sartrean concepts as "authenticity" and "bad faith." These works often
included, as well, a dimension of political allegory reflecting concerns that
were Ōe's legacy from the Occupation period and the anti-Security Treaty
struggle: the multiple dimensions of Japan's postwar dependence on the
United States, the attendant confused sense of cultural identity, the per-
sisting questions of war responsibility, the emperor system, and ultrana-
tionalist ideology.*

*Ōe's youthful fiction, however, was radically transformed by two events
in the year 1963: the birth in June of a first son with severe brain damage,
and a visit to Hiroshima in August to attend the Ninth World Conference
Against Atomic and Hydrogen Bombs. In 1964, Ōe won the Shinchōsha
Literary Prize for* Kojinteki na taiken *(A Personal Matter, tr. 1968), a novel
that describes a father's nighmarish struggle to embrace the existence of
his mentally retarded son. In 1965, an account of Ōe's confrontation with
A-bomb survivors was published as* Hiroshima Nōto *(Hiroshima Notes, tr.
1981), in which Ōe links his journey to Hiroshima with his despair over
the son "lying in an incubator with no hope of recovery." This coupling
of the motifs of the idiot son, symbol of purity and madness, and the specter
of nuclear apocalypse has since become a key feature of Ōe's major work.
Moreover, in the years since 1965, Ōe's fiction has displayed increasing ver-
satility of theme and complexity of structure as he has cut loose from the
conventions of the realistic novel to explore realms of the fantastic and
grotesque more appropriate for depiction of life in the era of nuclear war.*
Man'en gannen no futtobōru *(The Silent Cry, 1967; tr. 1974), the two-
volume* Kōzui wa waga tamashii ni oyobite *(The Flood Has Come in unto My Soul, 1973), and* Dōjidai geemu *(A Contemporary Game, 1979) are
long, multilayered novels with mythical, political, and epistemological
themes.*

*"The Clever Rain Tree" is a shorter, light work published just after Ōe
completed the novel* Dōjidai geemu. *The tale is set in Hawaii, where a
cross-cultural confrontation, an "East-West dialogue," becomes an occa-*

sion for the revelation of the limitations of human language and the precariousness of the distinction between imagination and perception (a distinction perhaps symbolized by the two differently shaped darknesses, one enveloping the other, associated with the clever rain tree). The pervasive, dreamlike tone of the work is characteristic of the mature Ōe, as is the colorful, parodic sketching in of a political context through allusions to American deserters from the Vietnam War, the Iranian revolution, and the taking of hostages. The image of the cosmic tree that appears in this story has been developed more extensively in his collection of stories, "Rein tsurii" o kiku onnatachi (Women Who Listen to the Rain Tree, 1982).

*   *   *

"You'd rather see the tree than these people, wouldn't you?" inquired the American woman of German descent as she ushered me from the room jammed with partygoers, along a wide corridor, and onto the porch where we faced a broad expanse of darkness. Enveloped in the laughter and hubbub behind me, I gazed into the damp-smelling dark. That the greater part of this darkness was filled with a single huge tree was evident from the fact that at the rim of the darkness the faintly reflecting shapes of innumerable layers of radiating, board-like roots spread out in our direction. I gradually realized that these shapes like black board fences were glowing softly with a luster of grayish blue. The tree—how many hundred tree-years old was it, with its well-developed board-roots?—in this darkness eclipsed the sky and the sea far below the slope. From where we stood beneath the eaves of the porch of this large New England-style building, even at broad noon one could probably see no further than its shins, to speak of the tree anthropomorphically. It befitted the old style of the building, or rather its actual age, that around this house whose sole illumination was so quietly restrained the tree in the garden formed a wall of total darkness.

"The local name for this tree, which you said you wanted to know, is 'rain tree,' but this one of ours is a particularly clever rain tree." So said the American woman, a middle-aged woman whom I called Agatha,

383

since we didn't know each other's surnames. . . Writing like this smacks of a romance set abroad, like those we see from time to time in contemporary Japanese novels, whose hero is a compatriot proficient in foreign languages. In my case, however, it was with no such leisure that I passed these ten days. I was attending a seminar sponsored by the University of Hawaii's East-West Center on the issue of "Reappraisal of Cultural Exchange and Traditions." As for my English ability, it was such that I mistook three delegates from India for delegates from Canada, and didn't realize until halfway through the conference that they were actually from the Kannada region of India. In fact, since the conference was dedicated to the memory of the Indian humanist Coomaraswamy, there were participants from various regions in India, fluent in many distinct forms of English. Listening to the presentation of a Jewish Indian poet from Bombay, for example—his manner of speaking was extremely Indian, yet there was something unmistakably Jewish about it—I was able to enjoy his sense of humor, but if I didn't question him about each point after his lecture, it was difficult to give my response in the following sessions.

The participant from the American mainland, the poet who defined an era as spokesman for the beatnik generation, would arrive at the meeting every morning with a youth who looked physically exhausted and psychologically scarred (at least to me he appeared in this pitiful state) and would cast tender glances toward the youth, who napped on the floor behind the round table where the seminar participants were seated, saying "He is my wife." Although the speech of this New Yorker so combined discipline and unpredictability in its unique way of unfolding that I could hardly follow his English, he elicited my comments on the so-called haiku of his I've inserted below. He even sketched on a napkin from the cafeteria the scene depicted: a snowy mountain glimpsed through the wings of a fly mashed on a window. In brief, he was determined to get an authentic critique from a writer from the land of haiku. Having thus become his friend, I could hardly sit through his presentation daydreaming of other things.

Snow mountain fields
seen thru transparent wings

of a fly on windowpane.

At the end of the schedule of meetings that day I returned to the student dormitory which served as our lodging—a girls' dormitory, at that—intending to rest before the nightly party, when I was accosted by an American, a man of small stature with damaged facial muscles, who seemed to be in great torment. He had apparently worked until five years ago assisting deserters from the Vietnam War in a provincial city on the Japan Sea coast. At that time he became aware that rumors were spreading among his co-workers that he was a spy for the CIA, so he quietly slipped off to Tokyo and returned to America from there. "I imagine the leaders of the movement still think of me as a spy. Even if I wanted to renew contact with them now, I can't remember their names myself. I've always been hard of hearing, which makes it difficult for me to understand the English spoken by the Japanese, to say nothing of Japanese itself. Actually, even when I was with the movement, this led to a lot of misunderstandings and I was often confused."

This garrulous young American had become so distraught over the insubstantial rumors that he was a spy that he was now in a private institution for the psychologically disturbed. There are many classes of such institutions here in Hawaii, from the very expensive on down. This fellow lived in the kind that charged little more than the actual cost of living, yet he still went out to work during the day to earn his expenses. But how was I to comfort this poor, tormented young American, this character whose small frame was completely covered with grime (apparently related to his work)? This thoroughly depressed man who kept cocking his head toward me like a bird as if to press his ear to my mouth, yet who still couldn't grasp with his bad ear what my English—a Japanese English—meant.

Engulfing the foreground of the darkness, only the expanse of the margin of the tree's well-developed roots was faintly discernible. . . It seemed that the middle-aged woman who showed me the tree also ran a private psychiatric clinic like those the tormented American had described, this one plainly of the higher class, in this spacious, old New England-style building.

There are often groups of so-called sponsors affiliated with public seminars at universities and research institutes throughout America. Usually late middle-aged or elderly women who have contributed no significant sum of money, they come as auditors to surround the seminar participants. Sometimes they put things in the form of questions, but they are also ready to express their own opinions. Then at night the sponsors take turns inviting the seminar members to their homes for a party. For those participants whose native tongue is not English, especially for those with my degree of language ability, these parties are a mortification no less severe than the days' seminars proper. Moreover the sponsors, having attended the day's seminar, beleaguer one with questions of which they never seem to tire.

The German-American woman whom people called Agatha was one of these sponsors, and her leading me out of the large adjoining rooms where the party was going on to view from the porch the tree in the dark garden was also related to something I had said that day at the seminar. Among the items in a collection of Coomaraswamy memorabilia on exhibit in conjunction with the seminar was a piece of Indian folk art, *Krishna in a Tree,* rendered in a minute sketch on a bound banana leaf. Naked women were calling to Krishna from the river below. "The bodies of these women are typically Indian in every manifestation," the beatnik poet who was also a specialist in Hindu culture stated at the outset. "This has been captured in such a way that the form of an Indian woman's body, especially the breasts and belly, is distinctive from that of women from any other country. And, in fact, when one travels through India one sees women of precisely this physical type." Comments from other areas of the Far East were solicited to reply to this, whereupon a group of Indian women who were auditing reacted against the American poet, and I articulated my thoughts by turning the discussion to trees.

"Regarding what Allen has said, I obviously agree with his point that the style of representing the human form in Indian folk art contains idiosyncracies that are typically Indian. I would even partially support the view that, conversely, the form of the body has itself been influenced. It is probably fair to assume that this means that the physiology of the Indian people determines the style of their folk art, which is a manner of speaking typical of Allen. However, since I myself am not qualified to speak from experience about the bodies of Indian women, I would like to see the same theories applied to trees.

"This black tree Krishna has climbed is undoubtedly what would be called an Indian bo tree in my country. It has certainly been depicted through the sensibility and techniques of the Indian folk art style. That is, its distinctive features are exaggerated, and yet the substantial feel of its trunk and curve of its branches, or again the way the tips of its leaves are elongated like a tail—these are all grounded in realistic observation. Nevertheless, the tree as a whole still strikes me as distinctively Indian. With this concrete example, I would like to propose a hypothesis paralleling Allen's idea. I feel there are close resemblances between a region's trees and the people who live and die there. Don't the trees of Cranach give every appearance of being the bodies of Upper Franconian people standing there?"

I also mentioned the particular fondness I have for trees and the names that identify them in various lands. "When I travel to a foreign country I take delight in seeing within that landscape the trees particular to that region. Moreover, it is only by learning the region's unique designation and thus for the first time really knowing the trees that I feel I have truly encountered them. As I said before, the Japanese call this tree of Krishna's a bo tree. For us, this is a form of expression completely different from its classification as *Ficus religiosa Linn*. As for its scientific name, I interpret it as an explanation of the tree, which is different from the tree's name. . ."

It was with such a set of prior circumstances that Agatha uprooted me from the party to lead me before the huge tree that occupied the garden in front of the building. Nevertheless, since dusk had already fallen when I had been brought to the house, even when I got off the minibus I had been unable to see the entire tree; as a matter of fact even now I was only peering into the darkness where the tree purportedly stood. In any event, Agatha had tried to teach me the local name for the tree.

"It's called a 'rain tree' because, when there's a shower at night, drops of water fall from its foliage until past noon the next day, as if the tree were raining. Other trees dry off quickly, but this one stores water in its closely packed leaves, no larger than fingertips. Isn't it a clever tree?"

At dusk of that day which had threatened to rain, there had also been a shower. The moisture I smelled coming from the darkness, therefore, was the rain that the dense fingertip leaves were causing to fall anew on the ground. By concentrating my attention in front of me and ignoring the din of the party behind, I could, it seemed, hear the sound made by the fine rain as it fell from the tree over a fairly broad area. As I listened, I began to feel that, in the wall of black before my eyes, there were two different shades of darkness. One darkness was something like a giant baobab tree, bulb-shaped; around its rim was a second vortex of darkness which fell away into bottomless depths, a darkness so profound that even if the rays of the waning moon had penetrated it no oceans or mountain ranges, nothing in our human universe, would have been visible. The immigrants who came to Hawaii from the American mainland a century—perhaps a century and a half—ago to build this house must have seen the same darkness on their first night, I mused. But was this darkness that yawned beyond the garden, ready to suck in body and soul of whoever looked at it, an appropriate setting for a home for the mentally ill?

Thanks to my habit of censoring my statements before I articulate them in a foreign tongue, I stopped short of putting this question to Agatha. It was probably just as well, since Agatha, as someone who lived in the building and was responsible for its residents, would no doubt have taken my words as a direct criticism of herself. Nevertheless, I realized that my perception of the two darknesses—the rim of the darkness shaped like the tree I had created in my imagination, and the darkness that engulfed it—was shared by the German-born American woman who stood just behind me. For I could clearly hear the long sigh, like an arrow of darkness released into the universe, that escaped from the sharp-chinned, oval face supported by her erect spine. We turned away from the tree that emanated the smell of water into the night and retraced our steps over the wide, wooden planks of the porch.

Agatha, like all the American women associated with this conference, was a realist, pragmatist, and activist in every sphere, and she could not restrain herself from infusing even the simple, quiet process of withdrawing from the dark garden with a sense of purpose. She came to a halt before one of the many first-floor rooms that lined the long porch and, bending slightly from the hips, peered in at something on the opposite wall with a truly affectionate gaze. Intrigued, I, too, peeked through the door and saw inside a wall covered with bookshelves, dimly illuminated by a lamp that hung from the high, plastered ceiling. (Soft lights, as opposed to the psychedelic lights I had often seen used in Hawaii, had also been used in the rooms where the party was being held, convincing me that this was, indeed, a facility for the mentally ill.) For someone of my height, it wasn't even necessary to bend as much as Agatha did.

As my eyes adjusted to the dim light after staring into darkness, I could see that an oil painting about six feet square was suspended in a most unusual manner, in midair, about halfway down the wall covered with bookshelves, hiding from sight all the books behind it. The painting almost seemed to have been hung at precisely the angle that would make it visible to someone peering in from the porch, as we were, or from the roots of the tree of darkness in the garden. Come to think of it, hadn't I noticed a steel chair, painted in a somber color, among the prolific board-like roots of the tree?

"A *Girl on Horseback*," Agatha intoned, apparently reading the title on the painting; I realized I was looking at a painting of a young girl seated on a saddle that sank deep into the flanks of a sturdy, chestnut farm horse. The girl was surrounded by gloomy, forbidding walls which could have been those of a prison or concentration camp, and were strangely out of keeping with the sporty atmosphere of horseback riding. It dawned on me that this *Girl on Horseback* was a portrait of Agatha herself as a child. I mentioned this and noticed in the dimness that blood seethed up beneath the thin skin of Agatha's face as she answered, "Yes, this is me when I was still in Germany, a girl on horseback, in the days before the truly frightful, unhappy things began to occur." Something intense and powerful in Agatha's burning blue eyes and in her cheeks, so flushed that heat seemed to radiate from the gold tips of her facial hair, prohibited me from asking what those "frightful, unhappy things" were. I knew only that Agatha had left her motherland, Germany (whether East or West, I was uncertain), and emigrated to Hawaii. Yet if I forced myself to make a connection between the two things, I could understand the meaning of the boycott of tonight's party by the European and American Jews at the seminar. (The Jewish Indian poet from Bombay, who deplored taking a single crab from the beach, viewed the lives and deaths of humans in the political context with the detachment of a Bodhisattva.) But some kind of wisdom which makes it possible for seminars and parties like this to proceed peacefully must come into play just one step before a person attempts to scrutinize and pass judgment on such an issue.

When we returned to the adjoining rooms where the party was taking place we discovered that, during our absence, a new central character had appeared and had taken over the role that was previously Agatha's. In fact, the bearing of this new figure contrasted sharply with Agatha's demeanor as hostess; he seemed to constitute a dominating center of the gathering, like a tyrant reigning over the party. He was a dwarfish man of about fifty, ensconced in a wheelchair, who at first glance might have been taken for a child dressed up like a witch for a play. His long, ivory-colored hair had been trimmed and shaped so that it turned under along the collar of his red satin jacket. His mouth, like a dog's, was the largest feature in his face, while his aquiline nose and double-lidded gray eyes had a proud beauty to them. The impression created when his powerfully vibrating voice issued forth from his large mouth was one of arrogance, yet he directed unflagging attention to the young people who sat at his knees and stood around his wheelchair. It was to the beatnik poet, standing directly in front of his wheelchair as if to block its path, that he addressed a steady stream of words. Yet it was clear that the exchange between the two was a sort of game or theatrical performance, and that the man in the wheelchair, if not the poet, was more conscious of his audience than of his opponent.

"The architect Komarovich—our brilliant architect! What high spirits he's in tonight!" Agatha explained brightly, as if displaying her proudest possession. Her voice had instantly adapted to the gay tone of the party before us; the note of exaltation, underlain by pent-up gloom, that suffused her words when she spoke to me about A *Girl on Horseback* had vanished. She left me behind and walked with long, brisk strides to join the young men beside the wheelchair, deftly skirting the legs and knees of those who were seated on the floor.

I stayed at my post beside the entrance to the room and observed the debate between the architect and the beatnik poet, which was beginning to seem like entertainment provided as the party's main event. In fact, if I were to give a perfectly balanced description of all that transpired that night, I would have to present the debate between poet and architect as a one-act play, consisting purely of dialogue without any action. This is because the hour-long debate, after which our soirée in the mental institution came to an abrupt end, consumed the major portion of the evening. However, as I mentioned at the outset, with my level of comprehension it was impossible to grasp precisely the multiple levels of meaning of this dialogue between the architect, with his strangely high-pitched, florid speech, and the poet, who barely opened his lips when he spoke, and whose words combined Manhattan-style sophistication with an unconventionality befitting an idol of the beatnik movement. The only way I could interpret the play of logic and illogic in their words was to follow one step behind, reconstructing whatever I could from bits and pieces of the conversation. Thus, in my own way, I managed to fend off boredom during the hour-long session.

What I have written here, then, is merely a recasting of a reconstruction I performed that evening, no doubt distorted both by memory and the passage of time. To keep myself from degenerating into tedious summarizing, I have interspersed my own perceptions of the atmosphere surrounding the talks. This is also because of the extremely "colorful" nature (to borrow a word used frequently during the seminar), not only of the debaters' performance itself, but of the responses of the guests at the party—who listened intently, and even seemed to participate without actually intruding—and of the waiters and waitresses who were serving them food and drink.

At the feet of the poet, who remained standing throughout the debate, sat three boys of fifteen or sixteen similar enough to be brothers, in the sense that the face and body of each one conformed to the poet's tastes. These boys, unlike the athletic youths of Hawaii, looked as if they had never been to the beach in their lives, and they sat with pale faces cast down, lost in thought. One was a boy who had followed the poet to the seminar that morning, looking as stunned as a virgin who had just been deflowered, and whom everyone tried not to look at. Surrounding these three boys and covering the floor were other young people who were admirers of the poet, among them a girl attired in a Judo outfit (though she showed no traces of physical exertion) who seemed to be trying to attract the poet's attention by acting like a boy. She was, of course, already quite drunk, and no sooner had she nodded vigorously in agreement with something Allen had said than her head would slump and she would doze off, only to struggle awake again, shaking her head as if she had been listening attentively all along.

Encircling the architect in his wheelchair on three sides, like stalwart supporters of his genius, Agatha and the other middle-aged and elderly ladies sat primly on sofas and chairs and cast stealthy, pitying glances at the drunken young woman of the opposing camp in her Judo suit. It was at the poet that they directed their unvoiced disapproval, and they let the architect act as their advocate, expressing the full burden of their moral sentiment. Needless to say, these matrons, whose silence formed a shield for the architect championing their cause, consumed more alcohol than the young people on the floor. Of the three types of drinks—beer, gin and tonic, and whiskey—being served by the bartenders, waiters, and waitresses (apparently students working part-time) in attendance at this midnight party, it was not beer but the more potent stuff that filled the glasses of the matrons, who looked for all the world like spinsters or widows in uniform as they sat in matching girlish frocks with lacy collars. With deft gestures, calculated to escape the notice of the other guests, they drained their glasses and then signaled immediately for refills. Agatha was no exception. In fact, the only people drinking beer at the party were the seminar participants, who formed the outermost flank of those surrounding the debate.

Although I assumed the young people catering at the party were students hired for the occasion, they were a mysterious bunch who seemed to have developed a unique style in their dress and deportment by training together as a group. The men all wore old-fashioned vests and silk shirts with puffy sleeves; the girls wore the same frocks as those of the matrons, covered with frilly aprons. All were pale, terribly thin, and showed signs of what, to a superficial observer like myself, appeared to be autism. For example, they weaved in and out of the partygoers without ever looking anyone in the eye, even when they handed you a canapé or a drink. And despite their graceful bearing, or perhaps even because of the excessive agility of their movements, I detected the sound of violent breathing, as if from sheer exhaustion, whenever one of them brushed past me. A strangely antique, musty body odor, which in no way contradicted their cleanliness, clung to each one. This seemed to mystify those seminar participants whose interest had not been aroused by the debate, and they whispered about it among themselves.

It was against such a backdrop that the debate between architect and poet took place . . . that is to say, the verbal offensive of the architect and the defensive maneuvers of the poet, who managed to deflect the attack without ever appearing underhanded. The following is a summary of what I was able to pick up of the attacker's argument:

"You are a passionate lover of boys and young men and this is a beautiful thing, in and of itself. It is a standpoint we hold in common. Yet it is clear that even here, at our very point of departure, there are insurmountable differences between us. Your passion develops in a direction that debases and corrupts the young. Mine uplifts and enlightens them. Perhaps you will say that you are introducing young people to dark, mystical knowledge and depths of feeling. Just now you insisted that carnal love was as central to human experience as spiritual love, since both were dark and mystical in their essence." (It was by taking the terse, acerbic rejoinders uttered jestingly by the poet and turning them upside down, in this manner, within the context of his own flowery and effusive speech that the architect was able to furnish his alcoholic supporters with a taste of victory. The poet, for his part, actually seemed to be enjoying his successive routs on the surface level of the debate, and made no effort to probe the deep-seated weaknesses of his opponent. Where he could easily have exposed the architect's argument for its imprecision or its fatuousness, he simply shrugged his shoulders and chortled like a Santa Claus.) "But carnal love and spiritual love must be like a spiral stairway, constantly ascending toward their bright, sacred essence. Especially that phiyscal and spiritual love which sees itself as educating the young. . ."

The architect went on to deliver a lecture—he had by now assumed the air of someone speaking from a podium—about the special features of this facility of the mentally ill as he, the designer of the building, had envisioned them, and about how the management of the facility was structured around his vision. "Those who seek refuge in this old house after fleeing the American mainland are the possessors of keen, delicate, ailing spirits. I felt I should provide each one with a place of retreat tailored to his or her own body. If there could be one hill, one valley, for every patient in this facility, what a wonderful thing that would be! Like the castles and estates that insane monarchs in Europe, suffering their various fates, made into hermitages in those wonderful eras of the past! The naked, wounded soul in America today is not even guaranteed a private dwelling place. Accordingly, I've devoted my energies to en-suring that, in this building at least, every person who seeks shelter will have a 'position' of his or her own. For my own 'position' I chose the lowest place in the building: my workshop is in the basement garage. And now, I'd like to ask you to take your cues from me, pretend you're going down to my workshop, right below the floor you're standing on, and from my 'position' try to imagine the 'positions' of the people who live in every partition of every room in this house. My structure incor-porates each one of these 'positions' in such a way as to give a sense of constant movement upward. This should strike you immediately. I planned and carried out the renovations of the interior with the aim of providing any individual (particularly a young individual) inside the assemblage of 'positions' with an awareness of existing on a stairway where the self was being elevated on a spiral course into the heavens. Those residents of the facility who are not young people have been assigned to 'positions' that make them a foundation for the constant movement upward of the young. They are primarily ladies in the later years of life who watch with admiring hearts as the children—our youth—ascend toward the sacred heights." (At this point the poet raised several objections. Although he found the conception inspiring, he wondered whether those in the lower "positions" would be happy. Fur-thermore, as one can see by looking at a pyramid, the number of people who can occupy "positions" at the top is extremely limited. Wouldn't this create antagonism toward the idea in society at large, so that the young people who participated might be subjected to abuse, rather than benefiting from their participation? This could even happen in the closed society of the institution itself. In response, the architect drew himself up with a mighty effort and assumed a godlike posture.) "You are a passionate lover of boys and young men. Yet you are afraid to ask society to sanction the path that leads them to the heights. This is why your love brings them to decadence and degradation. To hide in dark, low places where you pollute and befoul each other—it is this, and this alone, that arouses your passion for the young! The passion of a necrophiliac is no different! But between us there is a fundamental difference. What I have accomplished in this building I wish to propagate outside our 'closed society,' across the American mainland, throughout the world! I am launching an architectural movement to place young people everywhere in 'positions' on stairways of ascent. We must begin with schools, libraries, and theaters for children. The reason I have compressed and reduced my own body, once that of a normal adult, into the child's body you see in this wheelchair is in order to ready myself by seeing and sensing the world from a child's height, from a child's 'position,' from the eyes of a child's body and soul. My goal is to create a model of the entire world on the scale of the child's body and soul, and I am trying to live in the world as a physical and spiritual child, speculating day and night about the types of space and structure most suitable to architecture for children. My compressed and shrunken body itself will be a model for architects of the future!"

As the architect made his proclamation I scrutinized his body more closely: it did indeed seem possible that he had transformed himself into a dwarf by sitting in the wheelchair and compressing the area between his chest and his hips into two or three accordian-like pleats. The wheelchair was merely a device he needed to manipulate his external appearance. Now, raising his arms in their red satin sleeves over his head with a flourish, he became a rose-colored king with the mouth of a small, adorable dog, and the matrons behind him (made even more genteel by drink) let out a discreet burst of applause. Even his debating opponent, the beatnik poet with the face of a bearded Bodhidharma, shouted, "This man is fantastic! He's out of his mind!" Eyes twinkling behind thick glasses, he urged on his disciples, who joined without hesitation in the applause.

It was probably inevitable at this point that the guests at the party decided to tour the inside of the building to see how the architect's master plan had been implemented. With the wheelchair that carried the architect as our masthead, we filed out to inspect the part of the building that was the heart of the architect's vision: the rooms designed to impart a sense of upward motion. Since, aside from the area where the party was being held, the first floor consisted only of conference rooms and a library, we flocked to the stairway and began climbing toward the second floor. The young people who just minutes earlier had flaunted their silent antagonism toward the architect now bore his wheelchair aloft, supporting it on three sides. A mood of exaltation united us as we threaded our way through the vast structure, peering into one empty room after another and discovering, every time we turned a corner, a short flight of stairs. Empty rooms? More accurately, I would describe each room as an assemblage of boxes with bases at differing levels of height. Each of the large rooms of the original structure had been divided into four or five partitions of parallelepiped shape, arranged so that the unit as a whole gave one a sense of moving from a lower to a higher level. This was because, as one went from one of the large rooms to another, one repeatedly had the impression, created through an illusory use of color, of ascending beyond the level of the highest box in the room before (which would have been impossible in actuality). On the stairways, moreover, this illusion of ascent was reinforced by tangible reality, so that while climbing them I had the sense of being suspended in a lofty tower. As we went higher, I even began to wonder if we had been transformed into a herd of rats, racing up the stairs of this tower in the grip of some kind of group insanity. There were, in fact, some members of our band who found the emotion that united us disagreeable and dropped out of the procession.

As those of us who continued in the file reached the top floor of the building (the design created the illusion there was still one more room above) I could sense, outside the darkened windows of the square rooms of ever decreasing size, the dense leaves of the "clever rain tree" whose existence I had merely been able to assent to earlier in the evening. Or perhaps I should say that the rooms themselves seemed like birdhouses enveloped in a vast growth of leaves. We circled around the empty cubicles until we discovered that, in just one of the four partitions into which the corner room of the top floor had been divided, there was someone living.

As I mentioned before, there were a number of people in our group who had gradually become disenchanted with the atmosphere of the procession; still others were by nature apprehensive about the fragility of the wooden corridors and staircases, or had become bored with the unusual but repetitive formula according to which all the rooms had been renovated. Therefore, those who were left to approach the innermost chamber included only Agatha, myself, the Jewish Indian poet from Bombay, the beatnik poet, and the architect in his wheelchair, carried by two young men. I realize now that it was probably better that way. There, in that least accessible of all the rooms—a cubicle that appeared to jut right out from the wall of the house—we saw a woman about forty years old, crouching in a metal washtub which occupied almost the entire area of the floor. To judge from her facial expression alone, she might have been a close relative of those self-contained matrons who had gathered around the architect's wheelchair earlier in the evening, savoring his eloquence with their sips of alcohol. But from the neck down this woman, crouching there completely naked and with one knee drawn up, had daubed herself with a blackish red liquid. Now, turning the small, black holes of her eyes toward us, she smeared a single line of the dark, sticky substance across her narrow forehead.

The beatnik poet was silent, and even seemed impressed by the scene, while the always candid Jewish Indian poet made it known that he found the stench unbearable. This remark shattered the architect's mood of exaltation, and he explained glumly that the room the woman was now in was not her "position"; she had simply been moved here temporarily because of that night's party, and the change in surroundings had disoriented her. Agatha gave vent to the antagonism aroused by the poet's complaint even more bluntly. She told him that it was necessary for the woman to put her stale blood to some use, that no one could reproach her for this, and that she was perfectly capable of doing the same thing with fresh, living blood, but only at very special moments in her life.

Then, as if triggered by Agatha's words, a number of things occurred simultaneously. First the Indian poet, and a few seconds later I myself, came to a similar realization. In that instant of recognition, when we were also communicating to each other with our eyes that the beatnik poet had surely known everything all along . . . at that very moment when we understood that the midnight party had been organized entirely by patients in this mental institution (with the exception of the woman in front of us smeared with blood from her sexual organs) and that these patients were none other than the waiters and waitresses who had served us cocktails and canapés, not to mention the placid ladies sipping their liquor . . . an Iranian journalist who had been a member of the seminar came dashing up the stairs. He informed us that all of the members had decided to withdraw from the premises immediately.

My next clear memory is of the architect, so boyish-looking when he sat in his wheelchair, pulling himself to his feet in a single effort that made his body appear to double in size; I watched from behind as he hurried down the stairs, his surprisingly large body bent forward and supported by Agatha's shoulder. The beatnik poet, mindful not to disturb the woman covered with blood, waited until he had reached the floor below before bursting into peals of merry laughter. The Iranian then told all of us his story. It seemed that when everyone else had started climbing to the upper stories, he and an English teacher from the Republic of Korea, who had already sensed something strange in the air, had descended to the architect's workshop in the basement. There they discovered a scene straight out of an American gangster film: two enormous men in uniform were bound and lying on the floor. In the neighboring compartment, a bathroom, they found three nurses who were also bound. They worked out an agreement with the nurses and night watchmen whereby the seminar participants would return to their dormitories immediately by minibus, on the condition that they would not be implicated in any of the events of the evening. In addition, they requested that any reprisals carried out against the patients who had staged the rebellion would in no way involve the seminar participants. Since the facility was itself subsidized by the high fees paid by the families of the patients, however, it was unlikely that any significant punishment would be meted out to them. Finally, the Iranian warned us that if word that he and the Korean representative were involved in the scandal leaked out to the press, they might find themselves in trouble once they returned home. (This was several years before the Khomeini revolution.)

At that point, without further ado, we began to head toward the front garden, where the engine of the minibus was already humming. Far from bidding farewell to the inebriated women, moving unsteadily down the stairways and corridors in search of their "position," or to the young people, who still walked with their eyes cast down, we simply elbowed our way through them and boarded the bus. I saw no sign of the night watchmen who were supposedly presiding over our departure, and merely glimpsed the heads and shoulders of two nurses who towered over the throng of bent figures. But in my last moments in the building I heard, from the direction of the "clever rain tree" which had never materialized before my eyes out of the darkness, a woman cry out two or three times with sobs so loud it seemed her body was being ripped apart by grief.

Our bus, preceded and followed by young guests escaping on their motorcycles, sped over the steep, winding mountain road as if in desperate flight. But in the darkness inside the bus, reverberations of that sobbing voice seemed to echo all around us, and even the face of the beatnik poet (who had been laughing uproariously until then) took on an expression of pensive melancholy little different from the gloomy expressions of the Iranian and Korean representatives, who were brooding over the possible repercussions of the scandal in their native dictatorships. Yet for all that, I now find it strange that I never once looked back through the windows of the bus to the giant rain tree, which should have loomed up in its black entirety, no matter how dark the night, if I had only gazed into that part of the sky where the day was dawning. Strange, because I frequently picture to myself Agatha, who chose her "position" by setting her chair at the place where tree and earth came together, in among the board-roots that jutted out like great pleats in the ground; Agatha, who stared at the painting of A *Girl on Horseback* in the library across the porch, and looked up at the building designed to spiral endlessly toward heaven like an enormous twin of the tree . . . Agatha, whom I can still see in my mind's eye, although what kind of tree it was that she called her "clever rain tree" I shall never know.

THE SILENT TRADERS

Tsushima Yūko

Translated by Geraldine Harcourt

Tsushima Yūko's writing has grown out of a life of ordinary events, an extraordinary heritage, and an innovative independence. As Tsushima Satoko (her real name), she was born in Tokyo in 1947; she gained a degree in English literature in 1969, married in 1970, gave birth to a daughter and son, and had what she describes as "an ordinary divorce" in 1976. As the daughter of Tsushima Shūji (Dazai Osamu) and his wife Michiko, she grew up with the extraordinary literary legacy of the father she does not remember as she was only a year old when he committed suicide in 1948. She was also greatly influenced by her closeness in childhood to her mentally retarded elder brother, who died in 1960.

From early beginnings as a writer while still at college—her first published story appeared in Mita bungaku *in 1969—she gained increasing success by her late twenties and now supports her family by writing full-time (a fact worth noting in a society that is hard on single parents).*

Drawing on all these elements, a typical Tsushima work will take freshly observed domestic details—dead insects accumulated in a light fixture, say, or a bug being flushed down the kitchen sink—and give them a powerful significance as it develops such themes as blood relations, sexuality and the tie between the sexes that the birth of a child represents, death and the ties between the dead and the living.

These implications are often threaded through a deceptively loose structure reminiscent of the shishōsetsu *but which in fact sets up a resonance or impact all the more powerful because it is unforeseen. The story translated* here, "Danmari ichi" (The Silent Traders, 1982), is a striking example of this technique.

The "mountain men" whose silent trade provides the title were isolated, nomadic remnants of an earlier people driven back by agricultural settlement, and among the village dwellers any recognition of their existence was tabooed. The analogy adds a further dimension to the first-person story, while the symbolism of the nomads' invisibility to the settlement has been explored more fully in the novel Yama o hashiru onna (Woman Running in the Mountains, 1980).

Tsushima's fiction makes many such allusions to tradition and folklore (familiar to Japanese readers) that parallel her contemporary plots; for example, the collection Ōma monogatari (Ghost Stories, 1984) and a novel in progress which will interrelate Heian and modern characters.

Images such as light playing on leaves relieve the starkness of city settings and point up a clear contrast with the literature of urban alienation: this is a world of human connectedness, even if the connections are often tenuous (as in the many telephone conversations that figure in Tsushima's writing).

Water is another recurring motif. The novel Chōji (Child of Fortune, 1978; tr. 1983) has multilayered imagery of water, ice, and snow as the possibly pregnant heroine contemplates having the baby "to escape the molten lava of her own sexuality," and in the 1983 novel Hi no kawa no hotori de (On the Banks of the River of Fire), the author's most complex work to date, she matches a riverside city locale with the momentum of a father-daughter incest and an illicit love affair.

This is not to suggest, though, that the sex in Tsushima's books is decorously draped in metaphor, for at the same time she is attempting to describe sex from a woman's viewpoint in precise language.

Tsushima does not identify herself as a radical feminist, because she is "not part of the feminist movement," but her stereotype-breaking heroines do have a strong appeal for women readers. The 1980 serialization of Yama o hashiru onna in the Mainichi shimbun added considerable popularity to the critical recognition that had brought her the Tamura Toshiko Prize (1976), Izumi Kyōka Prize (1977), Women's Literature Prize (1978), and Noma Prize for New Writers (1979). "The Silent Traders" was awarded the Kawabata Yasunari Prize in 1983.

Women writers in Japan have traditionally been considered to form a "school" of their own, joryū *bungaku (which evolved in an entirely different way from the more recent feminist focus in Western criticism). Thus when Tsushima Yūko is acclaimed as a "representative woman writer" the boundaries of this praise are narrowly defined. Lately, however, Japanese critics have begun to cite her as a "representative writer" of the postwar or younger generation. In a literary establishment that sees* joryū *sakka or women writers as outsiders, this is visibility indeed.*

*　　　*　　　*

There was a cat in the wood. Not such an odd thing, really: wildcats, pumas, and lions all come from the same family and even a tabby shouldn't be out of place. But the sight was unsettling. What was the creature doing there? When I say "wood," I'm talking about Rikugien, an Edo-period landscape garden in my neighborhood. Perhaps "wood" isn't quite the right word, but the old park's trees—relics of the past amid the city's modern buildings—are so overgrown that the pathways skirting its walls are dark and forbidding even by day. It does give the impression of a wood; there's no other word for it. And the cat, I should explain, didn't look wild. It was just a kitten, two or three months old, white with black patches. It didn't look at all ferocious—in fact it was a dear little thing. There was nothing to fear. And yet I was taken aback, and I tensed as the kitten bristled and glared in my direction.

The kitten was hiding in a thicket beside the pond, where my ten-year-old daughter was the first to spot it. By the time I'd made out the elusive shape and exclaimed "Oh, you're right!" she was off calling at the top of her voice: "There's another! And here's one over here!" My other child, a boy of five, was still hunting for the first kitten, and as his sister went on making one discovery after another he stamped his feet and wailed "Where? Where is it?" His sister beckoned him to bend down and showed him triumphantly where to find the first cat. Several passersby, hearing my daughter's shouts, had also been drawn into the search. There were many strollers in the park that Sunday evening. The cats were everywhere, each concealed in its own clump of bushes. Their eyes followed people's feet on the graveled walk, and at the slightest move toward a hiding place the cat would scamper away. Looking down from an adult's height it was hard enough to detect them at all, let alone keep count, and this gave the impression of great numbers.

I could hear my younger child crying. He had disappeared while my back was turned. As I looked wildly around, my daughter pointed him out with a chuckle: "See where he's got to!" There he was, huddled tearfully in the spot where the first kitten had been. He'd burst in eagerly, but succeeded only in driving away the kitten and trapping himself in the thicket.

"What do you think you're doing? It'll never let *you* catch it." Squatting down, my daughter was calling through the bushes. "Come on out, silly!"

His sister's tone of amusement was no help to the boy at all. He was terrified in his cobwebbed cage of low-hanging branches where no light penetrated.

"That's no use. You go in and fetch him out." I gave her shoulder a push.

"He got himself in," she grumbled, "so why can't he get out?" All the same, she set about searching for an opening. Crouching, I watched the boy through the thick foliage and waited for her to reach him.

"How'd he ever get in there? He's really stuck," she muttered as she circled the bushes uncertainly, but a moment later she'd broken through to him, forcing a way with both hands.

When they rejoined me, they had dead leaves and twigs snagged all over them.

After an attempt of her own to pick one up, my daughter understood that life in the park had made these tiny kittens quicker than ordinary strays and too wary to let anyone pet them. Explaining this to her brother, she looked to me for agreement. "They were born here, weren't they? They belong here, don't they? Then I wonder if their mother's here too?"

The children scanned the surrounding trees once again.

"She may be," I said, "but she'd stay out of sight, wouldn't she? Only the kittens wander about in the open. Their mother's got more sense. I'll bet she's up that tree or some place like that where nobody can get at her. She's probably watching us right now."

I cast an eye at the treetops as I spoke—and the thought of the unseen mother cat gave me an uncomfortable feeling. Whether these were alley cats that had moved into the park or discarded pets that had survived and bred, they could go on multiplying in the wood—which at night was empty of people—and be perfectly at home.

It is exactly twenty-five years since my mother came to live near Rikugien with her three children, of which I was the youngest at ten. She told us the park's history, and not long after our arrival we went inside to see the garden. In spite of its being on our doorstep we quickly lost interest, however, since the grounds were surrounded by a six-foot brick wall with a single gate on the far side from our house. A Japanese garden was not much fun for children anyway, and we never went again as a family. I was reminded that we lived near a park, though, because of the many birds—the blue magpies, Eastern turtledoves, and tits— that I would see on the rooftops and in trees. And in summer I'd hear the singing of evening cicadas. To a city child like me, evening cicadas and blue magpies were a novelty.

I visited Rikugien with several classmates when we were about to leave elementary school, and someone hit on the idea of making a kind of time capsule. We'd leave it buried for ten years—or was it twenty? I've also forgotten what we wrote on the piece of paper that we stuffed into a small bottle and buried at the foot of a pine on the highest ground in the garden. I expect it's still there as I haven't heard of it since, and now whenever I'm in Rikugien I keep an eye out for the landmark, but I'm only guessing. We were confident of knowing exactly where to look in years to come, and if I can remember that so clearly it's puzzling that I can't recognize the tree. I'm not about to dig any holes to check, however—not with my own children watching. The friends who left this sentimental reminder were about to part, bound for different schools. Since then, of course, we've ceased to think of one another, and I'm not so sure now that the bottle episode ever happened.

The following February my brother (who was close to my own age) died quite suddenly of pneumonia. Then in April my sister went to college and, not wanting to be left out, I pursued her new interests myself: I listened to jazz, went to movies, and was friendly toward college and high school students of the opposite sex. An older girl introduced me to a boy from senior high and we made up a foursome for an outing to the park—the only time I got all dressed up for Rikugien. I was no beauty, though, nor the popular type, and while the others were having fun I stayed stiff and awkward, and was bored. I would have liked to be as genuinely impressed as they were, viewing the landscape garden for the first time, but I couldn't work up an interest after seeing the trees over the brick wall every day. By that time we'd been in the district for three years, and the name "Rikugien" brought to mind not the tidy, sunlit lawns seen by visitors, but the dark tangles along the walls.

My desire for friends of the opposite sex was short-lived. Boys couldn't provide what I wanted, and what boys wanted had nothing to do with me.

While I was in high school, one day our ancient spitz died. The house remained without a dog for a while, until Mother was finally prompted to replace him when my sister's marriage, soon after her graduation, left just the two of us in an unprotected home. She found someone who let her have a terrier puppy. She bought a brush and comb and began rearing the pup with the best of care, explaining that it came from a clever hunting breed. As it grew, however, it failed to display the expected intelligence and still behaved like a puppy after six months; and besides, it was timid. What it did have was energy as, yapping shrilly, it frisked about the house all day long. It may have been useless but it was a funny little fellow. Its presence made all the difference to me in my intense boredom at home. After my brother's death, my mother (a widow since I was a baby) passed her days as if at a wake. We saw each other only at mealtimes, and then we seldom spoke. In high school a fondness for the movies was about the worst I could have been accused of, but Mother had no patience with such frivolity and would snap angrily at me from time to time. "I'm leaving home when I turn eighteen," I'd retort. I meant it, too.

It was at that time that we had the very sociable dog. I suppose I'd spoiled it as a puppy, for now it was always wanting to be let in, and when I slid open the glass door it would bounce like a rubber ball right into my arms and lick my face and hands ecstatically.

Mother, however, was dissatisfied. She'd had enough of the barking; it got on her nerves. Then came a day when the dog went missing. I thought it must have got out of the yard. Two or three days passed and it didn't return—it hadn't the wit to find the way home once it strayed. I wondered if I should contact the pound. Concern finally drove me to break our usual silence and ask Mother: "About the dog. . ." "Oh, the dog?" she replied. "I threw it over the wall of Rikugien the other day."

I was shocked—I'd never heard of disposing of a dog like that. I wasn't able to protest, though. I didn't rush out to comb the park, either. She could have had it destroyed, yet instead she'd taken it to the foot of the brick wall, lifted it in her arms, and heaved it over. It wasn't large, only about a foot long, and thus not too much of a handful even for Mother.

Finding itself tossed into the wood, the dog wouldn't have crept quietly into hiding. It must have raced through the area barking furiously, only to be caught at once by the caretaker. Would the next stop be the pound? But there seemed to me just a chance that it hadn't turned out that way. I could imagine the wood by daylight, more or less: there'd be a lot of birds and insects, and little else. The pond would be inhabited by a few carp, turtles, and catfish. But what transformations took place at night? As I didn't dare stay beyond closing time to see for myself, I wondered if anyone could tell of a night spent in the park till the gates opened in the morning. There might be goings-on unimaginable by day. Mightn't a dog entering that world live on, not as a tiny terrier, but as something else?

I had to be thankful that the dog's fate left that much to the imagination.

From then on I turned my back on Rikugien more firmly than ever. I was afraid of the deep wood, so out of keeping with the city: it was the domain of the dog abandoned by my mother.

In due course I left home, a little later than I'd promised. After a good many more years I moved back to Mother's neighborhood—back to the vicinity of the park—with a little daughter and a baby. Like my own mother, I was one who couldn't give my children the experience of a father. That remained the one thing I regretted.

Living in a cramped apartment, I now appreciated the Rikugien wood for its greenery and open spaces. I began to take the children there occasionally. Several times, too, we released pet turtles or goldfish in the pond. Many nearby families who'd run out of room for aquarium creatures in their overcrowded apartments would slip them into the pond to spend the rest of their lives at liberty.

Rocks rose from the water here and there, and each was studded with turtles sunning themselves. They couldn't have bred naturally in such numbers. They must have been the tiny turtles sold at fairground stalls and pet shops, grown up without a care in the world. More of them lined the water's edge at one's feet. No doubt there were other animals on the increase—goldfish, loaches, and the like. Multistoried apartment buildings were going up around the wood in quick succession, and more living things were brought down from their rooms each year. Cats were one animal I'd overlooked, though. If tipping out turtles was common practice, there was no reason why cats shouldn't be dumped here, and dogs too. No type of pet could be ruled out. But to become established in any numbers they'd have to escape the caretaker's notice and hold their own against the wood's other hardy inhabitants. Thus there'd be a limit to survivors: cats and reptiles, I'd say.

Once I knew about the cat population, I remembered the dog my mother had thrown away, and I also remembered my old fear of the wood. I couldn't help wondering how the cats got along from day to day.

Perhaps they relied on food left behind by visitors—but all of the park's trash baskets were fitted with mesh covers to keep out the crows, whose numbers were also growing. For all their nimbleness, even cats would have trouble picking out the scraps. Lizards and mice were edible enough. But on the other side of the wall lay the city and its garbage. After dark, the cats would go out foraging on the streets.

Then, too, there was the row of apartment towers along one side of the wood, facing the main road. All had balconies that overlooked the park. The climb would be quick work for a cat, and if its favorite food were left outside a door it would soon come back regularly. Something told me there must be people who put out food: there'd be elderly tenants and women living alone. Even children. Children captivated by a secret friendship with a cat.

I don't find anything odd about such a relationship—perhaps because it occurs so often in fairy stories. But to make it worth their while the apartment children would have to receive something from the cat; otherwise they wouldn't keep it up. There are tales of mountain men and villagers who traded a year's haul of linden bark for a gallon and a half of rice in hard cakes. No villager could deal openly with the lone mountain men; so great was their fear of each other, in fact, that they avoided coming face to face. Yet when a bargain was struck, it could not have been done more skillfully. The trading was over in a flash, before either man had time to catch sight of the other or hear his voice. I think everyone wishes privately that bargains could be made like that. Though there would always be the fear of attack, or discovery by one's own side.

Supposing it were my own children: what could they be getting in return? They'd have no use for a year's stock of linden bark. Toys, then, or cakes. I'm sure they want all sorts of things, but not a means of support like linden bark. What, then? Something not readily available to them; something the cat has in abundance and to spare.

The children leave food on the balcony. And in return the cat provides them with a father. How's that for a bargain? Once a year, male cats procreate; in other words, they become fathers. They become fathers ad nauseam. But these fathers don't care how many children they have—they don't even notice that they are fathers. Yet the existence of offspring makes them so. Fathers who don't know their own children. Among humans, it seems there's an understanding that a man only becomes a father when he recognizes the child as his own; but that's a very narrow view. Why do we allow the male to divide children arbitrarily into two kinds, recognized and unrecognized? Wouldn't it be enough for the child to choose a father when necessary from among suitable males? If the children decide that the tom that climbs up to their balcony is their father, it shouldn't cause him any inconvenience. A father looks in on two of his children from the balcony every night. The two human children faithfully leave out food to make it so. He comes late, when they are fast asleep, and they never see him or hear his cries. It's enough that they know in the morning that he's been. In their dreams, the children are hugged to their cat-father's breast.

We'd seen the children's human father six months earlier, and together we'd gone to a transport museum they wanted to visit. This came about only after many appeals from me. If the man who was their father was alive and well on this earth, I wanted the children to know what he looked like. To me, the man was unforgettable: I was once preoccupied with him, obsessed with the desire to be where he was; nothing had changed when I tried having a child, and I'd had the second with him cursing me. To the children, however, especially the younger one, he was a mere shadow in a photograph that never moved or spoke. As the younger child turned three, then four, I couldn't help being aware of that fact. This was the same state of affairs that I'd known myself, for my own father had died. If he were dead it couldn't be helped. But as long as he was alive I wanted them to have a memory of their father as a living, breathing person whose eyes moved, whose mouth moved and spoke.

On the day, he was an hour late for our appointment. The long wait in a coffee shop had made the children tired and cross, but when they saw the man a shy silence came over them. "Thanks for coming," I said with a smile. I couldn't think what to say next. He asked "Where to?" and stood to leave at once. He walked alone, while the children and I looked as though it was all the same to us whether he was there or not. On the train I still hadn't come up with anything to say. The children kept their distance from the man and stared nonchalantly out of the window. We got off the train like that, and again he walked ahead.

The transport museum had an actual bullet train car, steam locomotives, airplanes, and giant panoramic layouts. I remembered enjoying a class trip there while at school myself. My children, too, dashed excitedly around the exhibits without a moment's pause for breath. It was "Next I want to have a go on that train," "Now I want to work that model." They must have had a good two hours of fun. In the meantime we lost sight of the man. Wherever he'd been, he showed up again when we'd finished our tour and arrived back at the entrance. "What'll we do?" he asked, and I suggested giving the children a drink and sitting down somewhere. He nodded and went ahead to look for a place near the museum. The children were clinging to me as before. He entered a coffee shop that had a cake counter and I followed with them. We sat down, the three of us facing the man. Neither child showed the slightest inclination to sit beside him. They had orange drinks.

I was becoming desperate for something to say. And weren't there one or two things he'd like to ask me? Such as how the children had been lately. But to bring that up, unasked, might imply that I wanted him to watch with me as they grew. I'd only been able to ask for this meeting because I'd finally stopped feeling that way. Now it seemed we couldn't even exchange such polite remarks as "They've grown" or "I'm glad they're well" without arousing needless suspicions. It wasn't supposed to be like this, I thought in confusion, unable to say a word about the children. He was indeed their father, but not a father who watched over them. As far as he was concerned the only children he had were the two borne by his wife. Agreeing to see mine was simply a favor on his part, for which I could only be grateful.

If we couldn't discuss the children, there was literally nothing left to say. We didn't have the kind of memories we could reminisce over; I wished I could forget the things we'd done as if it had all been a dream, for it was the pain that we remembered. Inquiring after his family would be no better. His work seemed the safest subject, yet if I didn't want to stay in touch I had to think twice about this, too.

The man and I listened absently as the children entertained themselves.

On the way out the man bought a cake which he handed to the older child, and then he was gone. The children appeared relieved, and with the cake to look forward to they were eager to get home. Neither had held the man's hand or spoken to him. I wanted to tell them that there was still time to run after him and touch some part of his body, but of course they wouldn't have done it.

I don't know when there will be another opportunity for the children to see the man. They may never meet him again, or they may have a chance two or three years from now. I do know that the man and I will probably never be completely indifferent to each other. He's still on my mind in some obscure way. Yet there's no point in confirming this feeling in words. Silence is essential. As long as we maintain silence, and thus avoid trespassing, we leave open the possibility of resuming negotiations at any time.

I believe the system of bartering used by the mountain men and the villagers was called "silent trade." I am coming to understand that there was nothing extraordinary in striking such a silent bargain for survival. People trying to survive—myself, my mother, and my children, for example—can take some comfort in living beside a wood. We tip various things in there and tell ourselves that we haven't thrown them away, we've set them free in another world, and then we picture the unknown woodland to ourselves and shudder with fear or sigh fondly. Meanwhile the creatures multiplying there gaze stealthily at the human world outside; at least I've yet to hear of anything attacking from the wood.

Some sort of silent trade is taking place between the two sides. Perhaps my children really have begun dealings with a cat who lives in the wood.

THE IMMORTAL

Nakagami Kenji

Translated by Mark Harbison

*It is appropriate that Nakagami Kenji should appear at the end of this an-
thology, for he is one of the new generation of writers, critics, and academics
who are preparing to succeed to the positions of Ōe Kenzaburō, Yoshimo-
to Takaaki, and Yamaguchi Masao in the vanguard of Japanese post-
modernism.*

*Much of Nakagami's reputation rests on early novels, deeply rooted in
his own experience, about growing up as a* burakumin. *The* burakumin
phenomenon is extremely complex: Nakagami identifies buraku *with the
ghettos of European and American cities, but discrimination against* burakumin, *or ghetto people, has no real ethnic or religious basis. Rather,
it is rooted in historical developments that vary from one locality to another,
and often, as Nakagami suggests, it arises simply from a shared perception
of "difference."*

*Misaki (The Cape), which received the Akutagawa Prize in 1976, and
Karekinada (The Kareki Sea, 1977) are brutal, naturalistic depictions of
the* buraku *in Shingū, a coastal city on the Kishū Peninsula in the Kumano
region south of Nara. Akio, the main character in these novels and in the
recent* Chi no hate shijō no toki *(End of the Earth, Supreme Time, 1983),
is not Nakagami, and Akio's father, his mother, his step-father, sisters,
brothers, half-sisters, and half-brothers are not Nakagami's. But the author
himself acknowledges that these novels are essentially I-novels, and his depiction of "the Alley" (roji), as the Shingū* buraku *is called in these novels,
could only have sprung from an intense personal experience.*

412

Nakagami was born in the Alley in August 1946. His mother, Kinoshita Chisato, registered him under her own name as an illegitimate child, her third by a man known as Suzuki. Kinoshita became Nakaue when Chisato married a local road gang boss, who adopted Kenji, but not his two younger sisters. After graduating from high school, an unusual feat in the Alley, Kenji left for Tokyo and began to call himself Nakagami. The complexity of kinship and familial relationships in the Alley, an important theme of Nakagami's work, is such that the hardback edition of Karekinada contains an insert with a diagram of Akio's family tree.

If the Alley is one wellspring of Nakagami's obsession, the "dark land" of Kumano is the other. Since the age of the Kojiki, Kumano has always been an "other world." In earlier periods, it was shunned as a place of unknown evils, unbound by the laws of the court and the state Buddhism of Nara. The hijiri and bikuni of Kumano, who traced their lineage to the semi-mythical wizard En no Gyōja, were revered as holy men and nuns, but they were also feared and shunned as non-people (saimin), wanderers in a sedentary society. Nakagami is fascinated with this tradition. The myths and legends of Kumano are a constant undercurrent in his work, and sometimes, as in "The Immortal," they are a dominant presence.

What makes Nakagami more than a burakumin version of the ethnic writer is his extraordinary talent and his voracious desire for knowledge. Though he never fails to mention his lack of a university degree, and often poses as an intellectual nihilist, his range of reference is awesome: Bakhtin, Derrida, Hasumi Shigehiko, Japanese literature, Irish folk tales, the legends of Bali. His prolific talent, and his identification with an outspokenly intellectual group of writers and critics, have propelled him into a unique position in the Japanese advance guard.

But Nakagami also has paid a price for his sophistication. His recent work has been condemned by critics who once supported him: "Too much Bakhtin and not enough of the angry, young burakumin." More important, it has forced him to question his own inspiration. He has renounced Misaki and Karekinada as "the work of a child," and Chi no hate shijō no toki is a deliberate deconstruction of the earlier Akio novels. Shortly after winning the Akutagawa Prize, Nakagami began to say that he has fallen into a dilemma, that he is trapped on a pendulum that swings between two extremes: in thrall to the Japanese monogatari, at the same time he is obsessed with demolishing *"the law, the system, the* monogatari *of Japanese literature."*

"The Immortal" is the first story in Nakagami's recent Kumano-shū *(A Kumano Collection, 1984), which embodies this dilemma. The author himself calls it a linked short-story collection, but, at least superficially, the selection and arrangement of the stories seem chaotic: traditional ghost stories with pre-texts in earlier literature interwoven through a collection of loosely linked I-novels that directly address the self-deconstruction of "I's" literary inspiration. The rich, evocative tone of "The Immortal" is posed against language that bares Nakagami's own soul.*

In "The Immortal," the monogatari *of Japanese literature certainly seems to dominate. The presence of Izumi Kyōka's "Kōya hijiri" (The Holy Man of Mount Kōya) as a pre-text in "The Immortal" is unmistakable. The images associated with Kumano (fire, the Nashi Falls, half-human creatures, crows) can be traced back to the dawn of Japanese history, and readers familiar with the Nō will recognize the structure and rhythm of the innovative dramatic plays of Kanze Nobumitsu (1435–1516), in which the* waki *(the hijiri) is the protagonist. But a close reading of the story will reveal that it is Menippean, carnivalesque: Nakagami turns his pre-texts on their heads, and in the process violates every single convention of the traditional supernatural tale. In "The Immortal," he deconstructs the law, the system, the* monogatari *of Kumano as brutally as he explodes his vision of the Alley in the I-novels.*

*   *   *

To the hijiri, it was not particularly strange to be pushing his way through a dense thicket as he walked on and on in the mountains of Kumano, thrusting aside the top branches of bushes whose leaves shimmered translucent in the sunlight like blazing fire. That is how he had come this far, walking on and on into the mountains. If Amida were peering down from above the mountains, it may have seemed nothing more than circling round and round in the same place, sometimes a profile, sometimes a full figure, like an insect wriggling in the earth beneath the torn grass. But even if that were true, he did not care in the least. *Walking suits me.* He had walked on and on reciting this to himself. And as he walked, he had sometimes reached the top of a mountain pass to find unexpectedly a village on the other side. Sometimes, when he had been in the mountains for a long time, he had suddenly found himself searching for a bamboo grove, wanting to eat something fire had passed through, and wanting to embrace a woman whose body had warmth. *There are always people where there's a bamboo grove.* He no longer knew when he had come to understand this in his bones. To the hijiri, the sound of wind blowing over bamboo leaves was the sound of his own throat, the sound of life rising from every pore of his skin.

The thicket had begun to slope gently upward, but the hijiri's breathing never became labored, and as he traced the faint path that remained where people or animals had trampled the grass, just as he had done up to now, he even raised his voice imitating the sound of the grass brushing against his garments . . . *jaarajaara jaarajaara.* . . He had done nothing to the hair on his face for nearly ten days now, and his demeanor was dark and malevolent. His garments, freshly washed ten days ago, had become filthy with dust and grime. *Jaarajaara jaarajaara.* . . Suddenly, what had happened ten days ago loomed up before him like a dream, and the hijiri closed his mouth, swallowing the sounds. Dense clouds roiled up covering the entire scene. The gentle slope of the mountain, which had seemed to melt into the sunlight striking it until just now, the stand of cypresses spreading out beyond it like outstretched arms, and the naked crags in the distance, to the hijiri's eyes like purple flames, all dimmed, as if their colors had been wiped away. For a moment, the hijiri felt pain bearing down on him. Raising his eyes, he spat loudly, and began to mimic the sound of the grass again . . . *jaarajaara jaarajaara* . . . as if he were chanting a holy sutra.

He had fasted often, abstaining from both food and drink, and besides a devotion to scholarship equal to others, he had been singled out by the person he revered as his master, who had praised him for his speed in learning the sutras. But perhaps because from the very beginning he had learned the sutras only as a child who had been abandoned by hill people, or valley people—or even perhaps by a monkey keeper in favor of the monkey—he always ended up chanting *jaarajaara jaarajaara,* like a lewd growling in the throat, instead of the phrases of the sacred sutras.

Reaching the end of the mountain's gentle slope, he entered a stand of tall cypresses and after walking a little further came out onto the ridge, which was thickly wooded with tall broad-leaved trees. He walked on, stooping so that the garments covering his large body would not be caught in the branches, and on the ground at his feet, where fallen leaves had piled up and rotted, a snake as large as his arm slithered away with a rustling sound to hide itself. There were sounds everywhere, like spattering raindrops—just behind him, something striking the leaves of the branches over his back. Startled, he whirled around, and then realized that he had stumbled into a nest of mountain leeches. He turned to retreat, but when he tried to brush away the branch hanging over his face, leeches fell from its leaves like gentle raindrops, a great number of them striking his head and tumbling into the collar of his tunic. Shouting out, he twisted his body backward, but the leeches, tiny as the seeds of a tree, stuck to his skin and would not come loose. The hijiri had encountered many such things as he wandered in the mountains. And whenever something like this happened, he was struck with wonder at himself, walking deeper and deeper into the mountains and even going through all sorts of hardships when there was no reason at all to be doing so.

He emerged from the cypress grove onto a precipitous cliff. When he looked down, he could see a swollen waterfall that seemed to rend the rocks, and a river. Catching the sunlight, the water shimmered like white silk, and the hijiri felt that even from a distance its beauty was breathtaking. He wanted desperately to dip out some of this water and drink it, and unable to contain himself began searching for a way down. After nearly an hour, he finally reached the bottom of the cliff. First, as if it were a perfectly natural thing to do, he thrust his face directly into the water and drank, kneeling on a moss-grown rock that received the spray of the waterfall. He drank with such force as to gulp down everything in the river into his stomach. When he had finally finished drinking, he washed his face and then his head in the water. Suddenly, as if it had just occurred to him, he plunged splashing into the swift current with all his clothes still on. Standing in water up to his hips, he washed his flanks, his neck, and his back, which were covered with marks where the leeches had sucked his blood. He had stopped the bleeding by covering the wounds with crushed blades of grass, and now the scabs softened and came loose in the water. Blood flowed from the wounds, seeming to dissolve instantly in the water. The hijiri was not surprised by a little blood. Perhaps because he had been in a village ten days earlier, he was fleshier than usual.

The hijiri walked through the water toward the waterfall, which shone with a white radiance like a length of silk. Reaching the base of the cascade, it occurred to him that if he was going to be beaten by this strand of silk, he would profit more naked than with his clothes on, and so he began to take off his wet garments. Just at that moment he heard a sound and whirled around. For an instant the hijiri doubted his own eyes.

Separated by the cliff from where he stood, a woman was dipping water from the river with a bamboo ladle into a wooden bucket. He wondered suspiciously what she was doing here, where there was not the slightest sign of a village, but rather than startle her by making a sound, he watched the weak movements of the woman's hands, bating his breath. She filled the dipper half-full, but apparently it was too heavy for her and she spilled the water. She plunged the dipper into the water again. He saw the ladle floating weakly on the surface, but it was only after the woman cried out and began running downstream along the bank that he realized it had been captured by the swift current.

The dipper was carried down to his feet, and when the woman realized that a hijiri was bathing himself in the small waterfall that plunged into the river, she turned her face away. The hijiri understood what the woman standing before him felt. Fear at having stumbled upon a man deep in the mountains, an ascetic attempting to purify his body in the descending torrent, was clearly visible on her face.

Picking up the dipper, the hijiri straightened his garments and walked through the water toward the trembling woman. Her hair was neatly gathered at the nape of her neck, and the white ankles he glimpsed beneath the hem of her kimono were slender. That alone was enough to evoke from the hijiri's throat the sound of grass rustling, the sound of treetops brushing against each other in the wind . . . *jaarajaara jaarajaara*. Slowly, he stopped in front of the woman, muttering that even

417

a scholar priest bound by high rank at the main temple would violate the commandments if he met a woman alone in the mountains.

The woman raised her face and looked at the hijiri, but now there was neither pleading nor fear in her expression. When the hijiri peered into the reflection of himself in her large eyes, there was even a suggestion of a faint smile playing on her white face. "Thank you," she said, reaching out to take the bamboo dipper. Her hands were too small for her body, as if they had remained unchanged since she was an infant. Staring intently into his face as if to confirm that his excited lust had faltered, the woman took the dipper in her tiny hands and said, "You must forget this." And then she began to climb quickly up into the brush on the mountainside, leaving the half-filled bucket where it had fallen beside the river.

For a moment, the hijiri stood rooted there as if in a trance. But after the woman's figure disappeared into the thicket, it occurred to him suddenly that she had not been a creature of this world. If she were a flesh-and-blood woman, he could rape her. But if she were an incarnation of Kannon, he could save himself from this existence if he but touched her gentle, infant's hands—this existence as a hijiri who could not live in the villages of men but neither was able to devote himself to scholarship. He plunged into the undergrowth after her, then paused to listen, and heard birds taking flight in the distance. He set off in the direction of this sound, without a thought for his soaked garments.

When he emerged from the thicket, the woman was kneeling beside a flat brushwood fence. The hijiri ran up behind her and stopped, standing over her. "Please leave me alone." Her weak, pleading voice seemed to emerge from her lips in a single thread, as if she sensed his rising passion. Here deep in the mountains, she could have escaped had she tried, and even as he lifted the cowering woman in his arms, the hijiri could not suppress the feeling that he was being deluded, though she closed her eyes and weakly gave herself up to him.

Exposing her naked body, he was both disappointed and relieved to find that apart from her hands there was no sign that she was more than human.

After he had sated his passion, he asked her why she was gathering water alone in the mountains, and if she lived here with her husband.

But the woman with the infant's hands only wept silently. He helped her up, but she closed her kimono and said only, "Please, just leave me as I am." The hijiri wondered if she was living alone here because of her stunted hands, to avoid inquisitive stares.

He had no intention of letting the woman go. The grass where she had sunk down was soft and gentle, and the hijiri thought it suited her white thighs. Drawn by their whiteness, he reached out to touch them, but she brushed his hand away, twisting her body back, and said, "Please leave me alone."

The sun was still in the sky but already turning red. When he lunged at her, the woman raised her arms to embrace him, pulling him down with her tiny hands. He thought that to a woman he must appear to be unimaginably crazed, and buried his face in her breasts, pressing his lips against her nipples and biting them lightly. Perhaps because this hurt her, the woman pressed her lips against his and sucked his tongue into her mouth. Just at that moment, he heard low voices around them. He tried to raise his head, but the woman held it down with her tiny hands and said, "Wild boars often pass by here." Not satisfied with this, he again tried to raise his head in search of the voices, but she pressed her body up against his and wrapped her legs around him. "It's only the cries of boar or deer running past toward the ridge."

When she insisted again, the voices did sound like animal cries. But deep in the mountains, with darkness suddenly falling over everything, the hijiri felt approaching danger. He sensed someone standing behind him and whirled around, but the woman wrapped her arms more tightly around his neck to stop him and said, "It is the noble ones." The hijiri threw off her arms and stood up, staring intently into the gloom.

The light that had lingered in the sky until moments before had begun to disappear, the mountains fading into nothing but shifting shadows, so he could not make out their features, but with sounds like the wind rustling in the brush, they were gathering one or two at a time to sit before him. For a moment, he thought he saw their faces, and he felt fear stabbing up from the pit of his stomach—yasha, night demons. Trembling, he pushed the woman away, and clutching his garments tried to run away. But the woman—where did she find the strength?—seized his hand in her own infant's hands and stood up facing him. "Do not

be afraid," she whispered. "No one thinks you are a savage like Ise no
Gorō." The hijiri had no idea what this meant, but she had drawn nearer,
and so he shouted out to the crowd hidden in the darkness, "I am nothing
like that," trying to tell them that he was only an ascetic who had happened to pass by this place in his wanderings.

"I won't bother you. I haven't even seen your faces."

From the darkness came voices that sounded like scornful laughter.

"I haven't seen anything. I don't know anything."

He was shouting, but when he heard laughter in what were clearly
human voices—had he said something funny?—the hijiri suddenly realized that he was shaking. *What am I doing standing here frightened out
of my wits and trying to make excuses for myself?* The hijiri saw himself
for the first time naked and shaking, unable even to throw off the grip
of the woman's tiny hands. He had valued his own life no more than
that of an insect. He had gone down into the villages, and claiming to
be a seer with long years of austerities, had wandered from place to place
curing nightmares, performing exorcisms, and even telling fortunes.
Sometimes, he had stolen the handful of rice that was all a family possessed. Once, when he had left the villages to wander again in the mountains, he had encountered rain, and before he could descend from the
peak he had become feverish. But thinking that he had no need of life,
he had simply fallen down against the base of a tree and lain there until
the fever passed by itself. The hijiri laughed at himself. He, who had
thought there was no particular reason to live, was now trembling in fear
that his life might be taken by these yasha devils.

"It is the noble ones."

The woman took the garments from his hands and put them on him.
And then, as if they had been waiting for her to finish, they all began
to walk, making a rustling sound in the brush.

"Come, let's be off," the woman said, taking the hijiri's hand. She
started walking, and the clumps of grass around him moved. He heard
the sound of many feet trampling the grass.

He did not know how long they walked. It seemed they arrived almost at once, but also that several hours had passed. Though he had
wandered endlessly here, the hijiri knew only that they were deep in the
mountains, far from the villages that dotted the seacoast. He had no

memory of the steep slope they were climbing or of the shape of the mountain that loomed up in the moon he glimpsed hanging in the sky whenever there was a break in the trees. They came to a place where he could hear the sound of spray, and a soft, cold mist struck his face, and he knew they were near a waterfall. "Just a little further now," she whispered in his ear. And as she had promised, they emerged from the grove of trees onto a broad, flat riverbank that opened before them in moonlight, which now covered the entire scene, and above it was a waterfall that plunged down from the heights with the sound of bells, aglow in the silver light. Next to the fall was a mansion, its lights so dim that it seemed uncertain whether it was actually there at all.

"The waterfall turns red, like flowing blood."

As if to show him, she pointed to the waterfall, which was drenched in the light of the moon. He heard a harsh, suppressed voice beside him:

"Have we not sworn revenge on the traitors of Tanabe?"

Voices of agreement rose all around him—"Yes" . . . "Indeed". . . Just then, a person of low stature appeared from the mansion holding two birds in his hands. Knocking the shrieking, flapping birds against each other, he shouted, "There, fight once more." Each time they were knocked together, the two birds kicked their legs out at each other and beat their wings, as if they were terrified of the impenetrable night.

The birds were brought together again and again, until finally one of them lost its strength and was no longer able to kick back at the other.

Apparently there was someone of noble birth inside the mansion, for the little man held the birds up toward it. In the silver light of the moon, which just at that moment hung directly overhead, their blood flowed black.

The voice of a woman weeping inside the mansion reached his ears. The little princess had been put to the sword, she said, and she herself had been forced to flee with the prince, who once had been promised the royal succession. Now they were reduced to living here in hiding deep in the mountains. These people, gathered under the cover of night—how many were there?—were only waiting for the right moment to rise up and attack in force. She spoke as though the capital were just on the other side of the mountain.

A soft, warm breeze was blowing. And with each gust the sound of the brush and the tops of the trees echoed like court music played by noble ladies-in-waiting. As if summoned by the voice of the woman crying inside the mansion, they assembled, pushing through the brush with the same mournful, haunting sound. Suddenly recalling the woman at his side, the hijiri looked at her face. Tears glittered in her eyes. He turned again to look at the people assembled in the silver moonlight and shuddered. Their outlines were hazy, and they could easily have been mistaken for the grass, or the branches of the trees, now only shadows in the darkness, but if he looked at them more intently, they were monkeys and wild boars. Yet they all had the shapes of human beings, no different from the hijiri himself. Some had human faces but the hands and feet of dogs. Whether they had become this way from being in the mountains for so long, or because the nobles living in the mansion had assembled a horde of yasha and devils, they were all weeping at the words of the woman inside. Some of them crouched with their hands together in prayer. Others stood covering their faces with hoofed hands. As he gazed at these creatures, the hijiri thought that it was because such things occurred deep in the mountains of Kumano that the hijiri and bikuni who wandered from province to province longed for and worshiped this land. He did not think that these weird monsters were phantoms. And neither did he believe they were the ghosts of the dead who had been defeated and had fled from the capital in this world. They were here now —the infant emperor who had been carried to the bottom of the ocean, and the slain princess whose blood stained the waterfall red.

When the hijiri stood up to leave this place, the woman with the tiny hands lifted her tear-streaked face and asked, "Where will you go?" In his heart, the hijiri replied that he had had nowhere to go from the beginning, that there was nothing for him but to keep going on and on, but he did not give voice to these thoughts and simply started walking. He sensed that the woman had risen and was following after him with weak, uncertain steps. *If you are some incarnation that is more than human, stay here and cry*, he thought. He was still immature, unfinished, and despite his wanderings and his austerities he could not yet perform feats like En no Gyōja, manipulating devils and flying freely through the air.

Even if he had been beaten by waterfalls and denied himself the five grains, none of it had been more than empty ritual.

Listening to the footsteps of the woman following him, he knew that sounds *jaarajaara jaarajaara* were rising around her. Were they made by the deformed creatures standing behind her, or was it just the wind blowing over the treetops?

He did not know the reason, but he felt ashamed. Unable as he was to live among other people, and at the same time wanting in his devotion to austerities, he nevertheless had an ordinary human body, unlike this woman and her monstrous companions. He could not accustom himself to life in the villages, and he was also incapable of true austerity. He knew that the woman was following him closely so as not to lose sight of him, and the sounds *jaarajaara jaarajaara* rose up even louder in his heart as he traced his way back through the brush from which they had originally come.

The rim of the mountain began to glow, and the hijiri stopped and turned back to the woman.

"Where are you going?"

She smiled and said, "I will see you on your way and then return to the noble ones. That is the way I live."

They had come to a place where the mountain jutted out to form a cliff, and so the hijiri sat down. The woman came up beside him.

"I no longer know how many years I have lived. The noble one mourns her lost children so. There it is."

Peering down from the cliff, she pointed with one of her childlike fingers. The wind blew through her hair, and to the hijiri her face was more lovely than anything he had ever seen before. He found himself looking down from the precipice, as if captivated by her gaze. It was there that he had suddenly wanted desperately to drink from the waterfall, and there that he had been inspired to enter the falls and be lashed by the cascading water. The morning sun had begun to rise, and the rim of the mountain sparkled in golden light. As if night had suddenly become afternoon, birds began to cry out all over the mountain, and the sound of the water reached his ears.

He began to climb down toward the waterfall. Suddenly, he thought that he had seen this thicket before. And it was then that the hijiri realized that the stand of tall broad-leaved trees he had walked through with the woman during the night was the place where he had been attacked by leeches. It seemed strange now that nothing in particular had happened to them.

As he climbed down through the brush the sound of the water pealing in the cold morning air and the woman's footsteps merged with the sounds *jaarajaara jaarajaara* that had begun to rise up again in his body, buzzing in his throat. He emerged from the brush and turned to help the woman, who had climbed down after him. Taking her into his arms, he lowered her from the mountainside and without releasing her laid her down beside the stream.

In the bright morning light streaming down on the riverbank, her naked body breathed colors of peach blossoms, and the downy hair that lightly covered her skin seemed aglow with the color of gold. As if to kneel before this beauty, the hijiri lowered his head and pressed his lips against her skin. He pressed his ear into the valley between her breasts, and the rapid beating of her heart assured him of the woman's arousal. He stripped off the garments he was wearing and stretched his body out beside her. It was enough to do nothing, enough that this woman was there breathing beside him, with her skin of peach blossoms bathed in morning light and her golden down—her red nipples, her navel, which seemed to him the center of this world, the burning shadow of her vagina, and the thicket of hair over it. Not resisting the touch of his lips, the woman opened her legs to the kneeling hijiri and gently stroked his back with her tiny hands. He took the fingers of those hands into his mouth, sucking them one at a time. The woman raised her hips to accept his engorged penis, and pressed her lips over his. He plunged into her, as if by doing so he were arresting the flight of an angel in a feathered mantle, holding her here.

The woman came forth again and again, and with her hands clutching his back, the hijiri thought she was too beautiful in the glaring light of the morning sun. *I don't want to let her go*, he thought. If she was an angel, he wanted to hide away the feathered robe that would carry her to heaven and stay here coupled with her like this forever.

After he too had come forth inside her and the vortex of passion within him had passed, he put his hand on her, and with his fingers stopped the semen that had collected inside and was beginning to flow out. "Stay with me like this forever," he said. The woman smiled, slowly shook her head, and stood up. She said that she would wash herself in the river, and began to walk toward it. As he watched her retreating back, the hijiri was seized with an evil thought. Chanting *jaarajaara jaarajaara*, the meaningless sounds with their lewd reverberations that he chanted instead of the words of the sutras, he saw a vivid image of himself wandering from village to village, from mountain to mountain, like a beggar or a thief, and he thought, *Shall I . . . jaarajaara . . . kill this woman?*—just as the hijiri he saw in his mind, unable to bear his own existence, had once killed a woman. He could see the semen that he had ejaculated into her flowing out and falling onto the sand. As if quite unaware that the hijiri staring at her back was contemplating something abominable, the woman piled her hair up on her head and stepped into the cold water.

The hijiri suddenly felt that the woman was about to disappear completely into the river and stood up to run after her. Looking up at the hijiri, who had come splashing through the current to stand beside her, she smiled and said, "The water is cold." He watched her plunge head first into the water with the same evil feelings and murmured to himself, *She is like the spirit of the morning soaking into your skin.* He splashed her, like a child playing, but she just smiled, not joining in his play. Her demure manner made him uneasy, and his expression became serious. "Come live with me in a village or somewhere.

"Who cares about the noble ones? Let's go to a village and plant fields, and rice paddies. I can exorcise the children's night demons, and I can make medicines for boils and sicknesses of the mind and sell them."

"I cannot go to a village where there are people."

"If you don't want to go to a village, here in these mountains is fine. I could hunt boar, or deer."

The hijiri approached the woman, who was covering her breasts with her infant's hands, and embraced her. He felt it unbearably sad that her skin had been chilled by the cold water, and hugging her more tightly, he thought he was going to cry.

"Stay with me. Live with me. . ." He knew how rash his proposal was. Whatever her circumstances, she must have some reason for being in such a place, and she knew no more about him than he knew about her. The hijiri felt that even now she might disappear from his arms, and put even more strength into them, pressing his stomach against her wet nakedness. His lips on the nape of her neck, he groaned, "Won't you save me?" He knelt in the water and kissed her breasts, pressing his lips between her fingers. She responded to his caresses, removing her tiny hands.

Lifting her in his arms, the hijiri walked toward the garments he had thrown from the stream. Perhaps because he had walked through the night, the roar of the waterfall echoed in his ears, seeming to spread out behind him, and the voices of the birds, more and more of them as the sun spread over the mountain, sounded clear and strong.

He could not suppress his rising passion—it was as if he had not yet embraced her even once. He put her down on a flat rock at the edge of the stream, and not even giving her time to warm herself, spread her taut pink thighs and entered her, unconcerned that the woman was arching her back in pain. But her pain passed quickly, turning to pleasure. She opened her mouth and stuck out her tongue for his and sucked it into her mouth. When he thrust his hips forward like a rutting boar, she closed her eyes and moved her tongue teasingly, as if to say that only she was giving pleasure. He felt himself an animal possessed of nothing but lust. And he thought himself incomparably repulsive.

He looked down at the woman, who had closed her eyes into gentle lines and released her coiling tongue, moaning in her ecstasy. He felt a hatred welling up that was equal to the love seething in his body. Still rutting like a boar, he grabbed her shoulders and butted into her again and again, grunting out loud. The woman just moaned. He knew that he had put his hand on her throat.

Certainly, he contemplated killing her. He put more strength into the hand he had pressed against her neck, and her body stiffened. He felt her vagina tighten hard around him and mounted higher, trying to thrust more deeply into her. The woman writhed in pain. He took his hand away from her throat. He thought he had understood everything from the beginning, and still naked, he raised himself and sat staring down at her body. She was watching his face. With the morning sun striking them, the stream, the rocks, and the woman's naked body were almost blinding. The brush beside the stream rustled in every gust of wind, and though the sound did not reach his ears, he thought he could hear *jaarajaara jaarajaara*. And though the woman by no means said any such thing, he imagined that he heard her tiny voice saying, "Please let me go. . . Spare my life"—just as he had heard when he killed the woman in the village. She had known he was little more than a thief and a beggar, but every night the village woman had called him "Holy man . . . reverend priest." And when she called him that, he could not bear it. When she called him that, he thought that however much he had fallen, he was still a hijiri, and in fact he had even begun to convince himself that his incarnation as a hijiri was only temporary, that he was really a holy saint, in no way inferior to Kōbō Daishi or Ippen Shōnin. *But it was a lie. I am inferior even to the grass, inferior even to a wild dog, a man who cannot live in the villages with other people, but lacks the wisdom to become a scholar priest. When she nestled her cheek against me and kissed me as if she were receiving it with a reverence that went all the way down to the toes of her feet, when she worshiped me that way, I felt as if I were being mocked, tormented, as if I were being gently strangled with silk floss. And in the darkness of the night, she cried out to me endlessly. "Ah! Save me! . . . Give me salvation! . . . Teach me the way! . . ." She moaned. She trembled. She threw herself on me as if I were the personification of all that was evil and without mercy, groveling and begging for salvation. And sometimes I felt that her voice was my own voice. I was pleading to myself for salvation and at the same time saying the same words in my heart to the woman. "Ah! Teach me! . . . Save me! . . . Teach me the path to paradise! . . ." From early morning that day, I sat in her house with the rain shutters closed, listening to the cries of a cuckoo. As I fondled her dusky nipples while she lay sound asleep beside me, I remember that I thought its cries sounded like "ako, ako, ako. . ." I rolled her nipple around in my fingers for a moment, and then, just as I had done long, long ago, I sucked it into my mouth. She cried out to me again. "Ah! Holy saint! . . ." The rain shutters were closed, and so I couldn't see her face, but the cries of the cuckoo echoed, "ako . . . ako . . . ako. . ." "Ah, holy man . . . reverend priest. . . Save me. . . Save me. . ." Her cries became louder, and with her moaning in my ears, my hand stretched out toward her throat. Save me. . . I was saying it with her as I put more strength into my hand. "Save me. . ." Even after I had released her limp body, her voice remained in my ears forever.*

The hijiri had said nothing to the woman.

His body empty, he stood up, and with the sound of the treetops fluttering *jaarajaara jaarajaara* in his ears, he began to walk toward his garments to put them on. But suddenly he changed his mind and turned toward the water. He stepped into it and then dived, submerging himself. Standing up again, he started to walk toward the waterfall, wiping away the drops of water on his skin with his hands.

Gazing up at the white cascade shooting bright rays of light in the sun, he felt that it was the same waterfall he had seen beside the mansion of the noble ones. It occurred to him that soon it should be stained red with blood, and he turned back to ask the woman with the infant's hands. But from somewhere a great flock of crows had gathered around her, as if to conceal her from him. They had come down near the spot where he had left his clothes and were now hopping around and flapping their wings on the flat ground near the river. Afraid that they would peck the woman's body, he scooped up a rock from the bottom of the river and threw it at them. One by one, they flew up, and squawking loudly to each other, circled over his head.

The hijiri finished putting on his clothes and turned to ask the woman one last time if she would live with him in a village. There was no one there. The hijiri thought he had known that from the beginning, too.

Notes on the Translators

MICHAEL C. BROWNSTEIN is an Assistant Professor of Japanese at the University of Notre Dame. He received his Ph.D. in Japanese from Columbia University in 1981 and is currently researching the evolution of Japanese literary thought during the eighteenth and nineteenth centuries.

ANTHONY H. CHAMBERS, a native of California, received his Ph.D. in Japanese language and literature from the University of Michigan in 1974. He is the author of several studies of the works of Tanizaki Jun'ichirō; his translations include *The Secret History of the Lord of Musashi and Arrowroot* and *Naomi*, by Tanizaki. He is Associate Professor in the Department of Asian Languages and Literatures at Wesleyan University.

BRETT DE BARY is an Associate Professor of Japanese Literature at Cornell University, where she teaches modern Japanese literature and film. She has translated works by postwar authors such as Hara Tamiki, Miyamoto Yuriko, and Ōe Kenzaburō, and also published articles on them. Her *Three Works by Nakano Shigeharu* was published by Cornell University East Asia Papers Series in 1979. She is now preparing for publication a manuscript on Japanese literature at the end of the Pacific War.

VAN C. GESSEL received his Ph.D. in Japanese from Columbia University. He has translated two novels and a short story collection by Endō Shūsaku—*When I Whistle, The Samurai*, and *Stained Glass Elegies*—and written critical articles on modern Japanese theater and Japanese Christian writers. He recently completed a monograph on postwar literature titled *Japan's Lost Generation*. He is Assistant Professor of Japanese at the University of California, Berkeley.

MARK HARBISON, a Ph.D. candidate at Stanford University, is presently studying in Tokyo and writing a dissertation on "Inter-textuality as Method in the *Shinkokinshū*." He has done a wide variety of translations from Japanese texts, including several volumes of Konishi Jin'ichi's *History of Japanese Literature*, and short stories by Nagai Kafū, Furui Yoshikichi, and Abe Akira. He is preparing a translation of Ōe Kenzaburō's *Atarashii hito yo mezameyo*.

GERALDINE HARCOURT, a science graduate, has been studying Japanese since high school. A native of New Zealand, she now lives in Tokyo. Among her published translations are Tsushima Yūko's *Child of Fortune*, Yamamoto Michiko's *Betty-san*, and Gō Shizuko's *Requiem*. Currently she is at work on a collection of stories by Tsushima Yūko.

CAROLYN HAYNES is a Ph.D. candidate in Japanese literature at Cornell University. Her article "Parody in Kyōgen: *Makura Monogatari* and *Tako*" appeared in *Monumenta Nipponica*.

AMY VLADECK HEINRICH received her doctorate in Japanese literature in 1980 at Columbia University, and has taught at Columbia, New York University, and Princeton. Her book, *Fragments of Rainbows: The Life and Poetry of Saitō Mokichi, 1882–1953*, was published in 1983. She is currently working on a comparative study of modern women writers and their place in the Japanese and English literary traditions.

ADAM KABAT did his undergraduate work at Wesleyan University. He has recently completed a master's degree at the University of Tokyo with a comparative study of the works of Izumi Kyōka and Mishima Yukio, and is now on a doctoral course there. He is also preparing a translation of a novel by Yoshiyuki Junnosuke.

STEPHEN W. KOHL is currently Associate Professor of Japanese and Chairman of the Department of East Asian Languages and Literatures at the University of Oregon. His primary field of interest is the interpretation and translation of modern Japanese literature. He is the author of over a dozen articles and translations, including *Cliff's Edge and Other Stories* by Tachihara Masaaki. He has also made a study of early relations between Japan and the Pacific Northwest.

WAYNE P. LAMMERS received his Ph.D. at the University of Michigan and is presently Assistant Professor at the University of Wisconsin. He has published a translation from *Utsubo monogatari* in *Monumenta Nipponica* and is preparing a collection of translations of stories by Shōno Junzō. He has also been an instructor of English language and literature at Iwate University.

KĀREN WIGEN LEWIS did her undergraduate work in Japanese at the University of Michigan, and is now pursuing graduate work in Japanese geography at the University of California, Berkeley. Her translation of Yasuoka Shōtarō's *Kaihen no kōkei* received the 1981 Translation Prize from the U.S.-Japan Friendship Commission, and was published as *A View by the Sea* in 1984 by Columbia University Press.

VIRGINIA MARCUS is a graduate student at the University of Michigan. Her annotated translation of selected stories from *Yorozu no fumihōgu*, a collection of epistolary tales by Ihara Saikaku, was published together with an introductory essay in *Monumenta Nipponica* in 1985.

TOMONE MATSUMOTO received her doctoral degree in 1979 from the University of Arizona. Her dissertation was a study of modern Japanese intellectual history, focusing on the career of Kamei Katsuichirō. She is currently teaching modern Japanese language and literature at Griffith University in Brisbane, Australia.

JACK RUCINSKI is a Senior Lecturer in the Department of Asian Languages at the University of Canterbury in Christchurch, New Zealand. His previous translations from Hori Tatsuo have appeared in *Poetry* and *Translation*. He has also published articles on Japanese literature and art in *Monumenta Nipponica* and *Orientations*. At Harvard University, he is presently researching illustrated books from the early Tokugawa period. He received his Ph.D. in 1978 from the University of Hawaii.

EDWARD SEIDENSTICKER is Professor in the Department of East Asian Languages and Cultures at Columbia University. His numerous translations of modern and classical literary works have placed him among the foremost interpreters of Japanese fiction and poetry.

CECILIA SEGAWA SEIGLE, a native Japanese, has taught classical and modern literature and language at the University of Pennsylvania, where she received her Ph.D. Her published translations include Shimazaki Tōson's *The Family*, Mishima Yukio's *The Temple of Dawn*, and Kaikō Takeshi's *Into a Black Sun* and *Darkness in Summer*. For the 1985–86 academic year, she is a Japan Foundation Fellow, and is writing her second book on Yoshiwara.

YUKIKO TANAKA was co-translator and co-editor of *This Kind of Woman: Ten Stories by Japanese Women Writers, 1960–1976*. Her Ph.D. dissertation at UCLA focused on narrative technique in the works of Kojima Nobuo. She has translated Kojima's novel *Hōyō kazoku* and short story "Happiness," and is now at work on a book on Japanese women writers.

JOHN WHITTIER TREAT received his doctoral degree from Yale University in 1982 with a dissertation on the literature of Ibuse Masuji. At present he is an Assistant Professor at the University of Washington.

WILLIAM J. TYLER, Assistant Professor of Japanese Studies and Director of the Japanese Language Program at the University of Pennsylvania, did his undergraduate work at International Christian University in Japan, and his graduate study at Harvard. His Ph.D. dissertation was on Ishikawa Jun, and he has published a translation of Doi Takeo's *The Psychological World of Natsume Soseki*. He is currently translating Ishikawa's stories and novellas, and preparing a study of Tōkai Sanshi.

ROBERT ULMER first left his native Toronto in 1973 to study in Japan. He received his Ph.D. in Japanese literature from Yale University in 1982. He is now working for the Japan Trade Centre (JETRO) in Toronto.

Selected Bibliography of English Translations

A number of the authors represented in the present anthology are appearing in English translation for the first time. Through the efforts of qualified and dedicated translators, however, a wide range of modern Japanese literary works has been made available for the interested reader. For translations published before 1978, the reader is referred to *Modern Japanese Literature in Translation: A Bibliography*, compiled by the International House of Japan Library and published in 1979 by Kodansha International. The selected list that follows is a compilation of translations in English which have appeared since the date of that original bibliography.

ABE AKIRA

"A Napping Cove" (Madoromu irie). Tr. by Mark Harbison. *Japanese Literature Today*, vol. 9 (1984), pp. 11–23.

ABE KŌBŌ

Secret Rendezvous (Mikkai). Tr. by Juliet Winters Carpenter (New York: Knopf, 1979). 190 pp.

"You, Too, Are Guilty" (Omae ni mo tsumi ga aru). Tr. by Ted T. Takaya. *Modern Japanese Drama: An Anthology*, ed. by Ted T. Takaya (New York: Columbia University Press, 1979), pp. 1–40.

DAZAI OSAMU

Selected Stories and Sketches. Tr. by James O'Brien (Ithaca: Cornell University Press, 1983). 248 pp. Includes: "Memories," "Transformation," "The Island of Monkeys," "Toys," "Das Gemeine," "Putting Granny Out to Die," "My Older Brothers," "Eight Views of Tokyo," "On the Question of Apparel," "Homecoming," "A Poor Man's Got His Pride," "The Mound of the Monkey's Grave," "Taking the Wen Away," "Currency," "The Sound of Hammering," and "Osan."

Return to Tsugaru (Tsugaru). Tr. by James Westerhoven (Tokyo: Kodansha International, 1985). 220 pp.

Tsugaru (Tsugaru). Tr. by Phyllis Lyons. *The Saga of Dazai Osamu* (Stanford:

Stanford University Press, 1985), pp. 271–385.

ENDŌ SHŪSAKU

A Life of Jesus (Iesu no shōgai). Tr. by Richard A. Schuchert (New York: Paulist Press, 1978). 179 pp.

The Samurai (Samurai). Tr. by Van C. Gessel (London: Peter Owen, 1982; New York: Harper and Row/Kodansha International, 1982; and New York: Vintage, 1984). 272 pp.

"The Shadow Figure" (Kagebōshi). Tr. by Thomas Lally, Ōka Yumiko, and Dennis J. Doolin. *Japan Quarterly*, vol. 31, no. 2 (April–June 1984), pp. 164–73, and vol. 31, no. 3 (July–Sept. 1984), pp. 294–301.

"Shadow of a Man" (Kagebōshi). Tr. by Shoichi Ono and Sanford Goldstein. *Bulletin of the College of Biomedical Technology, Niigata University*, vol. 1, no. 1 (1983), pp. 80–94.

"Something of My Own" (Watakushi no mono). Tr. by John Bester. *Japan Echo*, vol. 12 (1985), pp. 23–29.

Stained Glass Elegies: Stories by Shusaku Endo. Tr. by Van C. Gessel (London: Peter Owen, 1984). 165 pp. Includes: "A Forty-Year-Old Man," "The Day Before," "Fuda-no-Tsuji," "Unzen," "My Belongings," "Despicable Bastard," "Mothers," "Retreating Figures," "Old Friends," "The War Generation," and "Incredible Voyage."

Volcano (Kazan). Tr. by Richard A. Schuchert (London: Peter Owen, 1978; New York: Taplinger, 1980). 175 pp.

When I Whistle (Kuchibue o fuku toki). Tr. by Van C. Gessel (London: Peter Owen, 1979; New York: Taplinger,1980). 277 pp.

IBUSE MASUJI

Salamander and Other Stories. Tr. by John Bester (Tokyo: Kodansha International, 1981). 134 pp. Includes: "Pilgrims' Inn," "Yosaku the Settler," "Carp," "Salamander," "Life at Mr. Tange's," "Old Ushitora," "Savan on the Roof," "Plum Blossom by Night," and "Lieutenant Lookeast."

INOUE YASUSHI

Chronicle of My Mother (Waga haha no ki). Tr. by Jean Oda Moy (Tokyo: Kodansha International, 1982). 164 pp.

Lou-lan and Other Stories. Tr. by James T. Araki and Edward Seidensticker (Tokyo: Kodansha International, 1981). 160 pp. Includes: "Lou-lan," "The Sage,"

"Princess Yung-t'ai's Necklace," "The Opaline Cup," "The Rhododendrons," and "Passage to Fudaraku."

KAIKŌ TAKESHI

Into a Black Sun (Kagayakeru yami). Tr. by Cecilia Segawa Seigle (Tokyo: Kodansha International, 1980). 220 pp.

KANAI MIEKO

"Rabbits" (Usagi). Tr. by Phyllis Birnbaum. *Rabbits, Crabs, Etc.: Stories by Japanese Women*, tr. by Phyllis Birnbaum (Honolulu: University of Hawaii Press, 1982), pp. 1–16.

KOJIMA NOBUO

"Happiness" (Happinesu). Tr. by Yukiko Tanaka, with Elizabeth Hanson Warren. *Japan Quarterly*, vol. 28, no. 4 (Oct.–Dec. 1981), pp. 533–48.

"Shōjū" (Shōjū). Tr. by Elizabeth Baldwin. *Faith and Fiction: The Modern Short Story*, ed. by Robert Detweiler and Glenn Meeter (Grand Rapids, MI: William B. Eerdmans, 1979), pp. 213–26.

KŌNO TAEKO

"Ants Swarm" (Ari takaru). Tr. by Noriko Mizuta Lippit. *Stories by Contemporary Japanese Women Writers*, ed. and tr. by Noriko Mizuta Lippit and Kyoko Iriye Selden (Armonk, N.Y.: M. E. Sharpe, 1982), pp. 105–19.

"Crabs" (Kani). Tr. by Phyllis Birnbaum. *Rabbits, Crabs, Etc.: Stories by Japanese Women*, pp. 99–131.

"The Last Time" (Saigo no toki). Tr. by Yukiko Tanaka and Elizabeth Hanson. *This Kind of Woman: Ten Stories by Japanese Women Writers, 1960–1976*, ed. and tr. by Yukiko Tanaka and Elizabeth Hanson (Stanford: Stanford University Press, 1982), pp. 43–67.

KURAHASHI YUMIKO

The Adventures of Sumiyakist Q (Sumiyakisuto Q no bōken). Tr. by Dennis Keene (Queensland: University of Queensland Press, 1979). 369 pp.

"Partei" (Parutai). Tr. by Yukiko Tanaka and Elizabeth Hanson. *This Kind of Woman: Ten Stories by Japanese Women Writers, 1960–1976*, pp. 1–16.

ŌBA MINAKO

"Fireweed" (Higusa). Tr. by Marian Chambers. *Japan Quarterly*, vol. 28, no. 3

(July–Sept. 1981), pp. 403–27.

"Sea-change" (Tankō). Tr. by John Bester. *Japanese Literature Today*, no. 5 (March 1980), pp. 12–19.

"The Smile of a Mountain Witch" (Yamauba no bishō). Tr. by Noriko Mizuta Lippit and Mariko Ochi. *Stories by Contemporary Japanese Women Writers*, pp. 182–96.

"The Three Crabs" (Sambiki no kani). Tr. by Yukiko Tanaka and Elizabeth Hanson. *This Kind of Woman: Ten Stories by Japanese Women Writers, 1960–1976*, pp. 87–113.

ŌE KENZABURŌ

Hiroshima Notes (Hiroshima nōto). Tr. by Toshi Yonezawa; ed. by David L. Swain (Tokyo: YMCA Press, 1981). 181 pp.

SHIMAO TOSHIO

"The Sting of Death" and Other Stories by Shimao Toshio. Tr. by Kathryn Sparling. *Michigan Papers in Japanese Studies*, no. 12.

TSUSHIMA YŪKO

Child of Fortune (Chōji). Tr. by Geraldine Harcourt (Tokyo: Kodansha International, 1983). 186 pp.

"Island of Joy" (Yorokobi no shima) and "To Scatter Flower Petals" (Hana o maku). Tr. by Lora Sharnoff. *Japan Quarterly*, vol. 27, no. 2 (April–June 1980), pp. 249–69.

YASUOKA SHŌTARŌ

A View by the Sea (Kaihen no kōkei). Tr. by Kären Wigen Lewis (New York: Columbia University Press, 1984). Includes: "A View by the Sea," "Bad Company," "Gloomy Pleasures," "The Moth," "Rain," and "Thick the New Leaves."

YOSHIYUKI JUNNOSUKE

"Birds, Beasts, Insects and Fish" (Kinjū chūgyo). Tr. by M. T. Mori. *Japan Quarterly*, vol. 28, no. 1 (Jan.–March 1981), pp. 91–102.

"Scene at Table" (Shokutaku no kōkei). Tr. by Geraldine Harcourt. *Japan Echo*, vol. 12 (1985), pp. 42–45.

定価3,500円
in Japan